The Compromise

… a love story

The
Compromise

… a love story

a novel

Eleanor Scott Meyers
Claremont, CA, US
2018

**ESMeyers
PRESS**

The Compromise … a love story is a work of fiction. The main characters and some incidents are drawn from the lives of real individuals and from un-published stories and a memoir written by the two women whose personal stories inspired this novel, however the dialogue comes from the author's imagination. The names of the minor characters and most of the locales in this work are fictional and any resemblance to actual persons living or dead, events, or locales is entirely coincidental. Some liberties have been taken with geography, altering or renaming a few locations.

The Compromise … a love story
Copyright © 2018 by Eleanor Scott Meyers
All rights reserved.

Published in 2018 in the United States of America
by ESMeyers Press, Claremont, CA, US

Library of Congress Control Number: 2018909894
Meyers, Eleanor S
The Compromise … a love story/Eleanor S Meyers
ISBN 978-0-692-15296-6
eBook ISBN 978-0-692-16740-3

1. United States—mid 20th century—Fiction.
2. Lesbian History—United States—Fiction.
3. Women—History—United States—Fiction.
4. Great Depression—United States—Fiction.
5. Small town life—United States, 1900-2000—Fiction.
6. Midwestern Culture—20th century—Fiction.
7. Growing Old—Psychological aspects—United States—Fiction.
8. Kansas—History—Fiction.

Printed in the United States of America on acid-free paper

For information, email: author@esmeyers.com

Author photo by Carol Robb
Book cover art and *Self Portrait* by ESMeyers
www.esmeyers.com

❖

This book is dedicated to –
- those women and men who, by loving others of the same sex, helped create paths toward a more open and affirming society in the United States and beyond,
- and to my children.

Acknowledgements

While any mistakes in this work are mine alone, many people have provided important support through the years, including members of my extended family who encouraged me and the independent editor and friend, Ulrike Guthrie, who was the first to say "write this story." I want to thank these and other early readers who provided helpful feedback—including Lynn Rhodes, Janet Vandevender, Carol Robb, David Cisneros, Patty Contaxis, Judith Favor, Michael Nelson, John Wolfersberger, Kae Lewis, and the now deceased Vern Visick who personally knew the real-life family depicted in this work of fiction. Also, I am grateful to those in the Pilgrim Place writers group, the Joslyn Community Center writers group, and writer friends, BonnaSue, Dennis McDonald, Sally Simmel, and Jean Lind for insightful comments during the closing months of my work on this book.

A significant amount of the conceptual effort for this novel took place in the quiet beauty of the Cisneros-Bohlender family cabin in the mountains above Los Angeles. I will be forever grateful to this fine family.

I want to thank my neighbor, Joanna Harrington, whose comments on several drafts of this manuscript were critical throughout its development, and my daughter, Gaile, and son, Scott, who eagerly joined their mother's project providing advice and technical expertise necessary to achieve publication of this work.

Finally, without the constancy of Pat Hynds' friendship and generous editorial support, I'm not sure this book would have come to fruition. My gratitude to her is without measure.

"We humans will always require stories
in order to find out who we are."

Anonymous

One

The Confrontation

is loud and seemingly inappropriate laughter confused them as their puzzled eyes met surreptitiously around the close-knit circle. A few whispered …

"Why is he acting like this?"

"I don't know."

Everyone was there—friends, neighbors and family, elderly aunts and uncles, nieces and nephews circling out, generation by generation, from the family matriarch   forming a random collection of small-town folks who had set aside their everyday tasks in order to be present. Women in the quilters group at the Methodist Church postponed their monthly morning tea. George, the respected conservative Republican mayor, left his son, Tom, in charge of the gas station for the first time. And Bev, Ruth's hairdresser for more than twenty years, canceled her morning appointments. Life around town had ground to a halt.

Children could be seen chasing one another around the old cedar trees scattered over the cemetery knoll at the east edge of town. Those who knew this piece of land well were grateful for the morning breezes that had whisked away the odors from the region's refinery. Those same breezes now bathed the early spring air with fresh moisture from the night.

Adults gathered in small groups under the trees, their new leaves heralding the change of season. They talked quietly about the warm, heavy air and their calculations regarding rain, the condition of the winter wheat in the fields, and the bond for the proposed new Essex middle school on the upcoming ballot.

Except for those who had sensed something amiss, the small talk allowed many to disregard the bronzed casket set just above the fresh cut, dug into the dark Midwestern soil.

The brief service had ended; the time to depart had arrived. Yet a particular awkwardness continued to hold them, like surreptitious lovers not knowing how to walk away and return to their other well-ordered lives.

These folks made regular trips to the cemetery and knew the drill. They had anticipated conversation to halt as the minister opened his service book, read scripture, and said a prayer committing the loved one to the earth and back to God. They knew to stand around in a cordial and reverent manner, just a bit longer after the final "Amen." They also expected the pastor to make his rounds, shake the hands of the close family members, and then quietly disappear.

All that they expected—but not this ...

"My dad will not stay one more night under the same roof with that woman!" The son's loose and edgy laughter now took the form of a startling outburst, his words tumbling out haphazardly over the gathering.

At first, there was a deathly silence. Then an elderly woman, standing just beyond the edge of the small group, felt some confusion around her and shrilled, "W-w-what did he say?"

A few, barely out of reach of the son's voice, who had heard his passion but not his exact words began whispering to one another.

"Was he talking about Ruth?

"I'm not sure, but he sounded angry."

"Where is Ed?"

"Look, over there, with the children, as usual."

"Good. I trust he didn't hear that outburst!"

"Ruth heard it, I'm sure. She's over there, standing with Lillian, not far from the casket."

"I feel so sorry for her. Cassandra meant the world to her."

Taylor Thomas, the son of Ed and Cassandra Thomas, born right there in the late 1930s, grew up to make a name for himself as a professor at the college. Never known for strong language or strong emotions, he was seen as a son who helped his mother with her work and a teenager who played his trumpet in the City Band with his dad in the summers. He hung mostly with his neighborhood buddies, not the troublemakers, and stayed active in his church youth group. His divorce and second marriage thirty years ago had raised a few eyebrows back then, yet Taylor's success in his career made most folks feel quite proud that their little community had produced such a fine young man.

Yet on this morning, the son's angry outburst suddenly made those standing around the casket feel something unseemly was being forced upon them. Small-town secrets and questions had lingered about his family among these locals for decades, mostly as light-hearted intrigue. But, as happens, interests fade and whispered stories—or suspicions—tend to fall away, especially as friendships blossom.

Regardless of what any of them had thought about this family, today what they cared about was that Ed had lost his wife and Ruth her best friend. And only secondarily about the fact that only these two remained, who might be seen as an awkward pair, if the son's confrontation was to be taken seriously.

What was the son suggesting? That he could not countenance any thought of his father and his mother's longtime female partner continuing to live together in the family home? Did he think his family, represented by this pair, could not survive following his mother's death?

For most of their lives, this unique three-person family lived in an open, easy manner. And even proudly, as together and individually they experienced obvious respect within their rural Midwestern town. Now the fourth member of the family, their son, had violated the wider community's lifelong practice of quiet acceptance, their live-and-let-live attitude. But today they felt concern, fearing an unkind exposure regarding the lives of their grieving friends, Ed and Ruth.

At this uncomfortable moment, those who had heard the son's declaration about his father stood around in stunned silence, not knowing what to say or do. Could the lid, ripped off so unceremoniously, be put back on?

The son had drawn his line in the sand. Would it hold?

Two

The Question

t the cemetery, an uncomfortable silence reigned. Taylor's statement about his widowed father and "that" woman had shocked family and friends. However, those who suspected Ruth overheard what Taylor had said proved to be correct.

'My goodness,' thought Ruth absentmindedly. Buried in her grief and distracted from the conversations surrounding her, she had heard Cassandra's son speak in such anger. 'Is … is Taylor talking about me? About some kind of a problem … with Ed and me … living together? After over fifty years?'

She shook her head in an effort to clear her mind. 'Foolishness,' her first thought.

However, wounded from her loss, the question did begin to creep in. 'Could this be the dreaded moment I've not seen coming? Me, alone, really alone? After all these years, might this loving family now leave me behind?' Fear needled its way into her body.

Finding herself next to Cassandra's casket, surrounded by those she had grown to love and know as her family, and with the words of Cassandra's son ringing in her ears, suddenly and unexpectedly Ruth felt old. Very old. And overwhelmingly alone. She knew her life would never be the same. With Cassandra's death a piece of her had also died, yet Ruth had not felt afraid until now. She'd known that Cassandra, gone now at ninety-two, had been dying for some time. Ruth felt prepared for this moment, but not for her old fear ...

'Am I to be an orphan once again?'

But almost immediately she knew to put a stop to her silly question. 'Okay, enough of that! There's work to do.'

With years of practice behind her, work again would provide her salvation. The family, her family, would soon gather back at the house. She took her mind to the kitchen where she and Cassandra had orchestrated these family gatherings together for decades, recently, however, without Cassandra's help.

Ed surrounded himself with the children, the great-nieces and nephews all dressed in their Sunday best. The youngest, celebrating freedom from church pews, chased one another around the graves. Ed's watchful eye on them pleased everyone, young and old alike.

Ruth knew Ed would miss Cassandra, but she recalled with umbrage his thoughtless comment, "We all have to die sometime." He had spoken these shocking words many times in the past upon the deaths of their friends and loved ones. She prayed to high heaven that he would not say it today.

Yet, there, at the cemetery, standing next to Cassandra's grave, things Ruth had managed to avoid for years set loose, almost overwhelming her ... unspoken feelings fell heavily upon her, grief weighing her body down. This is what aged her that cemetery noonday, the burdens of all those years as her mind ran from here to there, from Taylor's words to Cassandra's grave, and yes, to Ed. 'What might Ed be feeling today?' she wondered. 'His life certainly hadn't turned out to be what he thought he'd said yes to back in Chicago almost sixty years ago.'

Ruth felt certain about Cassandra's love; however, as everything else around her appeared ready to shift, she struggled to find solid ground. Maybe Taylor knew something she didn't, that Cassandra's death would change everything for all of them.

And then, again, stubbornly, with heels dug into the cemetery ground, she moved to dispel her wild fears. 'How stupid I can be,' she admonished herself. There she stood, alone, yes, but surrounded by all these wonderful people — her family — including her good friend, Ed. Working to push all the unknowns aside, she felt Ed most likely had no idea about the emotions spinning around the two of them. 'Not a problem,' she told herself, 'Ed and I will be just fine.'

She checked her watch; time to go. Ed walked toward her, and together they said their farewells to friends from near and far. A few final shouted goodbyes and the sound of car doors closing echoed across the almost empty gravesite. Eventually, everyone tucked into one of the cars, they set out, headed back to town.

The funeral director had a car for Ruth and Ed. They thought Taylor and his wife, Nell, might ride with them but realized they had their own car. Ruth, still working to dispel Taylor's words over his mother's grave, quickly gathered in the grandchildren so she and Ed would have their youthful company.

As the long, black limousine headed out the cemetary gates Ruth said, "Sure wish you two didn't have to head back to work right away."

"Well, we won't leave until I've had a piece of your lemon meringue pie!" Steven offered, his wide smile playing with her. "I spied it on the kitchen counter early this morning."

"Yes, my dear, I made all kinds of pies this morning. In this family every one of you has a different favorite. You want lemon, your mom wants chocolate, your dad and Ed want gooseberry. Patricia is the only one easy to please," she said, while patting the young woman's knee. They laughed, easily enjoying each other.

But Cassandra, formerly the star of any gathering, they now left behind. She had made another of her well-rehearsed entrances, earlier at the church, in her best dress and with her hairdo carefully set by Ruth at the mortuary a few days ago. Both now finally covered by the coffin lid. Once everyone departed, workers standing near the back fence would come and close up the grave. Cassandra's last entrance and final exit. The family matriarch — gone.

As cars pulled out one by one through the cemetery gates and onto the highway, a new phase of life began, lives to be lived beyond Cassandra's strong presence. Oh, her words would certainly continue to ring in many of their ears. However, a time for shifts in the extended family had arrived. Cassandra, a woman who had never taken easily to change, might not approve of what lay ahead. Yet, their memories of this remarkable and in many ways unconventional woman of the plains, these would likely remain for the rest of their lives, exactly as Cassandra had expected.

Cassandra had trained Ruth and Ed well, and on this particular day that would be on full display. Within minutes of leaving the cemetery, once back home, Ed took his assigned welcoming post at the front door, and Ruth put on her freshly starched, ironed apron, ready to go to work. Leaving that unsettling moment behind her for the time being, Ruth could begin to relax and enjoy pouring herself into the final preparations for the family feast. Being in charge had never failed Ruth, and it would not now.

As the family began to gather, some of the womenfolk joined Ruth in the kitchen, putting on their own aprons, brought from home, along with buffet dishes they had prepared and brought to add to the meal.

"Mary Ellen, we need to sort those dishes on the buffet. The salads should be at the far end along with the relish dishes from the refrigerator. Bring that cake over here with the pies on the countertop. I'll cut the pies as we begin serving dessert, but maybe someone could go ahead and cut the cake now."

"Betty, while I carve this ham," Ruth continued, "you can take those buns and get them in the bun warmer on the stovetop. Put the burner on as low as you possibly can; just want to heat them, not burn them up! Then you can get the mustard and canned pickles out of the refrigerator. They're in the door, top shelf."

Marie came in carrying a large bowl of cut fruit.

"Where would you like me to put this, Ruth?"

"Over there, Marie, at the end of the buffet. I think there's still room. But leave space in the middle for the scalloped potatoes, and we'll need one of those hot pads from the top drawer to put under the casserole when I take it out of the oven."

As folks arrived, small groups gathered here and there around the house creating a richly layered family conversation, their words as sweet music to accompany both their loss and their joy in being together.

"I thought Cassandra looked so good, no longer stressed like these last few months. There was peace on her face today," said one of the older women. Others agreed. "Ruth fixed her hair the way Cassandra always liked it, didn't she?" Florence added.

"Sure smells good out here," Charles said, teasing the women as he dared to poke his head through the door into the kitchen, his arms anchored on the doorposts.

"Now, Charles, you stay put!" Ruth called out to him. "Marie, you may have to hogtie that husband of yours until we get this meal together. He's always chomping at the bit, can't wait for his dinner!"

Taylor and Nell put in a brief appearance. From the kitchen Ruth watched Taylor move through the house, acknowledging the older folks, shaking hands and thanking everyone for coming while saying that, pushed for time, they needed to return to tasks back home. As he stood next to his dad in the living room, saying farewell, Ruth caught hold of Nell and pressed a gooseberry pie, very carefully wrapped in foil, into her hands.

"For Taylor, his favorite," Ruth whispered. "Don't worry about the pie dish. You can bring it back someday, whenever you're down this way."

Once everything was ready, Ruth rang the dinner bell mounted on the kitchen wall. Folks began to find their way, lining up at the buffet—the younger ones first, watched over by their mothers, then the older parents, and finally the elders getting up slowly from their chairs, not wanting to stand in the line too long.

"Mary Ellen, why don't you fill a plate for Florence," Ruth said, "and Florence, let's put you right here at the big table. You can tell Mary Ellen what you want."

"Well, don't fill that plate too full," she said. "You know me, I can't really eat all that much, even when it all looks good and smells so delicious."

After everyone found their place, including the women who had been in the kitchen, Ruth asked John if he would say the prayer ... and almost as quickly as the energy had lifted, silence fell within the house, from the family room, through the dining room, and into the living room, with only a final "Shhhhh!" from an older sister to her little brothers.

"Gracious heavenly Father, we thank you for this day when we gather to remember one of our very own, Aunt Cass. She loved each one of us, her family, and took much joy in our gatherings. Give us now of that joy once again, as we share in this food around these tables in memory of her. And bless this food to our use and us to thy service. In Jesus' name, Amen." Standing next to John, Ruth placed her arm around his back and said, "Thank you, John. That was lovely."

As the noise level rose again, Ruth filled her own plate and took her place at the corner of the dining room table, next to the kitchen. From there, with help from Mary Ellen, she could keep an eye on who needed what, while the family enjoyed the afternoon meal and time together.

The youngest kids finished first and soon urged their Uncle Ed outside to read a story or watch them play tag, while three very sophisticated middle-grade girls sat under a tree, deep in important conversation. By late afternoon the women had finished cleaning up the kitchen. Mary Ellen made sure everything had been put away under Ruth's careful direction. Ruth made up leftover packages for Florence, Cassandra's sister, and Lillian, one of Cassandra's nieces, the two elders, women who lived alone. Ruth worried whether they had enough to eat each day. Her care packages would ensure something nourishing for tomorrow.

As it began to get dark, Ruth turned to their adult grand-children. "I'm not trying to get you two to leave," Ruth said, "but it is getting dark. However, you two will probably drive all night long. I could never have done that. But you're young and I guess you'll be okay."

"We're hoping to catch some of the burning of the grass-lands across the Flint Hills," Patricia said. "It's such a beautiful sight, one I rarely get the chance to see these days. When we lived in Hastings years ago, we used to see it each spring. It's a gorgeous sight, thrilling to see."

Eventually the kids took off as darkness enveloped the early spring sky. Ruth hoped the children would be fine as she and Ed placed two boxes with sandwiches and pie in the backseat of the car. Ruth, like Patricia and Steven, loved the land amid the famous Flint Hills of central Kansas. On this evening, she wished them luck in finding the nighttime sky filled with the beauty of the fires wiping clean the prairies, rejuvenating the land. As she stood in the front yard with Ed, waving them off, Ruth thought, 'Maybe Taylor's having thrown out some old, hot feelings today might clear some of whatever lies between us, just like the springtime fires.'

Taylor's first wife, Margaret, would arrive late tomorrow from Boston. Her work kept her from making it back in time for the service. Cassandra had asked her months ago to speak the eulogy at the service when the time came. So when it had come and Margaret could not get away from her work, she had written and faxed her comments to the church for the local pastor to read. Ruth looked forward to her arrival. She trusted Margaret would help her face the hard first few days ahead.

The last to leave finally said their goodbyes, sharing hugs with Ruth and Ed. Nothing seemed out of order to anyone. The family had come together, shared a bountiful and delicious home-cooked meal, sat around, and talked in their old familiar patterns. Finally, with the day almost gone, each one had hugged and kissed their way out the door, promising to stay in touch.

Later that evening, well after dark, with things back in order, a simple quietness and warmth from the long, sunny afternoon spread throughout the house. Ruth fixed a small chopped salad for Ed as she had done each evening for decades, part of his requested daily regimen. "I depend on a good amount of roughage every evening to keep my bowels open," Ed announced frequently, regardless of who might be within hearing range, to Ruth's horror. On this night, Ruth caught herself smiling while thinking of this as she chopped up even more roughage for Ed's evening salad.

A cold piece of something left over from the afternoon table would be supper for Ruth. Ed turned on the TV, set up the TV trays, one by his chair, the other by Ruth's, and they sat down to relax after an exhausting day. Now, only the two of them left to be at home together in the house. They sat watching TV and commenting about the weather in that easy evening comfort that had come to them living under the same family roof for so many years. Everything had changed and nothing had changed. Now all else — Ruth's questions and fears of the day — set aside in favor of the family routine and the simple pleasure of a quiet evening at home together.

This evening, as usual, Ed held the clicker, assigned years ago the responsibility to mute the TV for the commercials. The two of them talked easily about the service, whom they saw, and those they missed, sharing family news one or the other had heard.

"Did you hear that Marilyn is going to have another baby next fall?" Ruth asked.

"No, I didn't. Well, now, isn't that just mighty nice. I'll bet Marie and Charles are happy about that."

"Did you spend any time with John?" Ruth asked, with a look of concern on her face. "He didn't look at all well to me."

"We talked briefly. He didn't seem to have a lot of energy but said they were both doing okay. It was nice of you to ask him to give the prayer."

"I thought he did a good job — not too long, not too short, either. Maybe," Ruth continued, "whatever was troubling him has been taken care of by now."

"Well, I certainly hope so. Betty will let us know if things are not well there, I suppose."

Later Ruth did up the few dishes from their supper. Ed wiped down the TV trays and put them away, took out the garbage, turned off the outside light, and checked the locks on the back and front doors. As Ruth turned out the kitchen lights, they said goodnight and headed to their own rooms, having completed their end of the daily routines the two of them had practiced longer than they could remember.

As Ruth crawled into bed, she began reviewing the day. Unbidden, Taylor's words at the cemetery stunned her once again. She so wanted to free herself from them but was not sure how as her thoughts began to wander ... 'Given time, Taylor will see the two of us are fine together and stop his worrying' ... and, 'Of course, he's upset about his mother's death' ... and then this, 'But that anger, I've never heard him angry like that. That part does worry me.'

Determined not to let Taylor's words take root as they had earlier that afternoon, she found her release in the one thing she had confidence about: Ruth knew Ed would soon be sleeping away easily as he always did, still unaware of the concerns spinning around the two of them all afternoon. On that note she reminded herself to stay focused on what she knew to be real; thus, along with a deep, cleansing sigh, Ruth's heart gently turned to thoughts of Cassandra and the last few months of her life.

'Everyone said she looked so peaceful. It was true,' thought Ruth, 'Cassandra would have been glad it all turned out so well.'

Cassandra's death, Ruth knew, gave her love a gentle release from all those troubles she could find almost everywhere she looked during her last years.

'She just wore herself out from it all, from worry, from getting old, something she always declared she resented,' Ruth mused. The years of off-again, on-again illness had taken their toll. Tired from it all, Cassandra had merely stopped living. 'Certainly stopped trying,' as Ruth understood it.

Ruth had watched Cassandra literally giving up. 'I remember that night only a few weeks ago,' Ruth's thoughts continued as she lay there alone in the bed the two of them had shared for what felt like her entire life. So many memories, Ruth's gentle thoughts moving through time. 'Sitting with her in the hospital room, holding her hand ... I could actually feel her letting go. We talked very little, both content just to be together.'

And on this night, after the memorial service and all that the day had brought her, Ruth was exhausted. At several times in that long day, she had wondered if it would ever end. And yet, now, at the day's end, while others slept, Ruth could still look back and recall with clarity those precious moments as she and her sweet love faced together the approaching end of Cassandra's life.

Three

The Shame

'm tired … so tired … can't do this … anymore …," Cassandra whispered in the darkened hospital room as Ruth sat beside her bed, holding her hand.

"Yes, I know, dear." Ruth's soft voice shook, trying to hold her own emotions in check. She wanted to give Cassandra permission to go, even though it tore at her heart. A sense of loss overtook her, as emptiness crept into her own body, her arms limp as wet rags.

As daylight waned, quietness pervaded everything — the hospital corridor, the room — leaving behind the drab olive-colored walls. In the darkened silence, it was as if nothing existed beyond the two of them, as Ruth kept vigil for Cassandra. Everything appeared to hang in the air, waiting, quietly waiting, for a next word, a next breath, another tear softly dropping.

Finally, Ruth spoke again, "I love you so much, my dear," working hard to speak through her soft tears. "I will always love you … I already miss you so much … and I will miss you every day. You know that, don't you?"

Cassandra nodded, forming the word "yes" softly with her lips.

Ruth stood, smoothed Cassandra's hair from her forehead with her left hand, and then bent down to kiss her, the two of them too full of emotion and weakness for words.

Later, Ruth wanted to reassure Cassandra again that all would be well. "There is nothing for you to worry about sweetheart. The kids and grandchildren are all doing well." And then, knowing Cassandra as she did, Ruth added, "And you know you needn't worry about me or Ed. We'll be fine. You know that."

"Yes ... I know." Cassandra spoke as clearly as she could, trying to reassure the woman she loved about the now worrisome fact that her death would leave Ruth and Ed alone together.

And yet Cassandra's urgings that Ruth take care of Ed continued. Some time later, as Cassandra's breathing grew shallow, she spoke one more time to Ruth, with the last thread of her energy.

"Take ... care ... of ... Ed," she whispered. These would be her sweetheart's last words.

'It's unending!' thought Ruth, as she dropped her head onto her arm seeking whatever support she could find, while trying not to let Cassandra's words break her grieving heart. 'Always, it's always Ed. Her dying thoughts are going to be about Ed. Is she going to die still feeling guilty about the way she treated Ed?'

Ruth had so often heard her tell the story.

"I never intended to marry," Cassandra would say, perhaps feeling the need for some explanation for the situation in which the two women found themselves—she with a husband attached, "and I certainly would not have married Ed if I thought I had other options."

Sitting in that hospital room, day and night, Ruth had tried to sort and resort her sweetheart's troubled words around her concern for Ed.

'Why? Why her...almost-consuming...sense of responsibility for Ed? What is this? Could it still be from how she treated him almost sixty years ago? Is this guilt, or shame, or whatever it is going to remain until her very last breath?'

But at this point, regardless of the cause of Cassandra's distress, Ruth knew it was useless for her to try again to tell Cassandra not to worry.

On this final night in the hospital when it became clear that Cassandra would die soon, Ruth slipped away to make two calls. First she phoned Shirley, one of their neighbors, who had offered to help in any way she could.

"Shirley, it's Ruth. I'm at the hospital. They don't expect Cassandra to live through the night. Would you go over to the house and bring Ed to the hospital for me?"

"Of course, Ruth. Should I call him first?"

"No. I'll call him right now. He'll be expecting you. And thanks."

"Ruth, I'm so sorry. I love all of you so much."

"Thank you, Shirley. You've been such a good neighbor. I really appreciate it."

Then Ruth called Ed to let him know that Cassandra was slipping away and he probably should come. "Shirley will pick you up soon."

With Ed on his way, and Ruth back in the still darkness of the hospital room listening as Cassandra's breathing slowed even more, she sat thinking back over her life, Cassandra's and her life together. In her heart she could see Cassandra as she had first seen her decades ago, both of them young, moving toward one another and before long inseparable.

Earlier Cassandra, off in Chicago, had tried to create a life for herself far away from this small-town, Midwestern place, filled mostly with sky and, according to Cassandra, almost nothing else. Her plan didn't work; the Depression intervened and changed everything. It also brought Ruth's dear love back home, and eventually to her.

The women had loved each other and built a good life amid Cassandra's extended Taylor family, the Essex community, and their church friends. Yes, right here in the middle of this rural Kansas town, they had created a full life for the two of them, together. Now her sweetheart, Cassandra Taylor Thomas, lay dying. Yet, Ruth knew with sadness that, even after all these decades, her lover still missed and longed for the stimulation, glamour, and high life of the university and her wondrous city—Chicago. Cassandra had never hidden her feeling about that gaping hole in her life.

'Oh yes, we did have a good life together,' Ruth thought, her grieving mind softly running back and forward at the same time. In the face of Cassandra's dying, as she and Ed sat alone together in the hospital room that night, Ruth felt compelled to affirm it all.

While Ruth's thoughts consumed her, Ed had quietly slipped into the room and taken a seat on the other side of Cassandra's bed, now his head lowered and hands folded together in his lap as if in prayer. The two sat there together in silence through the nighttime hours, Ruth holding Cassandra's hand as her breathing slowly ebbed and finally stopped.

Death. A perfectly natural and amazing moment, one for which Ruth thought she had prepared, yet now it seemed almost unbelievable. Eventually acknowledging that Cassandra's breathing had stopped, Ruth stood, kissed her still-warm forehead, and gently closed her eyes. Then, while still not fully present in that room, off on her sad-hearted journey, Ruth turned to thinking, loving, and, yes, even smiling inwardly to herself, as she knowingly confessed.

'She's gone … gone from me. Yet, she never really was totally ours. And goodness knows, she surely never was totally mine.'

Yet in her heart, Ruth thought, 'But somehow I don't think I would change a thing even if we could start all over again.'

And then … regardless of Cassandra's worry, Ruth and Ed — as well as Cassandra — had known all along that following Cassandra's death, Ed and Ruth would go home together, and Ruth would take care of everything. However none of them probably had given any thought as to what others in their community might think of such an arrangement.

Four

The Truth

eanwhile, back in their homes after the funeral, stunned neighbors and family members remained puzzled about what Cassandra's son had said at the cemetery as feelings of discomfort blew through the community. Quietly, in twos or threes, they began to ask questions, now more curious and eager to know the truth about the Thomas-Peterson family.

"That guy was really angry! What's going to happen?" Toby asked his mother as he picked up his book and flopped onto the couch in the family room.

"Sweetie, don't pay it any mind. Most folks out there didn't even hear that. It's nothing."

"What?" Her husband stopped working to loosen his tie as disbelief spread across his face. "Do you really think what Taylor said won't make a difference?"

"I don't know, but for one thing, Ed seemed oblivious," she replied trying her best to stop this conversation in front of their young son.

"But what about Ruth?" he asked, unable to let go of it. "Don't you think she heard him? I saw her standing right there!"

"What if she did?" his wife replied, almost in a whisper. "What can she do about it?"

"Well, maybe we should be the ones doing something about it," her husband stated boldly.

"Like what?" now in her full, frustrated voice, totally ignoring their young son.

"Maybe speak to Ruth, try to see if we—or you, at least—if you can help her, let her know you care."

"But maybe the best way to help her would be to just keep quiet, to let it go," his wife continued. "I think those folks who did hear Taylor will soon forget this ever happened," she said, as she looked around, noticing Toby had left the room.

"Well, you actually know her better, knew both of them a lot better than I did. Maybe you're right, I need to let this go and quit worrying. But it felt more than awkward; you could have cut that air out there with a knife."

The public "event," and now the questions following it, set in motion ruminations rarely ventured about these three people, pushing folks to question their own memories about the two women, in particular. For most of them, Cassandra, Ed, and Ruth had shared a family household for longer than they could remember. These folks thought they knew this family well.

The musings around the community continued beneath the cover of a newly public but caring silence. Some wanted to take sides, yet the overriding social pressure had most of the town folk, especially Ruth and Cassandra's women friends, insisting, "Just let them be. They're good people. This will blow over soon enough."

However, the lid of curiosity had been lifted. Some newer folk began to ask what the old-timers remembered about how this all started way back when.

"George," Tim said to his buddy, sitting in the other chair at the barbershop. "How did all this come about anyway?"

"What are you talking about, Tim?"

"I know you're friends with Ed. Aren't you two in the city band together?"

"Oh, that," George said, "yesterday, at the cemetery," his voice belying his boredom with the topic. "Yes, I witnessed all the commotion."

"Did you know them before they all lived together? Where did they all come from anyway?"

"You sure are full of questions." George spoke wearied by it all. "I don't know all of it," he continued. "All I know is what everyone else around here knows, these three good people have been living together over there for decades. I don't even remember when I first realized they shared a home."

"But you did know that those two women were, ah ... shall I say ... living together?"

"Yes, everyone around here knows that, or at least may be thinking that."

"Really? Everyone knows?"

"Well, you know what I mean. It's that we all know these folks—Ed, Cassandra, and Ruth—like I said, good people. That's all. People around here don't really care." But then George could not totally resist. "You know, I might have been a bit curious early on, but I've known them for some time now and decided long ago this wasn't any of my business."

"Maybe you feel that way, but I hear tell some folks around here know a lot about where these people came from, and it's quite a story about all three of them!" Tim appeared intrigued by the whiff of a juicy story; however, for most, feelings of respect had surfaced by now.

"What differences can it make?" Shirley, the next-door neighbor, had said. "It seems to have worked. They've been great neighbors and good friends, all three of them."

And this. "Just think of all the contributions they've made to our community," Arthur, who had served on the school board with Cassandra, told his neighbor Ralph. "Why, we have that new high school because of Cassandra and Ruth. But I have to admit, I've never quite understood what goes on in that household."

Or this. "They've been together for decades; let sleeping dogs lie," overheard by Lillian in the grocery checkout line. She recognized the comment about her Aunt Cass and Ruth.

Many of their friends had merely asked, "How on earth could that son begin to think that everything would change with only this one death?"

A death has its way of bringing back stories languishing beneath the present moment, especially mostly forgotten stories that have become more like fiction. Some of the things people thought they knew about Cassandra and Ruth or about Ed and Cassandra lacked any basis in reality, yet some of what they didn't know had actually been there, right in front of them all along. Realizing this, these small-town folk sought to shake loose what they thought they knew from what they really did know, unearthing the half truths whirling around them all.

But stories about those who have gone before can be compelling. Probably few people knew how many threads made up the storied lives of these, their three friends — separately as well as together.

Cassandra Grace Taylor was born in 1903 in a rural farmhouse in southeastern Kansas just as winter set in at the farm and after a long, hard summer for her pregnant mother. Until Cassandra's arrival all of the first five children had been born to this pioneer family in a Nebraska sod house, but for Cassandra the Kansas farm would always be home.

Mr. and Mrs. Taylor, fourteen years apart in age, were miles apart in disposition. He, often gruff and feared by almost everyone, dominated the household, fiercely guarding his independence. She, a calm, submissive, faithful, and quietly competent wife and mother, knew well the hardscrabble life of a pioneer woman.

For Cassandra, family meant everything. The family matriarch at the time of her death in her nineties, she relished the title Aunt Cass perhaps more than those of mother and grandmother. Marriage or having children never interested her; however, Cassandra, the sixth child of seven, held a lifelong devotion toward her siblings and their offspring.

"I was brought up 'loosely,'" she said, boastful of her high sense of independence. "My younger brother Don and I terrorized our parents and siblings, and even the cows and chickens, as we romped to our delight all over the farm basically with not a lot of looking after, mostly because we could rarely be found and never corralled!"

With little affection for her deeply religious mother, Cassandra held the deepest respect and love for her father, who instilled within her the determination to live her life as she chose. "Never an easy child to raise," she would say, "I'm still not easy to manage. And I'm proud of it!"

To escape her mostly conservative Kansas upbringing, Cassandra, just before her eighteenth birthday, with her parents' reluctant agreement, ran off to Chicago and the university. She later asserted that, if her parents had had any idea of where and to what that train to Chicago would take her, her father would never have allowed it.

In Chicago, Cassandra knew for the first time what she had long suspected—that her early life had put boundaries on the possibilities she yearned for even as a young girl. Living among her new, brash, young women friends and lovers, Cassandra discovered a new freedom to be herself as she celebrated the gay urban culture, while at the same time stepping enthusiastically into a life of the mind. She lived as she had never lived before, relishing every moment, determined to live it fully.

Years later, once the euphoria of her Chicago days lay far behind—the economic depression of the late 1920s and 1930s changing lives, including hers—Cassandra's inclination to ruminate grew. Off and on, despair and a sense of failure would seep into her life as year after year the life she lived never quite seemed to add up to the one she thought she had found in Chicago.

Edward James Thomas was born in 1906, the son of a formerly aristocratic family and line of avant garde thinkers in New England. His father, a physician, became critical of traditional medicine and switched to chiropractic practice. His mother left her former life in upper-class society and her respected religious upbringing, becoming a convert to theosophy, a new marginal social movement that largely took her away from her husband and their children.

The marriage of these two highly independent, critical thinkers ended in divorce. The children were placed under the care of the maternal Grandmother Wright, in an early suburb of Chicago, while their mother traveled on behalf of her new movement.

The second child of eccentric parents, Ed gleaned from them a distinctive set of practices throughout his own long life. He rejected traditional medicine in favor of chiropractic care and took up a serious study of philosophical thinking as a critique of traditional Christianity. Having a highly individualized way of seeing and being in the world, Ed's controversial viewpoints eventually led to harsh family disagreements as his convert-like commitments would from time to time challenge the well-being of the household.

Ed slowed himself deliberately; a careful thinker, his unhurried demeanor could irritate those around him. People accused him of not being motivated, of lacking enthusiasm and the ability to get things done — all of which could have been true. However, Ed generally motivated himself, even if not in the ways others in his household desired.

As a young man, lacking resources for college, Ed found the intellectually stimulating University Church congregation next door to the University of Chicago his next-best option for thoughtful discourse. Once connected there, and continuously without work, he gladly accepted various part-time jobs that could be cobbled together for him at the church.

From the early 1920s, within the arms of his university-related congregation, Ed found a way of creating his life for more than a decade outside his own dysfunctional family. The congregation—its members, the university students and faculty who hung out at the church, and the staff, including the erudite pastor, Dr. Ames—became his family. There he found a place to think, belong, dance, eat, and work, surrounded by people he appreciated and enjoyed, seekers like himself.

Not known to initiate or provide leadership, Ed felt at home among people he respected, including the tall beauty, Cassandra Taylor, whom he admired for years, largely from a distance, and who proved herself quite able to initiate ideas for others, including Ed.

Ruth Peterson was born in 1910. No one knows for sure where her birth took place or under what circumstances. Brought from the East Coast to Kansas on one of the infamous Orphan Trains as a young child she landed in the county orphanage. She was adopted at the age of seven by the Peterson family of Essex, Kansas, dirt-poor farmers. The Peterson's had only one child, a nineteen-year-old son, Nate, who had not been to school, not married and was not likely to, and who worked the farm alongside his father. In those years this three-person Peterson family worked hard to make a meager living. Ruth felt convinced she had been adopted to provide someone to do the housework. She never balked at hard work after growing up saddled with long hours toiling on that farm.

Regardless of motives, the adoption proved to be a success for the child, for within this family Ruth was allowed to go to school. At this time, children of poor families like the Petersons at best completed sixth grade. However, with the support of her adoptive mother, Ruth managed to graduate. This successful step provided the seventeen-year-old with a country schoolteacher's contract for the coming year and the beginning of a long, successful teaching career.

In Ruth's early teaching years, while still a teenager, she faced the challenge of thirty (or more) students in all eight grades in her one-room rural schoolhouse, some of them older — or larger — than she. Teaching, work on the farm, and her church provided the central core of Ruth's early life. After her daily morning barn chores, on Sunday she looked forward to catching up with the young women she found at the church in town. Many of the women Ruth came to know were, of course, looking for available men. Marriage had never interested her. Instead Ruth intended to build a life for herself as a teacher and have the freedom to live her life as she chose.

As a young woman, Ruth faced a constant need to fix things for which there was little time, money, or know-how, whether at home, in the schoolhouse, or in public education. She came to be respected as a person with tenacity; a can-do woman willing to march into almost any setting and make things happen.

The shy, young orphan did come into her own as a talented and beloved teacher, a woman of stature in her community and, if grudgingly, within her traditionally male-dominated church. But she sorely missed having a real family. With elderly parents and no relatives other than the older brother, being a teacher and part of her small-town community had to provide for her what having a family might do for others.

And then Cassandra came back home from Chicago and within a few years moved to Essex with all her openness to life, and to Ruth as well.

Five

The Dead End

n the early 1920s, the city of Chicago bustled with commerce and trade, on the brink of becoming the major metropolitan hub of the Midwest. Riding a similar wave, the University of Chicago, with its growing academic acclaim and social prestige, helped to draw top students from around the country, including the bright and precocious Cassandra Taylor from the rural farmlands of Kansas.

Cassandra fell in love with the university and the big city. She easily immersed herself in her classes and the community of risqué women in her Hyde Park neighborhood. Given permission to question just about everything, Cassandra soared.

It was a heady time for young women like Cassandra flocking to Chicago where the suffrage movement had thrived. While many of her new college girlfriends had been involved in the movement, she had found little interest among the women back home and especially her mother.

"No one likely cares what I think," Cassandra remembered her mother saying when she asked her about women voting, something she heard about at school. "I don't think it says anything in the Bible about women being in charge. It's foolish. I don't have time to think about going a-voting. I've more than enough to do right here."

However, Cassandra did not consider it foolish to work for women to gain basic rights. Now, at the university she was drawn deeply into questions about the role of women in every facet of life. In fact, Cassandra's growing sense of her own identity came not only from her new women friends but also from her university studies where she discovered strong critiques regarding the traditional practice of placing social restrictions on roles for women within Christianity.

But upon graduation, as Cassandra sought a position in the workforce, the only options she could locate were in offices as a low-paid typist. Deflated as she returned from job interviews, Cassandra, who had refused to take typing in high school, found herself hobbled.

"Did you get the job?" Maggie asked.

"No, and I don't care. I'm not the least bit interested in working away on a typewriter in some man's office," she had asserted. "I wouldn't be any good at being a nurse or public school teacher either, or any of those so-called women's occupations, even if I were interested, which I am not."

She would soon find out her degree in Christian Education would not open doors, other than being the church secretary, a position she already held on a part-time basis in her own Hyde Park congregation — which did not require her to type.

As she and her women friends had lined up in caps and gowns to receive their diplomas, instead of a sense of accomplishment, Cassandra felt dismay. Her friends seemed at least to have options, even if merely going back home. However, Cassandra had moved far past her upbringing on the family farm and in the rural church.

"Me? Back home? Now, after this? Why I'd feel trapped, like being hogtied to an old fence post!" Desperation rang in her voice as she talked with her sweetheart, Maggie, begging her to stay.

Finally, when Maggie told Cassandra she wasn't going to stay in Chicago with her, she felt defeated, even while Maggie tried to explain her decision. "Cassandra, I can't make any money writing. I'm just starting out. It will take years. It's clear you can't make enough to support yourself, let alone the two of us. Besides that, my parents wouldn't allow it. They expect me to return home."

Sad and puzzled, Cassandra thought to herself, 'Surely my parents will not expect me to run back home.'

Early in her life, Cassandra's family had learned to expect her to do what she wanted to do. During her years in Chicago, Cassandra had honed more fully, if unrealistically, her hopes and dreams. She wanted a life lived among intellectually engaged and personally exhilarating women, and in a big city like Chicago. There would be no returning home for Cassandra.

Maggie returned home, along with many others. While focused on what she had had during her college years, Cassandra had failed to notice that her life would never be the same once her cohort of women friends departed. Melancholy filled her days. As a young student, she had come to love the gay, flapper-girl life among her new, raucous women friends dashing into the city to see shows and running to campus meeting halls for women's gatherings. But now what?

While having a vision of what she wanted in her life, she had to face the question of how to get there from where she stood. Creating a life could no longer be merely an abstract idea.

Monday

Dear Peg,

Maggie wrote that you have found a job in New York. Are the women you are living with as interesting as our crowd here on Woodlawn Ave? But how could that be!

As for me, I'm still here and still looking for a 'real' job, but there is nothing around here for a woman interested in questions about the meaning of life! Still working at the church, thank goodness. But what I make there, even if I am enjoying the work, doesn't really cover my rent. So I have to find something else and soon I fear.

Give my love to Bobby, if the two of you are still together. Maggie seemed to think that you gals are doing well as a couple. I hope so.

Love,
Cass

While missing her girlfriends, Cassandra moved faint-heartedly through her days. The meager pay from her part-time job at University Church helped while she continued to share rented rooms with a shifting set of younger women students.

At the church that winter, she was asked to add to her present secretarial duties assisting the cook in planning and preparing the congregation's traditional weekly Friday evening and Sunday noon meals. But, of course, Cassandra knew almost nothing about meal planning, let alone cooking.

✤   ✤   ✤

From an early age, Cassandra had laid out a careful plan to stay out of the kitchen. Daily, she found myriad reasons to remain after school: offer to clean the blackboards, pound the erasers clean on the stone wall outside, or help out in the small school library. "I wanted to live in that library!" Cassandra often remarked, "Definitely not in the kitchen back home!"

When back home at the farm, Cassandra also had strategies for avoiding kitchen work. "I had a favorite tree, an old bur oak, where a lovely set of limbs provided a good hiding place. I'd drop my book down the front of my pinafore (held tight there by my bosom), tuck my skirts into my drawers, and climb up there and read until dark."

And ignore repeated calls on warm evenings from the back porch …

"Oh, C AH A – SSANNNN - N - D R A A A A - AH!"

If the weather was too cold or rainy, Cassandra made for her hidden attic corner, just below a vent that provided enough light for reading, propping herself up against an old trunk—with her coat on if necessary.

"Where is that girl?!" she could hear her mother's voice on the porch or from downstairs. By hook or crook, Cassandra met her goal. She managed to leave home at age seventeen, having spent hardly any time in a kitchen.

Nonetheless, with time on her hands and need for more income, Cassandra took on the expanding job in the church kitchen and discovered, much to her surprise, that she enjoyed meal planning and cooking for a large crowd. The longtime cook, Mrs. Nelson, had aroused her curiosity about every aspect of meal preparation.

Over time, Mrs. Nelson came to rely on Cassandra's help with meal planning, ordering supplies, and, increasingly, more of the cooking. After about a year, her mentor retired and Cassandra assumed full responsibility for the meal program, while continuing to be church secretary.

Soon Cassandra also needed an assistant in the kitchen. Several young people hung around the church, often looking for work, including Ed Thomas, the part-time janitor. "I wonder," Cassandra said in conversation with the church pastor, "if Ed might like to help me in the kitchen? What do you think?"

"Well, he really seems to enjoy hanging around here. He has proven to be a reliable worker and I know he could use the extra income. Ask him. See what he says."

That afternoon, Cassandra found Ed cleaning the floor in the sanctuary and mentioned her need for some help in the kitchen.

"Do you think you might enjoy making bread?"

"Well, I guess so," Ed replied, his forehead wrinkled in thought, "but someone would have to teach me how to do it."

Ed easily picked up the tricks of working with yeast bread and also appeared to enjoy it. Cassandra taught him to make various kinds of bread and eventually all kinds of desserts, exactly as Mrs. Nelson had taught her. However, while Ed proved a reliable helper in the kitchen, the young woman remained totally unaware of the source of Ed's enthusiasm for his new work assignment.

Soon, through her management of the kitchen, Cassandra had discovered two special things: her talent for quantity cooking and her ease with being in charge.

As for Ed, he seemed totally willing for her to be in charge of him.

Enjoying the two part-time jobs at the church, Cassandra began to think she might be able to manage the transition from student to that of resident worker in her Chicago neighborhood, but even with the increase in salary, the income proved insufficient.

Still grieving the loss of her girlfriends, Cassandra had no idea of the depth of their concern at leaving her behind. Unimpressed with her hard work for low pay at the church, they urgently wrote back and forth behind her back. Peg and Bobby in New York City and Maggie in northern Michigan shared a growing fear of Cassandra stuck in the old neighborhood. They knew this would not serve her well in the long run. During the course of the years since the girls had scattered, several schemes to get her out of Chicago had failed. But this group of women did not give up easily.

Wednesday

Dear Cass,

I just heard of a job opening that I think might fit you well. There's a small church college with a job opening up in my neck of the woods ... a bit to the west from my place. I think you should come up here and have a

look. I could meet you there; we could have a short visit.
Missing you too!

Love,
Maggie

In the spring of 1928, Cassandra agreed to the travel to northern Michigan only because she yearned to see Maggie.

However, this effort paid off. The following July, she received an offer for a job in Collingwood. The college needed a woman to act as assistant dean of women students and to plan meals and oversee the student dining hall. The job did not pay much but would provide room and board. As a dean, Cassandra would live in the dorm among the young female students.

Soon her friend Maggie wrote ...

"So, are you going to take the job in Collingwood? I
know it isn't the best job in the world for you, but jobs
for women like us are very few it seems. At least it is
a full-time job and you will have housing provided ...
and you will almost be in my neighborhood."

Cassandra wrote back:

"Yes, Maggie, I've sent in my acceptance letter. Now
I just need to get myself organized for the train trip
up there early next month. And I don't know which
will be worse ... knowing that you are there in the
north woods while I've been here in Chicago without
you, or knowing you are way up there when I am in
Collingwood ... still many miles apart!"

Finally Cassandra reluctantly moved on. She had hung on to Chicago, yearning to hold on to what she had experienced there since her arrival years earlier. Even though she would in her later years refer to herself as a "wanderer," in truth, Cassandra never really wanted to wander anywhere other than back to Chicago.

Cassandra's next three years at the small college in the rural northern Michigan town were bone hard. She missed her vibrant University of Chicago neighborhood and the glamorous urban scene. In Collingwood, she found life at the small college and surrounding rural community harsh. But little did she know that first winter just how jarring life could become.

In October 1929, following her first full year in Collingwood, the shock arrived. With the stock market crash, the tiny world of Collingwood, Michigan, came to a standstill, and then began to plummet, spiraling downward to far below anything that Cassandra could have imagined. As the already fragile local economy diminished drastically, basic necessities, including food, became scarce.

While suddenly faced with serious constraints to providing food for so many, Cassandra stepped forward as a judicious planner and resolved there would always be something to eat on her dining-room tables. In the fall she begged at nearby farms for leftover corn, in the spring for spoiling vegetables, and in the summer, for fallen, partially spoiled fruit from the orchards. "The students may not have had fully nutritious meals but no one starved," she related years later, with tears in her eyes. Cassandra's years in Collingwood taught her much about the possible cruelty in life.

However, living in the women's dorm provided the opportunity for friendships. She developed a close relationship with

Alice, the dean of students, who lived next door, their dorm rooms joined by an inside door. As their friendship deepened, Alice and Cassandra created a small suite by leaving the door open between their rooms allowing for a closer and pleasant relationship to develop.

After three years, Cassandra and Alice both left at the end of the spring semester, with some suggesting their departures resulted from a perhaps inappropriate relationship. However, Cassandra, while declaring her love for her friend, told Maggie, "I just cannot live any longer in such an isolated place."

Cassandra moved to Milwaukee where she had found a temporary job in the kitchen at a group home for children. However, when the job ended, in desperation Cassandra moved back to her family home in Kansas. She found a job working as the matron for the high school girls in the Wichita orphanage, where she also had responsibility for the dining room in the children's side of the home.

"The work was something I felt I knew how to do; however, my heart was never in it, nor in being back home," Cassandra confessed to Maggie, still far away in Michigan. As a woman in her late twenties, used to being on her own, and longing for a much different environment, she felt lost.

Rural Kansas could no longer hold her, and within the year she fled back to Chicago, renting a tiny, shared apartment in the old university neighborhood. Taking up her relationship with the University Church and her beloved pastor, Dr. Ames, Cassandra went back to work in the church kitchen. The community meal had become the local soup kitchen for the needy in the formerly thriving Hyde Park neighborhood.

Cassandra was well-prepared for her new challenge providing meals under the devastating economic conditions on

Chicago's south side. A creative genius at stretching supplies, Cassandra found her way by making everything from scratch. She used seasonings to vary the monotony of dishes like creamed hard-boiled eggs on toast, or potato soup made with water instead of milk, which she served with butter and sugar sandwiches.

Bread made by Ed Thomas had become the staple of almost every meal. Ed had remained in the church kitchen making bread as Cassandra had taught him years ago. By now he could make bread with almost anything: oatmeal and lard, or ground wheat with water and salt, or from corn meal, a bit of lard, and the water used to cook the beans.

Ed could not have been happier to welcome Cassandra's return to take charge in the kitchen.

Cassandra eventually found a second part-time position in downtown Chicago at Marshall Field's department store, where she became a hostess in the famous Marshall Field's Tea Room. With two part-time jobs and still not enough income, she lived off leftover food brought home from her days of work at the tea room and the church soup kitchen.

For someone who had experience working with food in various kinds of settings, Cassandra stood in awe of the famous tea room, filled with elegance in every way. She had discovered that she enjoyed planning and preparing food for large numbers of people, but this fancy tea room took her breath away. She easily began to feel right at home amid luxury beyond anything she had experienced.

Cassandra had returned to Chicago, yet, bereft of her former life, spent her time working for little pay, managing her meager resources, and adapting to rotating roommates in her small, two-room flat. The old days of frivolity and wild parties, dressing up and going out dancing with her girlfriends—all far behind her.

"Without much of anything other than work in my everyday life," Cassandra recalled when talking with her daughter-in-law, Margaret, one day, "I fear I spent most of my days, and nights, dreaming about that glorious downtown tea room. I was enthralled with the carefully prepared delicacies being delivered to the tables for the women who dined there. Those were not my best years, but at least I lived in Chicago, partaking—in a small way—of some of the delights of the city."

During this downturn in Cassandra's life, Ed Thomas finally expressed his interest in being a suitor. He seemed friendly and a bit different from other men she knew, something she couldn't decide if was in his favor or not. He did seem to have a mind and enjoyed using it. Importantly they shared some intellectual critiques of contemporary religion by their mentor and pastor, Dr. Ames. Other than Dr. Ames, Ed had become the only tie, however loose, to her former halcyon days in Hyde Park. Although he was never part of her circle of friends, Cassandra saw Ed as part of the landscape for which she yearned.

"Cassandra," Ed said, clearing his throat, "would you be interested in taking a walk this afternoon during our break in the kitchen? It's a very nice day."

"Not today. Perhaps another time. Today I want to go over the figures for the budget and plan my order for tomorrow."

But when Ed suggested on a later day that they plan an outing to the local park, taking a lunch basket they could prepare in the kitchen, Cassandra saw an opportunity. The picnic didn't interest her but something else did. She took the opening to make a counterproposal.

"I have an idea. I've never been a guest downtown at the tea room. I think that would be fun. Maybe one day next week we could do that when we are not scheduled to prepare a meal, and I have my day off downtown."

"Well, now, that sounds just fine," Ed said.

Eagerly Ed agreed to her plan. Finally he would have an afternoon with Cassandra fulfilling a long-held hope to have time alone with her. He really didn't care where they went as long as they went together.

The following week, on their day off, Cassandra put on one of her best dresses, hat and gloves, and took the "L" train into Chicago with Ed. Upon their arrival, she suggested a walk from the Loop over to the lakeside before they went for tea.

The cool breeze off the water felt good on that early spring afternoon to Cassandra who spent too much time in a basement kitchen over hot stoves. Ed knew this lakefront from his childhood, but Cassandra had grown up far from water, other than the small ponds that would pool up in the creek after a rain. She craved a real lake.

'Ah, this must be what an ocean looks like,' she thought to herself, as the lake disappeared into the far, low horizon.

'Oh, if I could only take hold of her hand!' Ed thought, his desire for her rising to new heights … 'or maybe sit on that bench over there, close enough that our bodies would actually touch!' Perhaps feeling more flustered than he expected, he moved to his fallback position — conversation about religion.

"What did you think of Dr. Ames' sermon on Sunday?" Ed began, energetically. "It really made me think we don't really follow the Jesus of the Bible as a model for our everyday lives."

"Oh, I don't know ... I have no idea how someone would decide what that might be or look like." Cassandra spoke in a lazy fashion, more interested in watching the waves on the lake; "And you know, I'm not sure there was such a person—Jesus 'of the Bible,'" she said, as she tried to hide a yawn.

But when she noticed the look on Ed's face, Cassandra took a more definitive stance. "But I do think Dr. Ames is exactly right pointing to all the silly rules church folks have made up, rules about what people can and can't do—especially on a Sunday. Ridiculous!" That was more than she had said all afternoon.

However, no heresy in her words for Ed; in fact, Cassandra's strong feelings fascinated him. She impressed him by how easily she expressed herself, and he loved her even more at that moment.

Their conversation continued over afternoon tea in Cassandra's famous tea room. Ed, buoyed by the opportunity to discuss his thoughts about Professor Ames' controversial ideas, might have missed noting her primary focus on the tea room, instead of the conversation—or him.

Undaunted, Ed continued, "I've just read what Professor Ames says about the church's wrong-headed prohibitions regarding dancing. Do you agree?"

"Well of course," Cassandra, suddenly back in the conversation, concurred. "Dancing, not dancing, has nothing to do with religion. Some folks just got it in their heads that dancing wasn't proper. Ludicrous!"

"Oh yes, indeed." Ed responded with uncharacteristic energy. "I'm glad we have dancing for the young folks at church on Sunday evenings. I think dancing can be extremely healthy."

"Well, of course dancing is healthy." Cassandra almost spit out the words showing her disgust for such silliness. "Even on

Sundays!" She raised her volume while thinking how absurd it was, "It's amazing what some people get all fussed up about. Well, anyway, dancing has certainly never bothered me. I'm just not any good at it," she offered naively, having no idea how Ed might have steered the conversation.

"So is that why you generally stay in the kitchen during the social times at the church?" Ed asked.

Then Cassandra did not really know what to say. He obviously had noticed she never wandered out to the dance floor.

He broke into her thoughts. "Because if you don't know how to dance, I'd be pleased to teach you."

Later, they would dance together once or twice on a Sunday evening in the church basement as part of their work preparing the meal for the young adult group. She enjoyed it, but it would never hold the delight that it held for Ed. Her attention was given primarily to the food table and overseeing the kitchen cleanup crew. Cassandra had early on determined that no germs would lurk in her kitchen.

It was the following late fall when the soon-to-be-infamous letter arrived from one of Cassandra's sisters back home telling her of an opportunity for a job in Halton, a few miles west of the old family farm.

Saturday

Dear Cass,

I hope you are well and still have that good job you like so much in Chicago. Seems like I never have the time to write, but we do think about you most every day and hope you are doing good. Letter writing is *not what I like to do but all of us have been talking about something going on here we want you to know. Remember the old hotel at the corner of Main and the highway? Well, that is what we want to tell you about. It got sold not long ago. The man that bought it wants somebody to buy the dining room in there. Last time we were in town and picked up a newspaper and I saw this little ad about it. I will put it in this letter. When you read about the $75, don't worry so much. Not that $75 isn't a lot of money. But Mama says she could pay that for you. It looks like they want a married couple but maybe you could talk with this person. At least you would get a place to work, a place to live, and your own food. Now that's a real job isn't it? Anyway, like I said, we been talking and talking about this and I just thought your ears might be burning and you would not even know why.*

Your lovin' sis,
Pauline

Cassandra knew that hotel and its dining room. Her mind set to thinking, 'Yes, at the most important intersection in the heart of town ... could surely draw customers easily at that location.'

And then, a question came to her mind, 'Hmmm-m ... interesting ... wonder why the man who bought the hotel doesn't want to own the dining room?'

And, of course, Cassandra did not have $75, and her mother knew it. But the fact that the job in the dining room meant the owner could live rent free, she found compelling.

Then she read further "… for the couple who bought the business," and slapped her hand to her forehead.

'Of course! The job isn't for just a woman with the skills to cook and manage a dining room—someone like me, obviously. It's for a married couple.' Disappointment overwhelmed her as she read on, noticing how the advertisement lined out who would do what: "the wife to manage the kitchen and the husband to be the janitor for the hotel lobby and hallways as well as assisting in the dining room," as she finished the sentence in the ad angrily, "blah, blah, blah!"

But after a deep breath, she thought, 'Well, Cassandra Taylor this is the world you live in. Guess you'd better get used to it.'

She could picture the old hotel and its dining room, remembered having eaten there on some special family occasion. One of the few places to eat out in Halton, it had a captive dining clientele among those living in the hotel.

But then her mind took a turn to another quite different thought. Having come to love the tea room at Marshall Field's, Cassandra drifted into a dream …

'Maybe, just maybe I could find a way out from this dead-end life of mine. Maybe … just maybe … I could own and operate a tea room.'

'Yes. Yes, that just might work,' she said to herself as she crawled into bed. Tired from a long day, she finally gave into dozing off to sleep, with her last thoughts … about a tea room of her very own.

Six

The Compromise

ndeed, that next morning, Cassandra sat at her desk at the church office dreaming of her own tea room and the one maddening impediment: 'The simple-minded hotel owner thinks he needs a married couple.'

The gentle knock on the partially opened door brought her out of her daydreaming as Ed stuck his head in wanting to know if the oatmeal had arrived. "I've got time this morning to put down some yeast bread for the evening meal," he said.

"Oh yes, of course. Yesterday's order is right there, Ed; the oatmeal's in that first box. Sorry. I'm a bit distracted this morning. Go ahead and take the two boxes down. I'll bring the rest and help sort it out. I did post the menu for today on the bulletin board before I left yesterday."

"Yes, I saw that. Okay, I'll look for you later then," he said giving her a big smile as he gathered the supplies.

'Okay,' she said to herself, skipping right over Ed's brief interruption. 'So … it really has to be a married couple? Tarnation.'

Chafing, she couldn't turn off her mind. 'That tea room is perfect for me … and if it has to be in Kansas, so be it. And if I have to have a partner,' her thoughts continued, '… well, I'll have to figure this out.'

But she had work to do. "Oh, my goodness, the morning is slipping away. This'll have to wait," Cassandra said to no one as she stood, picked up the large sack of flour, and headed for the stairs, while her anger at the advertisement walked with her down the steps and into the kitchen.

Later that evening, exhausted from a long day at work, Cassandra sat on her bed to remove her shoes and rub her sore feet. Even as she thought of the full day she and Ed had shared in the church kitchen, her mind struggled on with her personal dilemma when suddenly, startled by her thoughts, she sat bolt upright.

'Ed … what about Ed as a partner to this venture? Why didn't I think of Ed?' For Cassandra, it was a bold and disturbing question, but she had stumbled upon something right before her all this time: Ed Thomas.

'Ed does janitorial work and provides excellent help in the kitchen. And,' she said to herself with a sigh, 'he also meets the requirement for a husband. And,' with dismay she continued, 'it's also true, this man has already professed interest in me, obviously quite a bit more than my interest in him, but he is a good worker and a kind person—everyone likes Ed Thomas.'

Cassandra, unexpectedly in need a "suitor," suddenly realized she already had one, standing next to her in the church kitchen every day.

'I have absolutely no doubt I, or the two of us if it has to be that, can manage this job, have a place to live and our meals, plus if we're careful and work hard, earn some income.'

After all her agonizing to find a possible way forward, and now thinking she may have found one, she still felt conflicted. Something held her back. She lay awake that night, puzzled by feelings she could not name.

'Am I afraid? Afraid of what? Of getting married? Why would that be? Nothing really needs to change all that much ... we get married, move to Kansas, have a job, not unlike the jobs we have here.'

But fear, uniquely uncomfortable territory for Cassandra, had put her at odds with herself. Bound up by her past as well as her dreams, she tried to acknowledge a growing suspicion that the thought of marriage itself frightened her. Yet, continuing to resist, she felt compelled to question such a thought.

'Why would getting married unnerve me so? It's a logical plan, and it could work,' she struggled to convince herself. However, in the long, dark hours of the night, fear and hard questions continued to pour out of her.

'Can I really do this?' she asked.

'Of course, I can!' she answered, attempting to hold on. 'But ... should I do this? I've never thought I'd marry. Would marriage really work for me? And what about Ed? Could such an arrangement work for him? What would he expect?'

Cassandra's efforts to make up answers to such questions quickly became rather messy in her mind.

'Am I interested in sex with him? No.'

'Do I want to have children? Definitely not.'

'Am I interested in his crazy family? Not really.' These along with all the other things she did not want to talk about with him seemed only to draw the contours of the dilemma even more tightly around her.

Finally, she could feel herself painfully caving in, "Oh I've got to stop this!" she said as she broke into a sob. Feeling disoriented, her body grew heavy, paralyzed by the anguish she felt in facing such a choice, feeling forced to compromise herself and others—especially Ed.

As the flood of worries continued to sweep over her, she stood and paced the floor in her small room. "Maybe I can't leave Chicago! I've tried before; it doesn't work, because I don't want to leave. And especially not to go back home—with a man. No, God forbid, with a husband and my old girlfriends thinking I've lost my mind."

"Maybe I am losing my mind," she cried out, as she dropped onto the bed, bent double, sobbing while holding her shaking head in her hands.

But finally, feeling she had passed through her "valley of the shadow of death," she stretched to get hold of herself, got up to find her hanky and blow her nose. Calmer, she walked over to the window in her still, dark room. While quiet tears fell down her face, she leaned against the window frame.

"I feel so alone," she whispered to herself. Watching the dim, flickering glow from the single lamppost below on the empty street, Cassandra, surrounded by sheer silence, found her mind clearing.

'I am running in circles. I must get myself off this awful merry-go-round of figuring out my life … and right now I'm not sure I have any other choice but to take this job. And to do that I will need Ed Thomas.'

Finally, realizing she had made a decision, she did not waver again. She knew Ed would arrive early in the morning to put down the dough for the day's bread. She would meet him there as he came in, tell him about this opportunity, and they could talk about it together. She would find out how he might take to the idea of sharing the job in Kansas.

That was it; her choice made. She would not lose any more time.

Early the next morning, without a moment of sleep, she arrived in the kitchen just ahead of Ed.

"Well, this is a surprise," Ed said as he smiled, pleased to see her. "You are here awfully early, Cassandra, but it's nice to see you."

"I wanted to talk with you about something. My sister sent a notice from the paper about a job she thinks I and a friend might share. Here," she said, handing Ed the clipping.

But she did not give him a chance to say anything or look at the advertisement.

"It's a hotel dining room in Halton, Kansas. It's for sale. It would cost $75 but Mother is offering to pay that. Look at what they want. It reads like what the two of us already do—or almost. Plan menus, cook, serve, keep the place clean."

"And," she continued almost without taking a breath, "look there closely, do you see? Right here," as she leaned toward Ed, pointing to the advertisement. "We would have our own tea room."

Who cared that the ad did not actually say "tea room?" Cassandra could already see it in her mind exactly as she saw the beautiful downtown Marshall Field's Tea Room. Tired of struggling to make her life work—and failing—she decided to do something about it. Maybe this opportunity to follow a new dream might work. She paused, but again not long enough for Ed to speak.

As for Ed, he alternated between looking at the beautiful woman before him and at what she had placed in his hand.

He could see her clearly, but his mind seemed to be whirling so that he could not make out a word in the advertisement. He had, in fact, given up trying, far more interested in merely watching Cassandra and listening to her voice.

"There are some issues that would have to be solved. But here's the point. If we take on this job we know we can manage, we would have a tea room of our own, could make a real living, and have a place to live. All we would have to do is move to Kansas."

Here Cassandra paused, but only briefly.

"Except, there is one other thing that seems to be a condition of employment. This job is for a married couple. We would have to get married."

There. She had said it.

Suddenly she felt there was nothing left for her to say. She did not speak, but her mind and thoughts had not stopped. 'I can only hope he sees this is a business proposition,' she said to herself, hoping to bolster her own concerns, 'and at a time when neither of us seem to have any other good options,' something she was still angry about, she realized.

She waited, nervously, to see what he would say.

'What?' Ed could hardly believe his ears. 'Did Cassandra say what I think she said?' he asked himself. '… the two of us getting married?' This startling turn of events had Ed's eyes opened a bit wider, but her proposal, or whatever it was, sounded fine to him.

"Well, Cassandra, this sounds, ah, really … well, actually … sounds just fine to me." He paused, trying to think of how or if he might try saying what was in his heart.

"Cassandra, you're a smart and hard-working woman, and I am very fond of you. I think we make a good team. I guess

I really don't care where we live. Never thought of living in Kansas. Well, of course, I've never been there, but I'm willing to go with you."

"Well, that's settled then," Cassandra said and turned on her heel to go back to her office. "I'll write a note to Mother to let her know we'll buy the dining room and take the job."

As she left the kitchen, throwing these few words back over her shoulder, Ed stood still. Then he began to look around the room as if trying to recall how and why he had come to be standing there. Finally, shaking his head, he found his apron, put it on, and turned to making the bread dough, still a bit puzzled and wondering exactly what Cassandra, off in her office, might be writing to her mother.

No puzzlement in Cassandra's office, however.

Tuesday

Mama, tell the man that we will buy the Dining Room. Ed and I have talked about it and are willing to take this on. Thank you for offering to pay the cost. That makes this possible. Let me know when he wants us to arrive in Halton. When I know this, we will begin to make our plans.

Your daughter,
Cassandra

Given this bold opening by Cassandra, she and Ed would find themselves together more than before as they began to think about and make plans for the approaching move to Kansas.

Filled with her growing dream of the tea room, she spent a lot more time observing closely everything about the Marshall Field's Tea Room. Eventually she told one of the cooks about her plans, and the woman happily shared even more of the tea room's secret recipes. Cassandra buried herself in making plans.

As for Ed, his mind was filled with a dream of Cassandra as his wife, without any real curiosity about Kansas, her family, or the old hotel in Halton. An amorous man who had waited years for such a moment now dreamed day and night of holding this woman in his arms. Yet with his now heightened desires, Ed still could only hope for a small kiss at the door when he walked Cassandra home after work. His thoughts of philosophical conversation had slipped away; Ed looked toward the promise of their wedding day.

Within a few months, without the benefit of what might be called romantic moments, Cassandra and Ed married early one Friday afternoon in a tiny chapel adjoining their church. Dr. Ames officiated, the church organist played, and church soloist sang for the small gathering. There were a few friends from the church and Ed's younger sister and brother who came with Grandmother Wright, to the ceremony.

Mrs. Wright paid for the catered meal attended by those at the wedding and managed by members of the congregation. As the celebration ended, the bride and groom were delivered to a downtown hotel by a friend who had an auto. Cassandra had taken special care to select the best hotel, one famous for the dining rooms.

The Stevens Hotel, built right before the stock market crash and feted as the largest and best hotel anywhere around the globe, filled an entire city block in the heart of Chicago. All three thousand rooms had private baths and the several restaurants within the hotel vied for guests' differing tastes. However, by now, the hotel was failing, much of its former glamour lost on many, but not Cassandra. She had heard of their famous dining rooms and wanted to be there to explore possibilities for her own restaurant-to-be in Halton, Kansas.

The newlyweds spent a first, rather awkward night together in their hotel bed. Ed, so eager for the lovemaking he had dreamed of, was caught for a moment by Cassandra's passionless compliance. In his accommodating manner, Ed told himself it was their lack of experience, thinking, 'I'll need to give her time to become comfortable with our being together.'

Early the next morning, after breakfast in one of the famous hotel dining rooms, they left, but not before Cassandra had tucked the menu carefully in her purse. They took the "L" train back to the university district, where they would share her room—and bed—in the small, apartment, along with Cassandra's female roommate. And the two of them went back to work. Within a few months, they made their way to Kansas in an old car, pulling a small trailer, with their few worldly possessions.

Upon their arrival, the couple received a joyous welcome. On a beautiful spring afternoon, the Taylor family gathered for a picnic to celebrate the newcomer, Aunt Cass's husband. Ed, naturally gregarious, enjoyed the gathering and especially the food prepared by the women. He soon discovered these rural folks had gardens and raised chickens, so despite the Depression and longtime drought, he experienced a feeling of plenty around the family table. He hardly knew where to begin. There were piles of fried chicken, many vegetable Jell-o salads, and bowls heaped with potato and egg salad, plus homemade bread and cakes of every kind—and homemade ice cream to put on top! Right away, Ed began to feel at home within Cassandra's large Taylor family.

However, it was with far less enthusiasm that Cassandra and Ed had taken a first look at their new home and workplace. For the first time in Cassandra's daydreaming about this job and her tea room, reality raised its ugly face. The old building with its small, bare dining room jolted her. The room's only promising feature, the several windows wrapping the corner of the building, were large, but covered with old paint and years of grime. And the much smaller attached room, the kitchen, depressed her beyond words.

With a deep sigh, Cassandra turned and in her strong voice said, "Well, let's get started fixing up this mess! We have customers waiting for the dining room to reopen."

So with that, Cassandra put on an apron and took charge of putting her new kitchen into shape for the work ahead. The next day she started cooking for the men who lived in the hotel as best she could.

A lover of books and ideas, Cassandra, a graduate of the University of Chicago, now prepared to become the breadwinner for her family. Having learned to enjoy working with food, and given her natural inclination to industriousness, she eagerly took to creating a successful dining room in her small Kansas town.

In the early winter of 1936, south-central Kansas continued dry and dusty from the long drought as wheat farmers just to the west of Halton struggled to survive. Yet jobs for migrant workers were available in the local refineries around Halton, as the demand for gasoline increased, given the talk of war in Europe. Many refinery workers lived in the Halton hotel and took their meals in Cassandra's dining room. This meant she and Ed had hard, steady work, and, as she had planned, food to eat and a place to live.

"My goodness. How those men can eat." Cassandra would exclaim, even while she enjoyed the challenge of filling them up with good-tasting food after their long, hard day's work. "Every day I make great amounts of mashed potatoes and gravy for the men to pour over big slices of homemade bread, regardless of what else I serve," she told her mother.

She took charge of the dining room, planned menus, and did most of the cooking while searching for economical ways to purchase the supplies she needed. Ed cleaned the hotel lobby and hallways, including their own one-room apartment at the end of the first floor hallway. He also worked hard getting the dining room cleaned and the windows scraped and washed, and he assisted Cassandra in baking the bread and making desserts.

When Cassandra's father passed away not long after they had arrived, she moved her mother into the hotel room next door to theirs. Along with her mother's support in the kitchen, and occasional help in the dining room from her older sisters and nieces, they were beginning to eke out a small living. But it took hard labor and long hours, and even then, there was need for more income.

In an effort to meet her financial needs, Cassandra created a catering business for local and area dinner parties, adding greatly to her weekly workload. Cassandra's new friend, Ruth, began to drive over from Essex now and then at the end of her teaching day to help in the kitchen.

"Ruth. Oh, the days she would turn up, what a godsend!" Cassandra reminisced years later with Margaret, almost in tears. "She brought critical help on many days."

Continually exhausted, Cassandra and Ed were grateful for the little hotel room down the hall. There they would fall into bed late at night only to rise in the dark, early morning hours to put down more bread and make other preparations for the day ahead.

The couple's exhaustion, as they fell into bed together, was often compounded by Ed's slowly formed, frustrated passion. "Cassandra, my dear," Ed said as he gently massaged her shoulder and back, "I know you work hard all day but I can't tell you how often I look forward to holding you when we come together as we are now ... and how difficult it is when you push me away, refuse my desire to comfort you in our lovemaking."

"I'm sorry Ed," she said as she turned to look at him, "but I just do not have much strength by the end of my long days of work." She paused, then continued, "I'll try to be more respectful of your needs, but tonight I need to rest." As she turned back to face the wall, she added, "By the way that cake you made today was lovely. The men really enjoyed it."

In the spring of 1938, Cassandra faced a new, private crisis. Devastated by the discovery of her pregnancy, she suffered while trying to think it through by herself. 'I've never wanted to have a baby ... and now I certainly can't have one! I have to work, be up and on my feet long hours every single day. And the money. We can't afford this!'

Absolutely nothing about her situation fit with having a baby. Alone in the bathroom, her one place of any real privacy, her tears poured out until she thought she would die, 'Dying, yes! That would fix all my problems.'

Cassandra had learned during her days in Chicago that women did find ways to end pregnancies. However, locating such help in tiny Halton, Kansas, with family and small-town neighbors around every corner, she knew would not work.

'Kansas City ... I might find help there. But how am I going to find that help, get there, and really take care of this?' Without anyone to confide in, she felt defeated before she could gain information and perhaps help.

'This was never supposed to happen to me ... but what can I do? Really! What, oh what on earth can I do?' she cried pitifully into her hands until she was all cried out. Eventually she got up, washed her face, and went back to the kitchen.

Constantly upset, she was sick for weeks with a cold and flu and steadily losing weight, yet she forged ahead with the work. Eventually finding herself without options, she finally told Ed and her family of the pregnancy. Ed seemed surprised but pleased; he, along with her family, had been concerned lately about her health. Learning of the pregnancy helped to explain what they had watched but their concerns continued. Cassandra was miserable. It was a long, hot summer and dry, never-ending fall and early winter.

That December, after she had hosted the traditional, large Taylor family Christmas dinner in their newly named Taylor Dining Room, Cassandra gave birth to a son in the closing days of 1938. She stated proudly she had cooked for two parties the day before the birth and had begun working full time again in less than two weeks. She easily turned the baby over to the young, unmarried nieces living nearby, and her mother tended the baby in the hotel when necessary.

Life went on much as before with few complications from the unplanned family expansion. But now, Cassandra had her next plan staunchly in place: there would be no more pregnancies for her. Cassandra, generally reluctant regarding sexual encounters with Ed, from the beginning of her pregnancy had refused even infrequent sexual contact. She declared to Ed this was too much for her, given illness and the weariness pregnancy brought to her. But her new edict stated clearly that sex between them had ended, never to resume.

Years later, Ed told Margaret, "I couldn't believe Cassandra at first … thinking how could she not desire even the smallest of intimacies, but it soon became clear to me that she meant what she had said, and an important part of my life with her, as a husband, had ended."

At the same time, life moved on for Cassandra almost as if nothing had changed. But, in truth, her declaration altered nearly everything. She had turned a corner and began again to create a life for herself as she sought freedom from most of the responsibilities of motherhood and being a wife while her friendship with Ruth continued to grow.

However, in Cassandra's mind, nothing had shifted about their contract as she had understood it: they would work ahead together, trying to make ends meet, doing the job they had taken on as a team, even if that job did not provide a living.

By the early spring, Cassandra told Ed, "We're not making it here. I hear the government is hiring men in Salina. Maybe you should look into that."

Clearly, they needed income. The new Civilian Conservation Corps of the Department of the Interior had opened a work camp in the next county seat. Ed signed on with the CCC workforce while Cassandra added Ed's work in the hotel to her own workload. But, within a few months, the work with the CCC ended in that area, and, without other options, Ed returned to Halton and the hotel where together they continued to eke out a meager living.

The following summer, in August 1940, Ed, probably with Ruth's help, secured a job at the American Legion in Essex, ten miles south of Halton. He hated to leave Cassandra behind and initially had concerns about the drive. However, raised in big cities where the skyline consisted of buildings, he came to enjoy the daily drive to Essex, watching that huge, colorful sky swoop down to meet the rural landscape, day by day at sunrise and again at sunset.

Ed continued doing the janitorial work at the hotel in the early mornings and late evenings. Cassandra carried the dining room work and her increased catering load primarily by herself, while family members took care of the baby. Ruth and others in the family would help her when a workday required more than she could manage alone. At the same time, Mother Taylor's health declined rather quickly, and not long after her mother passed away, Cassandra lost the dining room itself. The hotel had been sold, and the new owners wanted the dining room under their own management.

"Maybe this is a good thing, Ed," Cassandra said with a sad but hopeful tone. "Being pushed out of here will give us an opportunity to find another way of earning a living. Working our fingers to the bone here in this old hotel, I now have to admit, is never going to accomplish that." She sat down, drummed her fingers on the table for a while and then looked up at Ed and said, "Why don't we pack up and move to Essex. Ruth thinks she knows of a house to rent not too far from your job at the American Legion, there on the east side of town. Maybe I can help you with your job and begin to turn that kitchen into a place that serves real food, not just bar food."

"Well, now, I've been thinking about that for quite a while myself, ever since I started to work there. Essex is still a small town, but it's bigger than Halton."

"Well, I guess Essex is as good as any town for me to build a catering business," Cassandra said.

Thus in the summer of 1941 Cassandra and Ed made the move, leaving behind her short-lived dream of a tea room. While she began to help Ed with some of his duties in the kitchen at the Legion Hall, he took over all the janitorial work and tending the bar. Cassandra worked hard to expand her catering business, now looking to Essex for most of her clients. Ed, and also Ruth, continued to help as her catering business grew.

Soon the toddler, adored and cared for by the regular customers of the club, came to feel at home in the Legion clubhouse. The men delighted in letting the three-year-old try to drink the foam off their full beer mugs, getting bubbles in his nose and making him sneeze.

All together, the customers were not sure if they should be horrified or entertained by watching the mostly unattended toddler crawl in and out of the dumbwaiter that carried food and dirty dishes between the basement kitchen and the first floor club room. It appeared, however, that the child relished his secret hiding place.

"Fortunately," Cassandra told Taylor when he became a father himself, "you were a good and easily managed child for we were way too busy to pay you much mind."

Cassandra's catering business thrived in Essex. She kept busy preparing meals for luncheons and dinners in the large American Legion Hall or other local hospitality rooms. She often needed to call for help from sisters, nieces, and, of course, her friend Ruth.

Cassandra and Ruth became a team, working together and enjoying their growing friendship. Most folks in Essex knew Ruth well; they had watched her grow up to become a respected teacher and faithful member of the local church. And it seemed to most around town that Ruth almost single-handedly managed to hold things together at her family's farm where the aging Mr. and Mrs. Peterson, along with the older brother, pretty much stuck to themselves and were not that well-known. When Ruth wasn't teaching or working at the farm, the town folk thought of her as always alone. Many were glad she had found a well-deserved new friend.

Years earlier, around the first time Cassandra left for Chicago, Ruth began driving an old Model T, purchased by her parents and held together with baling wire, so she could live at home on the farm and get herself to high school in Essex. Many rural students boarded with a family in town. But when Ruth's father finally gave in to her mother about Ruth's schooling, he did so with one stipulation.

"If you are gonna insist that girl keep goin' and goin' to school, she's got to still do her part out here! There's more work than we can manage. You hear me!" Mr. Peterson drove a hard bargain. "That girl can just git herself back out here and take care of things, and she'll haf to git the barn chores done before she takes leave of the place in the mornin'." He continued. "I'm not likin' the sound of it at all."

Ruth had no choice. She would have to comply with her father's demands if she wanted to continue her schooling. This did not surprise her; she expected it, if he gave in at all, which had been far from certain. "I was willing to do whatever I had to do in order to go to high school, and I was already used to all the farm work," Ruth had told Cassandra.

They bought the old car, and Ruth taught herself to drive it.

From Ruth's earliest school days, she wanted to become a teacher. Four years later, she graduated from high school and left home for the first time to attend eight weeks of summer school at the Teachers College. While there she worked for her room and board and also made the trip home on weekends to work at the farm.

That fall, she began her first teaching position as a country schoolteacher in a nearby, one-room schoolhouse, allowing her to live at home. She learned quickly she would have to find her way forward teaching by the seat of her pants, much like Cassandra would do when she began working with food.

Back then, with the country deep in recession and after several years of teaching in rural country schools, Ruth earned a coveted teaching position in town. The salary remained the same as it had been in her rural school, $900 for a nine-month teaching term, but at least in town she only had to deal with one age group, second grade at first, in one room. Perhaps more importantly, she left behind sweeping the floor, keeping two outhouses clean, and carrying the coal and managing—and cleaning up after—a recalcitrant coal-burning heating stove. Old Goliath, as Ruth had named it, remained infamous for frequently belching black coal dust all over her one-room schoolhouse. Pleased with her new assignment, Ruth especially celebrated having left Old Goliath behind.

Ruth's work at the farm mushroomed as her mother's health declined. The laundry, cooking, morning chores in the barn, especially the milking and feeding, plus separating the cream for selling and use by the family, all fell to Ruth. She was up well before dawn and all too often long into the night.

Weekends were for catching up, doing the laundry, working in the garden and putting up food from the harvest.

Ruth found in the Essex church one place of social contact beyond her work at the farm and the schoolhouse. This congregation would eventually serve as the center for the lifelong friendship between Cassandra and Ruth—and, of course, Ed.

Cassandra and Ed had been somewhat involved in the Halton congregation during their few years there. But with meager time and money, the two of them seldom had the freedom to attend and build new friendships. However, Ruth and Cassandra had found each other at one of the church women's regional meetings and had easily become friends, given Ruth's help with Cassandra's catering business, first in Halton and then in Essex. The two women enjoyed every minute they could carve out to be together given their busy lives.

In the late fall of 1941, following Cassandra and Ed's move to Essex, they found a home in Ruth's church where the pastor was nothing like Dr. Ames of University Church in Chicago; however, their lives had changed. With the bombing of Pearl Harbor in early December and the entry of the United States into the Second World War, having a community gathering place proved to be important. To everyone, their past and present experience of years living beneath the weight of the Depression and the long drought, the people of Essex now added the additional stress from the uncertainties of war. With many of Ruth's students and Taylor family nephews having left to join the military, off in harm's way, the three adults went to church seeking solace along with their neighbors, and to pray for peace.

During this difficult time, Ruth and Cassandra, like women everywhere in small towns, relied on their friendship. Brought together by shared burdens and wartime fears, the two women soon found their happiest hours together in kitchens and among other women at the church. Ruth and Cassandra were finding love. Now, every day before they parted, the two created a plan for the next day and dreamed of being together again — tomorrow.

Seven

The Love-at-Long-Last

aundry day!" Edith shouted out, as the back door slammed shut behind her. Mabel, her next-door neighbor, was hanging the final pieces of laundry on the line, well ahead of Edith. "What would the two of us do on a Monday if we weren't doing the laundry?" Edith added as she put her heavy basket down under the clothesline.

"Oh yes," Mabel said, laughing. "Well, in truth I can think of a few other things that I really could do today but probably won't get to with all this wash on the line!"

Suddenly, changing the tone of her voice, Mabel said, "Oh, by the way, did you hear about the Millers?"

"No, what's happened?" Edith asked as she walked toward her neighbor.

"I'm afraid Dewey is ill again."

"Oh, no," Edith replied, "not again. Maybe we could put together a supper for them?"

"Good, let's do that. Come over for a cup of coffee later, we can plan a meal. Meanwhile, I'll run over and tell Shirley we'll bring in their supper."

"Okay. I'll see you after I get all this laundry on the line," Edith replied.

It was commonplace for women neighbors to build friendships, become lifelines to one another in times of difficulties. But for Ruth and Cassandra, something in addition was taking place as they began to find joy and friendship working together in kitchens.

"When you get resettled in Essex, I'll be able to help you a lot more," Ruth assured Cassandra in the weeks before the move.

In the years to follow, the women would have decades together with their cooking pots and pans, and among their women friends. Soon after the move to Essex, the two became inseparable, together in kitchens and participating in their women's groups. On most days, Cassandra and Ruth would be seen together alone in Ruth's car as they were going and coming from catering meals and social gatherings.

"Oh, thank goodness that is over!" Cassandra said as she almost crawled from weariness into the front seat of Ruth's car.

"However, my sweet," Ruth replied, "we did put on a great feast for those folks. Did you see Darrell dive into that pie? My goodness, you'd think a good piece of homemade pie had never crossed his lips before!" Ruth, also tired from the long day's work, gained renewed strength when with Cassandra.

"I'm almost too tired to even smile, honey. But yes, I did see that."

In this way, their earliest intimate moments most often took place in Ruth's car. Through this sharing of work and pleasure, the two women's lives soon came to feel, for them, like a real life, their life, one they were living together.

In truth, both Ruth and Cassandra preferred the company of women. Even more, they had both, for as long as they could remember, yearned for a close, intimate woman partner. Now the two felt they had forged a special bond, one to which they soon found themselves committed.

Eventually, they told each other of their dream to spend their life with a woman. Maybe, for them, naming it helped to bring it about. Without regard to what others might think, for Cassandra and Ruth, being together mattered. And, in looking back, it is as if the folks in their little town did not seem to care all that much one way or the other.

From that night—the first night they spent together at Cassandra's—they knew they had stepped over an important threshold. They were in the kitchen at the American Legion doing the final cleanup from a big dinner Cassandra had catered that Friday evening with Ruth's help. It had been a long day for both of them.

"Ruth, it's so late and you're too tired to make the trip back out to the farm," Cassandra said. "Please, come home with me. Stay with me. I'll give you one of my nightgowns."

Ruth was stunned to silence, Cassandra's words having caught her off guard. But then she turned to look at her. There Ruth could see the softness in Cassandra's eyes, a look that calmed Ruth's racing heart.

"Well, I guess I could drop into that bed in the guest room and get up early enough to get back out to the farm in time to do the morning chores," Ruth replied with a bit of evident reluctance, testing the water, for she had not said what she wanted to say.

Turning and stepping toward Ruth, Cassandra said, "But I want you to sleep with me." She spoke tenderly but also as if pleading as she leaned her head close to Ruth's, her hands holding Ruth's shoulders, drawing her near. "Please, dear, come home with me and to my own room," she whispered into Ruth's ear. "Together we can rest and put this long day behind us."

Ruth, breathless, nodded her assent. The two stood there in the middle of that huge kitchen, soaking up the pleasure; together, their arms around each other. No other words needed.

Ruth knew, of course, that Cassandra had her own room and that she and Ed did not sleep together and had not done so for some years. And yet, at that moment, suddenly things had shifted. It may have appeared to be something simple; a tantalizing invitation, or merely an obvious next step. But, in fact, their first night together would become an earth-shaking, life-changing moment for the women, and also for the lives of others in this family and beyond. Their lives changed—Cassandra's, Ed's, and Ruth's—and also the life of the young child, Taylor.

But now, on this night, without a single thought about anyone or anything else, Ruth told Cassandra of the first time she had seen her.

"My dear," Ruth said as they lay in bed, talking about this big step they had just taken, "I fell in love with you on that first day … the day I saw you at the church women's gathering in Halton, not too long after you arrived from Chicago."

"Yes, I remember; I saw you as well, way on the other side of the room."

"I can still recall the feeling in my body when I spotted you … that tall, gorgeous woman across the crowd. And while I stood looking at you, because I couldn't take my eyes off you, you looked up and our eyes met. You took my breath away."

Ruth lost her breath all over again that night as she and Cassandra were finally together in one another's arms. It soothed them deeply and in an amazing and new way. Their tiredness from the long day fell away as they held and melted into each other.

From that day, the two women were often together for the night in Cassandra's room. Did others notice? Of course, Ed noticed; his wife, in her room just down the hall, having invited someone else into her bed, what he pined for and had been denied. How could he not notice? By now Ed had grown used to the two of them being together at the American Legion and in the kitchen at the house almost daily. Watching them, he had seen this coming, ruing the day. Having been forced aside years ago, he had seethed alone in anger; now, hurt again, his pain, anger and helplessness pressed down upon him.

Yet Taylor had grown used to Ruth, along with other women in his home, and wouldn't have paid much attention to this change at the house — at least not yet — but that time would come.

Did others outside the immediate family notice or care? Probably some eventually began to notice — and conjecture about — Ruth's overnights at the Thomas household. But given it didn't seem to affect their lives, folks exhibited little interest regarding women they knew and respected. In the early 1940s, people in Essex, and throughout the nation, had other things a bit more worrisome on their minds than who might be sleeping with whom in the house over on South Street. Most individuals have private lives, and Cassandra and Ruth now also had theirs; their life together was private, but not hidden.

However, in the Midwestern Bible Belt, and maybe especially in small, rural communities like Essex, Kansas, old teachings could persist: "The Bible teaches homosexuality is a sin!" Even when rarely spoken, such ideas lurked, sub rosa, within the culture. Public talk about the relationship between Cassandra and Ruth most likely was held in check by folks' discomfort talking about sex in general. However, such so-called Christian teachings were not unknown to Cassandra or Ruth.

"Cassandra," Ruth, with old fears rattling inside her head, asked one evening as they lay in bed together, "have you heard it said that homosexuality is a sin?"

"Oh, honey, let's not even think about such pure nonsense," and, without giving it a second thought, added, "I've always been guided by knowing what is right and what is wrong and if others aren't, that's their problem, not mine … or yours, my dear." Eventually, it would become clear that Ruth had been wounded by such pernicious and pious declarations, from which she carried fear and guilt, but at that moment, she felt free to live within the confidence of the woman she loved.

The women felt secure in their conviction about their lives being drawn together, and with no one inquiring about their plans, they just continued to live their life. Yet, it was always possible that eventually someone would ask. That person—and the first and only one to ask—turned out to be the daughter-in-law, when she was the new wife to their son, Taylor. It happened one holiday weekend, in the winter of 1960, when Taylor and Margaret were back home in Essex for a visit.

❖   ❖   ❖

Supper was over. Ruth was fussing with the turkey carcass in the kitchen, while Ed and Taylor had gone into the living room where his dad wanted him to look at the footstool he'd been repairing. Margaret and Cassandra sat together at the dining room table visiting and enjoying a second cup of hot tea.

When the two of them started to get up to help in the kitchen, Ruth said, "Now you two just sit right back down there and enjoy your tea and conversation. Mom's been on her feet all day."

Cassandra and Margaret looked at each other, smiled, and sat back down. It was then that Margaret, who enjoyed her two mothers-in-law, took the opportunity to ask, "Mom, I've never heard either of you say anything about how you came to be keeping house together, you and Ruth. I love you both and am curious how this came about?"

It was a simple question, but any answer to it likely not simple.

Ruth, scraping the leftover vegetables into a glass bowl, paused and looked up briefly at Cassandra, caught her eye, and then continued her work as Cassandra turned toward the young woman sitting with her at the dining room table. The story Cassandra told went something like this:

"Ruth was having a hard time, about to have a nervous breakdown trying to take care of her mother and her brother and the farm while also teaching. Then, after they both died so close to the same time, she was devastated and at her wits' end, out there working on that old farm by herself while commuting back and forth to teach in town. I told Ed, 'Someone has to help Ruth get through this tough time, and I think we should ... we are her friends.' He agreed so we called and told her we wanted her to move in with us for a while until she got things settled. She moved in, and before we knew it years had passed, and it was clear she was here to stay. And by that time, I would not have wanted to live without her."

Many years later, during the time following Cassandra's death, Margaret was in Essex with Ruth and Ed for a week, helping them in whatever ways she could, when this old conversation between Cassandra and Margaret came up. Ruth laughingly acknowledged to Margaret that Cassandra's little story had made her smile. "Yet it was true," Ruth said easily, "as the years passed, neither of us wanted to live without the other." Ruth added, with a giggle in her voice, "However, there were days when I thought it actually might be impossible to live with her! She was one gloriously stubborn woman."

Then, in a softer voice, Ruth added "… and beautiful, and smart, and a deeply caring and committed woman. When she said she would do something, everyone knew she would do it or die trying. So when she said, 'Come live with me at the house; I want us to be together,' I knew she meant it or she would not have said it. I also knew she would figure out how to make it happen."

Ruth naturally had her own version of how she and Cassandra came to live together. To hear Ruth tell it, their lives slowly and steadily, through the early years, began to come together as they shared time in kitchens, first in the Halton dining room, then in the Essex American Legion. "Being together, love just happened," Ruth said.

Once Cassandra and Ed lived in Essex, Ruth began by staying with Cassandra on the nights they worked late. She still had large responsibilities out at the family farm, especially since her father had died years earlier at the time Ruth had established herself as a teacher in Essex. However, after Ruth had to put her mother in the nursing home, Cassandra put her foot down. "Ruth, with your mother not in the house, you must not stay by yourself at the farm with Nate. I will not stand for it." She was insistent. "If you still have to do the housework, you can run out there on the weekend and do that work." This plan removed a lot of stress from their lives as Ruth moved in with Cassandra to stay.

Little fanfare accompanied this shift. Tired of finding ways to be together, they simply wanted to share their lives fully. Cassandra and Ruth wanted what most lovers want, that their lives become complete and that each day, every day, be made up of their love for each other.

Cassandra simply announced it. Period. While the story told by Cassandra to her daughter-in-law did loosely acknowledge real happenings, the missing part lay at the core of the story: the two women fell in love and wanted to be together.

Cassandra loved her wonderful old house on South Street with its four bedrooms upstairs. Cassandra and Ruth had the bedroom at the top of the stairs, then Ed's room next along the hallway, and Taylor had the room at the end of the hall, leaving the small guest room alcove for Grandmother Wright and, in the years to come, for the youth minister from the nearby seminary who lived there on weekends while working at the church.

Through the years, the work at the American Legion for Ed and Cassandra had become somewhat unpleasant, no longer providing a good environment for Taylor's after-school time and less conducive to the kind of work Cassandra wanted to do. With Ruth living at the house and contributing to the household budget from her teaching salary, plus Cassandra and Ruth's expanding catering business, they had finally stabilized the family income.

Cassandra talked with Ed, and they decided to resign. He found work as a bookkeeper at a local machine shop, and

Cassandra had no trouble filling the calendar for catering meals. She planned the menus, together the two did the shopping, and then Cassandra would get the cooking started during the day while Ruth taught her classes. In the late afternoons, the women completed the meal preparation together and delivered or served the meals, often, at first, with Ed's assistance.

Soon they all realized the bookkeeping job did not work well for Ed. When one of the small stores on Main Street became vacant, he asked the women what they thought about developing a music store in that location. He already had attracted a sizable business in instrument repair among the town's music students. The idea of selling instruments and then offering ongoing servicing and repair seemed like a good idea.

Just at this time, Ed and Cassandra had come into a small inheritance from one of Cassandra's bachelor brothers. They decided to use the money to fund the opening of the music business on Main Street. Almost instantly, his work took Ed from the house all day minding the store and often in the evenings with bookkeeping and instrument repair. While never a financial success, the music store provided Ed with the pleasure of interaction with children and music. From those years in the store, Ed established an instrument-repair business he managed, in a small shed behind the house, well into his 90s.

In the spring of 1953, no one had expected that Ruth's brother, Nate, still relatively young, would take sick and die so quickly. Suddenly the land and the farm, which Ruth had helped the family to purchase once she was teaching, fell to Ruth's responsibility. She quickly found a neighbor to care for the livestock in exchange for boarding their own stock in the pasture and barn. Nate had already stopped doing the fieldwork, renting out the acreage to neighboring farmers to till and harvest in exchange for livestock feed. Now Ruth had to face the huge task of getting the farm and house organized and ready to be sold. There would have to be an auction to sell the farm implements and livestock, as well as the sale of the house and most of the furniture.

In Essex, springtime had arrived and the school year would soon be over. Cassandra had a plan. Of course. Cassandra always had a plan. This time she proposed the two of them move out to the farm for the summer and "that way," as she said, "we could do the work together to prepare for a sale in August. Just think, we can have a wonderful garden, do a lot of canning, and enjoy the time amid the summer songbirds, fruit trees, and flowers."

"Oh, Cassandra, you're always the romantic one!" Ruth said, while shaking her head. "You have such fond memories of your early years on the farm, but remember, dear, you left the farm when you were seventeen. Maybe you've lost touch with all the work there is to do out there." But Cassandra seemed quite thrilled that such an opportunity lay before the two of them.

Back then, Ruth could see Cassandra's dream, and parts of it appealed to her as well. However, Ruth thought she could more clearly see the work involved. This kind of dream-building described well the way much of their life together took shape, with Cassandra dreaming up things for them, or more likely, for Ruth to do.

Ruth, said, while laughing between her words, "Sweetie, I see I've lost this round. Your creative mind is way out there ahead of me again ... you're making summer plans for everyone in the family. And when I say everyone I mean, everyone — beginning with me."

Cassandra and Ruth moved out to the farm when the school year ended. They sorted, cleaned, and together worked their way through the early weeks of summer. They enjoyed a lot of what they both had hoped for, precious time for the two of them living alone out there far away from the daily routines back at the house with the men. This brought freedom to their days and sheer delight to their nights, a little bit of heaven on earth.

They worked in the garden, canned fruit and vegetables, cooked for themselves, and without the need to cook for others, ate only when hungry. They relished the cool morning breezes while sitting with their morning coffee on the porch. Together they fell in love again with the sound of the wind in the trees, the wonderful feel and smell of laundry hanging on the line, and the joy of the porch swing together at sunset.

Ed and Taylor came out for supper a few times. Ed rarely could get free from the music store, and Taylor, now a busy teenager, also had a life full of plans with his buddies. Fortunately, the women did not need to worry too much about Taylor. They knew him as dependable and were glad he had good neighborhood boyfriends his age. Sometimes the boys picked up odd jobs together, but mostly they entertained themselves. Taylor seemed easygoing and pretty satisfied with whatever came his way, and he had a lot of doting aunts and neighborhood wives and widows, or women from the church, surrounding him with love and attention.

Frankly, both Ed and Taylor enjoyed the hiatus that the women's move to the farm allowed. Those two women could keep up a steady buzz throughout the summer with all their canning and other chores. This time, the men did not have to find ways to tiptoe around all that female energy. The women seemed to relish the work they poured into the summer months, even if they did complain.

Many in the family came and went throughout the summer giving them a hand and some good advice, including one of Cassandra's older sisters who came out with her farmer-husband, staying several days to help pull things together in preparation for the big auction.

After the sale, Ruth hired a local farmer to move the household goods and furniture the women had chosen for the house in town. They had decided to keep a set of good dishes and other kitchen pots and pans they knew would be useful in Cassandra's catering business. They had also selected some of the nicer furniture pieces, such as an old but beautiful handmade drop-leaf table, some straight-back chairs with leather seats, Ruth's mother's cedar chest. Oh, and the old family clock. These were the things that found their way into the family home on South Street in Essex.

Most importantly, Cassandra and Ruth kept for themselves the beautiful bedroom set, a large dresser (which Cassandra used for the rest of her life), a highboy chest (that became Ruth's dresser), and a bed frame and headboard. The women splurged and bought a new mattress for their bed and a new bedspread. Their room became a place of beauty in the house which they enjoyed showing off to their friends while it felt so new. Cassandra, in particular, enjoyed the feeling of luxury in their fixed-up, lovely bedroom.

Their room at the top of the stairs was a sanctuary for the two women. They celebrated the northward and eastward windows with their cool evening breezes that provided comfort following a warm day. It was in this room where they enjoyed getting up together with the sun during the summer months, eager for the plans ahead for their day.

With Cassandra's help, Ruth had put much behind her. The old Peterson home place with its farmhouse and barn, the fields, and the small tree-lined creek that ran through the western quarter—now gone. The land, buildings, tractor, and farm equipment, plus the animals—all sold, along with most of the family furniture. Ruth kept only what she wanted and thought they could use. Most everything had been handed over to the auctioneer. With the proceeds from the sale, Ruth created what she called her rainy-day fund at the bank, a small cache of funds that would become important to the family through the coming years.

Finally, back out at the farm, with only about ten days left before the beginning of the school year, Cassandra and Ruth locked the door to the farmhouse for the last time and moved out, making way for the new owners. They had had a full but rewarding summer.

The women were exhausted and, with the heat of August bearing down on them, they escaped to Colorado. There they rented a small cabin in the mountains outside Colorado Springs for a much-needed rest. Cassandra would, as usual, relish the time to read her books while Ruth rested, taking morning and afternoon naps all week long.

However, back home and before winter had fully set in, Ruth's mother also succumbed. She had been an invalid for years, wasting away in the nursing home without knowing anyone. Her illness and age caught up with her, and she passed on quietly. With no known family left, Ruth turned with even more gratitude toward her new family. Through Cassandra,

Ruth gained not only a life partner but the large and fun extended Taylor family. Cassandra's brothers and sisters and their children, the nieces and nephews, and their husbands and wives and children, the grand-nieces and nephews, of the Taylor clan had easily welcomed Ruth as one of their own. Now Ruth had a home, knew what it meant to be loved, and have a real family.

Thus Cassandra and Ruth, and also Ed—if sometimes below the surface, grudgingly—continued to enjoy life in their small Kansas town and in the old ramshackle home, which they continued to share with Taylor until he left for college. For all those years it was the local church that formed the center of their family life. Ed and Ruth sang in the choir and attended Thursday evening choir practice together week by week. Ed participated in a regional church men's group while Cassandra and Ruth became involved leaders of the state-wide Women's Fellowship as well as their small local church Women's Circle which generally met in their home. Taylor stayed active in the senior high youth group until he left for college. From time to time, Cassandra and Ruth held positions in the church as deaconesses or on a committee, the only positions women were allowed to hold. Ruth sat on the Church Foundation Committee, an organization she helped establish. She was appointed the chair over and over again, even though she was a woman, because as folks said, "Ruth understands managing money."

After the war years, Cassandra and Ruth helped to found a couples' Sunday School class they named the Keystone Class. Of course, they were the only female couple but it was a fun group of folks about the same age and whose children were no longer youngsters. Cassandra was asked to teach the class, which she did for more than twenty years, until she said she lacked the energy to continue.

Then Ruth took up where Cassandra left off and taught the class for the next thirty-plus years with Cassandra sitting proudly in the front row until her death. Between the two women, they taught and wrangled with that wonderful group of folks about the Bible, religion, politics, and local, regional, and national church controversies for more than five decades.

Their Keystone Class and the Women's Fellowship provided the lifeblood to Cassandra's and Ruth's lives. Faithfully, these tightly knit folks supported one another through the ups and downs in their personal lives, the births, deaths, marriages, divorces, and other tragedies and illnesses. These men and women also argued together on Sunday mornings, during the hour before worship, about the push and pull between their more conservative selves and their more liberal ones.

Never timid in speaking, and with her ideas in general out ahead of the rest of the group, Cassandra spoke her mind, even when she expected her words heretical to mainstream thinking, maybe especially heretical to country-folk thinking.

Once in awhile, one of the men would shout out from the back row in the middle of a class discussion on a Sunday morning, "Now Caaasaaandrah, is that what they taught you up there in that high fauuu-luuu-ting Uuu-niii-verr-sii-ty of Che-caaaugh-gee?" Always a tension breaker, Mervin, in particular, knew exactly when to lob it into the fray.

This couples class, including farmers, teachers, professional folks of all kinds, was the best-educated group in the church at that time and had stubbornly grown old together until almost everyone who had been a member had died or become too infirm to participate. For decades the lay leadership of the church primarily came from the members of the Keystone class and when the end drew near, so did an important era in the life of the congregation.

At the same time that Cassandra and Ruth led their class, Ed taught a small group of the older men. They faithfully read the scripture lesson together, verse by verse, slowly and deliberately, week by week. Ed had his own particular and more liberal bent on religion and scripture and, had he had a more lively audience, would have loved to delve deeper and broader. However, he proved himself content to help provide time for these older men to be together and talk about the Bible.

He, like Ruth with the couples group, taught his class until the men had passed away or couldn't get out and about, even with help. Ed and Ruth outlived almost every member that had been in the church at the time they had joined.

These two Sunday classes, going on under the same church roof and studying the same biblical text, could not have been more different. However, once the three adults returned home and were sitting around their Sunday dinner table, a rich conversation would ensue. Galvanized by their experiences in the earlier class discussions, they could stake out different positions and argue somewhat boldly about the implications of the day's scripture. Especially Cassandra, of course, with Ruth sometimes disagreeing with her, but it was Ed who greatly enjoyed speaking his thoughts, though the word bold is not normally used to describe anything Ed Thomas generally did or said.

So their life together continued, with Ed working at the music store during the day and on many evenings, and later at the Kansas Turnpike, as a toll taker. Cassandra and Ruth kept busy as well. Ruth had, by now, been teaching at the high school for many years and had expanded her responsibilities in public education in Essex and beyond. Cassandra continued her cooking during the daytime and often catered meals in the evenings with Ruth's help.

Ruth and Cassandra continued to develop their lives outside the home. First one and then the other was elected to the School Board, and, as Ruth's work in the National Teachers Association expanded, the women began many years of summer travel to national NEA and AAUW meetings. Their first trip in 1954 was by train to a national women's meeting in New York City, a city that thrilled them — they went to the theater to see Margaret Truman in a play and heard Eleanor Roosevelt speak at the U.N. They trained north to Boston and south to D.C. to see some of Cassandra's old college girlfriends. None had married and all fell in love again with Cassandra, and now also with Ruth. Together Cassandra and Ruth on many days found it hard to believe their good fortune at the life they were living. They loved it … almost all of it.

Frequently Cassandra could be found speaking for Ruth or storming out of the kitchen totally fed up with her. From the beginning of their relationship, neither wanted to live without the other, and they alone were the ones who understood just how normal their coupled, everyday lives were as lovers and partners. They wanted only to have a lifetime together.

Cassandra had always wished for a close woman friend and that wish was granted in her friendship with Ruth. Those in the family and in their small town who knew and cared about them had the chance to watch as the two women fell deeper and deeper into a matured and settled love, becoming indispensable to one another.

At the time of Cassandra's death in 1995, in a conversation with Margaret, who visited with Ed and Ruth the week she died, Ruth told Margaret, "I had always wished for a close woman friend and a family, and in Cassandra Taylor, I found both. Cassandra Taylor Thomas was the most beautiful and interesting woman I have ever known. The thought of living without her was always too painful ... and yet, of course, I'm having to learn to do exactly that," she said with tears in her eyes.

This love at long last, found by the two women, held within it true beauty, yet it came wrapped in a larger not-always-beautiful reality within their immediate family. It was a love they had legitimately sought after from authentic needs to live out who they truly were. However, once Cassandra made her compromise, others became caught in it's tightly woven web, including Ed, Ruth, and Taylor — the effects of which are still waiting to be understood.

Eight

The Triangle

O ne day, after a particularly challenging moment around the Sunday dinner table at Cassandra, Ruth and Ed's family home, Cassandra's niece called.

"Do I need to worry about you three?" Lillian asked her Aunt Cass. "On some Sundays when we're together around the dinner table, Ruth — but particularly you — can be somewhat harsh with Ed. Yesterday was certainly one of those days as you railed at him about putting gravy on his ice cream."

"We would never set out to make you uncomfortable, Lillian, but you know as well as anyone, Ed can be so exasperating. Ruth got up early to make that ice cream."

"Maybe that bothers you more than the rest of us, Aunt Cass. I enjoy being around him, but some days you sound like he's not smart enough for you."

"Lillian! I'd never say something like that. Ed comes from good stock," Cassandra went on to say, piqued by her niece's words. "His parents, while perhaps a bit eccentric, were intelligent, and Ed has a good mind. I certainly would not have made any pretense of interest in him had this not been the case. But I'm sorry I made you uncomfortable on Sunday … yet it is true, I hate to see him ruin both the leftover gravy and the ice cream!"

Few people, including his wife and Ruth, gave Ed credit for having a quick mind. However, Edward Thomas was not dumb. And more importantly, he equaled Cassandra in self-determination and surpassed her in having a calm, purposeful demeanor. Cassandra invariably acted quickly and vigorously, while Ed was determined to move thoughtfully, managing his feelings with care. Cassandra, though filled with self-confidence, actually felt insecure and was often mired in melancholy about life itself, while Ed habitually focused on others, happily engaged in thinking about the unknowables of life.

Such propensities led Ed to a quiet and well-defined, if somewhat distracted life, as if someone were driving the car, his right foot softly on the accelerator and his left toe resting gently on the brake, making his way along in life, taking time to think things through carefully, somewhat unaware of what lay ahead and with a lack of practicality regarding the future.

Thus, while clearly passionate and resolute about life, Ed was also caught between his big dreams and his down-to-earth everyday living. This lover, who greatly enjoyed the company of women, with great patience had quietly pursued the woman he admired. Spellbound from the first time he saw her at University Church during her early college years, his dream grew year by year—for well over a decade—until he had achieved his goal, largely without much initiative on his part, for creating a life with Cassandra Taylor.

Eventually, one early morning in 1935, in the basement of their Chicago neighborhood church, Cassandra had made her proposal to Ed. Suddenly it seemed his dream had come true. Soon Ed awoke to find he had merely caught hold of the fringe of a dream and a woman he really did not know, whose truer, deeper yearnings were not for such as him.

When others inquired about his family, Ed would say, in a thoughtful manner, something safely descriptive, he "felt fortunate" to share a home with "two talented women," then mention his "beautiful wife" and "another woman, who has become like an adopted sister to me." This triangle in which he found himself certainly brought him sorrows, but also a family and, toward the end, a great friendship.

However, while he had more or less sought out the wife, early on in their marriage his wife had chosen the "other woman" for herself. Even with such a disconcerting beginning, through the years Ruth and Ed did become convenient friends. The two could easily spend evening time together enjoying a television drama or spirited sports events, while Cassandra would read by herself in the front room.

Uncomfortable talking about his feelings, Ed's life as the third member of the household presented him with daily challenges. Along the way he decided to live his life as well as he could within this reality: 'I will not dwell on things I cannot change,' he thought, 'even if I want things to be different.' Ed had the capacity to thoughtfully observe his life with his own questioning gaze, which became an act of interminable patience on his part.

The three of them developed a sociability that Ed, as well as Ruth, enjoyed as part of Cassandra's extended family and in their small town. Ed had grown up in major urban centers, but, after a few short years in rural Kansas, he easily and often claimed to anyone who would listen, "Well now, I guess what some call small-town living suits me mighty fine."

Much of what Ed could list as experiences that brought him contentment in his life came as a result of living in that small community. Edward Thomas, in Essex, Kansas, became a much bigger player than he could have ever been in Chicago where he grew up, or Boston where he had first lived. Here, through the years, Ed had earned a place of honor and an enjoyable social life by playing his musical saw for hundreds of school children and by helping to make the city band a success.

At times, some neighbors and friends had questions about Ed and his life in the house on South Street, for he had a way of endearing himself to almost everyone in the community. Because they cared for him, they also worried about him, wishing that his life would go as well as possible.

"Everyone knows that the two women Ed lives with are very strong and outspoken," one neighbor said to another. "Now don't get me wrong. That Cass and Ruth, like Ed, are terrific people. They bring a lot of wonderful talent to our little community; but, nonetheless, those gals may be a bit of a challenge at home." The neighbor smiled, in agreement, while nodding his head.

Questions lingered within the family and beyond. Did Ed fail as a husband to Cassandra? Some would likely say, "Yes, obviously he did." Others, including Ed himself, and maybe also his wife, might actually say otherwise. Patiently living on the fringe of his marriage, Ed sought to be a helpmate within the household, out of his love for Cassandra.

Having taken up his father's teachings about nutrition and daily exercise, Ed was adamant to keep himself agile, physically and mentally, so that he was able to contribute to their life together. Yet, contrary to his stated goal, Ed's efforts in these ways could drive the women crazy.

Time was precious for the women, who repeatedly had more to do than they could get accomplished in one day. To them, Ed's exercices wasted time day in and day out, something they could hardly bear.

"Edward! You surely have had enough of those exercises," Cassandra would shout back into the house as she opened the kitchen door to leave, "Ruth has everything in the car. We must go now!"

Or, "Now, where in tarnation is Ed?" Cassandra might shout from the front seat of the car, her door still open. "Probably doing his morning exercises!" she would say to no one, merely letting off steam.

Scarcely impressed by Ed's disciplined efforts, the women found it difficult to hold anger toward him, because he worked diligently not to add to the women's displeasure and was rarely found unprepared for the moment of departure.

Although Ed took special care of his body, Ruth and Cassandra erroneously tried to convince themselves for a few years of Ed's declining health. Sometimes making onlookers suspicious such statements might have implied they wished it might be true.

"So how is everyone on the old home place?" Taylor or Margaret, from their home in Hastings, would inquire during a regular phone conversation.

Ruth, or Cassandra, whoever happened to answer the phone, might say, "We are all doing pretty well, it seems; however, we are rather concerned about Dad. He doesn't seem at all well. Not sure what it might be, and, goodness knows, you couldn't get him anywhere near a doctor's office! Guess we'll just have to watch and see how things go."

This unusually eccentric man also gave a lot of daily attention and planning to meeting his "body's nutritional needs," as he would say to anyone who expressed interest. Ed easily and frequently told of his appreciation for how Cassandra and Ruth supported him in this important effort, which they did, yet all the while growing weary of his descriptions of food in relationship to his bodily functions. However, to his credit, he rarely, if ever, commented on the women's apparent lack of respect for what he so fervently believed.

Yet, and often to the delight of the women who loved to cook, Ed confessed to having a sweet tooth. "Oh this looks wonderful," Lillian said as they waited Sunday at the dinner table for Cassandra and Ruth to return to their seats after serving the dessert. "And Ed," Lillian continued, "I know how you feel about eating sugar, but you are almost drooling!"

"Well, Lillian," Ed said, his eyes concentrating on the dessert plate before him, "maybe I'd hoped you wouldn't notice. But it's true, Cassandra and Ruth frequently soothe my desire for sweets and lovely gravies, which I enjoy so much and would never prepare for myself." Those around the table could see, without a doubt, Ed enjoyed eating his forbidden fruits, regardless of his convictions about nutrition.

Ed's life bore the marks of significant teachings from both his parents. While his father instructed him about the care of his body, his mother had taken over the instruction about the care of his soul.

As a young boy, and often left behind by his mother as she moved out into the wider world on a mission to spread her new commitments to theosophy, Ed puzzled over his mother's zeal for her new religion. But once Ed became a teenager, he took up his own study of the matters his mother had been trying to impress upon him about the nature of this life and the hereafter. Ed's determination to figure things out for himself became a genuine quest. Through hard work, and without the benefit of anything beyond his high school education (and then learning to type), Ed slowly began to develop his own ideas.

Using largely self-taught methods, Ed managed to provide for himself a fair, if narrow, education in religion and philosophical thinking. Eventually he found a long-sought-after dialogue partner for this effort in Margaret, his daughter-in-law, who had an interest in religion. When she was visiting, Ed could hardly wait for the rare opportunity to talk about his work.

"I have made," Ed explained to Margaret as part of his introduction of himself to his newly arrived daughter, "a life-long effort in the study of logic and what Dr. Ames, of the University of Chicago, called a new orthodoxy. If you are not familiar with Dr. Ames, one of his primary interests was to move believers beyond traditional religious practices rooted in what he defined as superstition."

"And what have you concluded from your efforts?" Margaret inquired.

"Well, I've come to the conclusion that my mother's beliefs at points are misleading. She was a convert to theosophy, but my study leads me to quite different ideas, more in line with Christianity, but with certain critiques of the ways this religion is practiced."

Ed, a slow and careful reader, appeared to some as if he spent his life senselessly plodding along in circles, year after year with his books. However, Edward Thomas had a plan and stayed with it.

"First," he offered, "I read as carefully as I can, in small portions, the most important and timely texts on the subject. Then I type out my responses to what I've read. This helps me digest as thoroughly as I can the intended meanings, plus my interpretation and possible critique of the ideas as presented." Margaret was intrigued by her father-in-law whom she would soon come to lovingly refer to as "Dad."

Even though Ed's rather straightforward process was carefully planned and required laborious effort on his part, he found it fulfilling. Perhaps some of his pleasure came from the women's befuddlement at all of this, which may have heighten Ed's sense of accomplishment, as Margaret observed with a smile.

Ed's study time and typing had a consistent impact on the women, who could not bear all the time he spent musing, rereading, and typing. "Forever typing!" as Ruth or Cassandra said frequently to each other, their voices filled with aggravation. Yet the three rarely talked about this until Ed prepared a few small pamphlets he called tracts, to pass out among their friends and family.

"Seems like Mom and Ruth are upset with you about these pamphlets you have been handing out," Margaret said, during one of her visits, as Ed handed her one of his small, new publications.

"Yes, I fear at times," Ed admitted, "I've made Ruth and Cassandra quite frustrated, or maybe I should just say angry, when I've attempted to pass these out. They shudder to think that I might be trying to force my thoughts on anyone else. So now I am learning to be discreet, waiting for people to inquire, even though this has proven to be infrequent, except for you, Margaret. I greatly enjoy your asking about my current projects or writings when you arrive for a visit."

Ed continually had his eye out for ways he could assist others. For instance, he discovered that during Cassandra's pregnancy, if he did the vacuuming, she would be greatly relieved. For the rest of their lives together, he did all the vacuuming. Also, he regularly prepared his own breakfast, thinking … 'this way I can free up the women to get on with their busy lives without having to prepare a morning meal.'

Perhaps the reverse was also true: that the 'always busy' women in Ed's life left some resentment—or anger—behind for him as they dashed here and there around town taking care of so many and so much, and Ed was not the only one noticing this.

"I don't know how Ed puts up with those two women running thither and yon to manage every event in this town and take care of all those in need," Leo, the neighbor who watched this unfold for years from his front porch, told his neighbor across the street, also a keen observer in the neighborhood, "People sometimes refer to Ed as a saint. Maybe trying to live with a saint might parcel out a few challenges itself!"

Some might say Ed lived a rather difficult life. Many knew of various family quarrels, quarrels that would arise between husband and wife or between the husband and the wife's lover, in addition to disagreements between the two women. Often, however, when points of tension would arise, the dividing line would be drawn between Ed and the women, even if they were having their own private squabble.

When this happened, Ed worked hard to control his feelings, and when things became too uncomfortable, he would quietly leave the room, turning to his desk and typewriter.

Any kind of direct confrontation brought Ed distress, and he felt removing himself worked pretty well, thus 'letting them fight it out between themselves,' or so he thought.

The women had a very different strategy—they would just explode. This generally cleared the air for the two of them. However, for Ed the thought of himself exploding, even when angry, would require more emotional energy than he felt he could bear, especially if he might be pushed to say what he thought or felt.

On some occasions, however, Ed did get caught, trapped in a high-velocity family quarrel among the three of them and, if this should happen in front of others, the pain it unleashed bit into him hard. This is exactly what happened on one hot, late summer evening, during one of Margaret's visits.

Something ignited a disagreement between Cassandra and Ruth out in the kitchen while they were finishing up their evening chores. Anger erupted and rolled out into the living room where Ed and Margaret sat visiting, and Ed, as was typical, became the focus of the blowup.

Earlier Cassandra and Ruth had been busy trying to finish up in the kitchen, with Ruth also wanting the pleasure of helping Margaret give the children baths. Having Margaret and the children underfoot for several days pleased them greatly but did take its toll.

Perhaps Ed made some simple comment about getting the little ones ready for bed. If he did, it could have easily taken place without Ed understanding how a word of his, at a time when they were exhausted, could trigger old, habitual disagreements between himself and the women. He could not recall anything he had said, and Margaret, who had settled the children into their beds upstairs, had heard nothing unusual.

However, something had happened that gave an overly tired Ruth an opportunity to express disapproval. And suddenly there she stood, in the living room doorway, hands on her hips, giving Ed a lecture in a loud, angry voice.

"You do not need to tell Cassandra or me anything about how to take care of our grandchildren! No one in this household agrees with you — all you do is cause trouble! And to tell the truth, I'm tired of hearing your opinions about anything!"

Grumbling to herself, she turned as abruptly as she had arrived and more or less marched back to the kitchen, where, from what Margaret and Ed could hear, Ruth and Cassandra continued their own argument.

A few minutes later, Ed and Margaret, somewhat paralyzed and still sitting in stunned silence, heard Ruth stomping up the stairs where she actually slammed the door to her and Cassandra's bedroom.

All this made Cassandra angry, and not one to hold in any emotion when it came to how Ruth and Ed did or did not get along, Cassandra then stormed through the living room, ignoring Margaret, while throwing angry words at Ed.

"I will never understand you! You know how upset Ruth gets when you act this way! Now look what you've done!"

Ed did not reply, but sat stoically, head lowered like a trapped animal, as Cassandra dressed him down. When Cassandra had had her say, she turned and followed Ruth, in a huff, up the stairs. For them, the evening had ended — and probably much too late to suit either of them.

A deafening quiet careened through the house.

Neither Margaret nor Ed had made a move. They sat, eyes averted, in silence at the two ends of the couch where they had so recently taken up what for Ed promised to be a treasured conversation.

Finally, after a prolonged silence and a deep sigh, Ed gathered himself together and, like a tried and exhausted old man, slowly stood up, his hands on his knees, helping to lift him from the couch.

"Well, it's probably time for my bedtime also," he said and started to leave the room.

Margaret could see and feel his hurt. She had no idea what to do or say. Stunned, she felt powerless, yet before he reached the door she found her voice with words that came in the form of a question.

"How do you stand it, Dad?"

Ed stopped in the doorway, his back to the room and Margaret. He could not remember such a public humiliation. Then, slowly, he turned his head back and looked, noticed something in Margaret's eyes, and then spoke words that did not sound anything like the man Margaret knew.

"Sometimes I have to grit my teeth ... in order not to scream ..." his words terse and honest while looking sideways just short of letting their eyes meet. Then he turned slowly ... and left the room.

As he walked away, with his shoulders drooped, Margaret couldn't move. She heard him in the kitchen, then in the bathroom, eventually on the stairs. All she could do was sit there, listening and thinking about the person she loved, someone totally broken open, a piece of his private life so utterly exposed.

That night might have been unusually grave. Yet Ed had struggled with himself often through all these years, likely unaware of the costs to him for his many efforts to manage his anger and the guilt that followed. Being denied Cassandra as a sexual partner so soon after they married had been both a physical and emotional struggle for him. Cassandra, the beautiful woman for whom he had yearned for years, one day became his wife yet had continually held him at a distance. It had to be a formidable hurt, then as now.

As Ed said, he had found a few special ways to actually touch her like rubbing her feet. But what about all the rest, the sexual intimacy that Ed naturally craved?

"Being cut off from any real intimacy," Ed confessed to Margaret years later after Cassandra had passed away, "left me feeling bereft, even at times betrayed. At least for a few years, while we lived at the hotel, we shared the same bed. But even there, Cassandra refused what I so desired. I don't know which is worse, but I'll never forget when we made the move to Essex and had enough rooms for her to have her own bedroom. A significant part of my life ended that day."

Any real physical contact with Cassandra came to a halt, all he had dreamed of when he fell in love with her suddenly ended.

That was bad enough; then Ruth arrived.

Ed found it difficult to speak disparagingly in any way of Ruth, for they had become true friends, to the surprise of some. Early on, when Ruth would stay only during weekday nights, sleeping with Cassandra, snippets of conflict could erupt. And even back then, it was hard to discern the shape of the conflict, what had brought on the eruption.

"In those early days," Ed continued, "I frequently felt, along with anger, which I'm sorry to have to admit, that perhaps I was just naïve or confused."

"I can understand that," Margaret said.

"Eventually, I came to realize that Ruth and I had been placed in competition for Cassandra's affection. Obviously"

Ed admitted, "I still wanted her affection, at least some of it. I actually think I was willing not to have Cassandra exclusively for myself, given the situation. However, back then, and for many years, it felt to me Ruth was determined Cassandra would be hers alone."

None of the three escaped these conflicts, each caught in a highly developed web of unmet desires, misunderstandings, and fears.

Ed might have told Ruth he already experienced very little in the way of Cassandra's affection, but that was not the issue. His mere presence in the house proved to Ruth that she needed to control Ed's access to Cassandra, and Ruth made a fairly good lifelong effort of that as long as Cassandra was alive. Ed, always trying to figure it out, probably could see the handwriting on the wall and worked hard to make peace, beginning with himself.

"I learned," he said, "how ... well, how to be as invisible as possible in my relationships at home. This holding in my thoughts, my urges, my frustrations did take a certain toll on my energy." Ed went on to acknowledge, with hesitation, the anger he felt, saying, "While not proud of my anger, I felt it understandable that I might feel that way.

"Yes, it is, Dad."

"When we married I made a lifetime promise, for better or for worse, even though I never expected this, but a promise is a promise. Most of all I wanted for us, Cassandra, Ruth, and me, to be able to survive as family. And," he said with a big smile, "I guess you would have to say we have actually managed to do that ... for my wife is now gone and here Ruth and I are, still together, our little family intact."

Again, Margaret agreed with Ed, joining his smile. She knew when Ed's primary strategy, to be kind, failed, in order to help maintain some kind of equilibrium, Ed tried to stay out of a lot of it (by typing in his room) or, when caught, to make some kind of a silent exit.

"I know, without any doubt, I frequently chose to walk away as quietly as I could while in some kind of giving-up hidden rage. I don't think I could ever really yell at anyone, but that doesn't mean I don't know what it feels like to want to yell," he struggled to say. "So, yes, when the losses felt too painful, I got up and left the room."

"Do you think you've been more angry than not over all these years?" Margaret asked.

"Well, that's a good question, but I don't think so. However, it brings another question I have had on my mind for some time. You know," he said, "how the women disapproved of my typing?"

"Yes, I am fully aware of that, Dad!" she said with a tender chuckle and smile.

"Well, do you suppose it could be that the force of my fingers hitting those old upright typewriter keys might have been a display of my anger? It's merely a thought," he added.

Still smiling, Margaret said, "Dad, I tried to use your type-writer once and those keys are hard to push down! But maybe it could have been a way for you to let off some steam."

"Well, I don't know." Ed said apologetically. "Were my wife still alive, I know I would not have wanted anyone, least of all me, to be saying many of the things that I have now said. These comments I have made about our life together—Cassandra's and mine, as well as the three of us ... well ..." bowing his head over his hands folded in his lap, deep in thought, then continued, "... I don't know ... I just don't know," he finally said.

From Ed this was a profoundly honest statement, for he would never have created such an unguarded moment, rarely if ever risked exposing Cassandra, or his own feelings about her, or their life together as a couple or as a family.

Finally he lifted his head and said, looking directly at Margaret, "My greatest hope and purpose was never to disturb or dismay Cassandra in any way, but only to love her. For I really did love her and always will, regardless." Again he paused and, when he spoke again, said with a slight smile, "and of course, we have our son ... yes, we did manage that wonderful event."

Nine

The Son & Heir

n impatient frown tightened on his mother's face. "Where have you been?"

Without giving the child a chance to stammer out a reply, she said, "Go sit in that corner," lifting her hand out of the soapy dishwater and pointing to the backdoor in the basement kitchen. "And you are not to move until I tell you to."

Worried, she thought, 'It's getting late. Ruth's meeting at the school must have gone longer than expected.'

Then having forgotten about the child, out loud she said, "What on earth ever made us think this was going to work today?" Cassandra's large dinner party was scheduled to begin in only a couple hours.

She had planned carefully. Ed would be back soon from the ice plant. 'It's going to be a late night here, with the serving and cleaning up. Ed can walk Taylor over to Dray's house.' Thinking it through settled her mind. 'Dray can put him to bed there until we finish up here.'

'Ruth! Where in hell's bells are you?' Her mind running as she wiped the back of her hand across her forehead. 'My goodness, it's hot in here,' she thought. Yet, as she wilted over the sink of steaming dishwater, she continued to scrub the stack of pots and pans before her.

She took a moment to glance over her shoulder to check on Taylor. He had found some small stones around the back of the doorjamb to play with. Entertaining himself. 'Good,' she thought. 'He's a good kid ... wouldn't have time to worry about one who wasn't.'

Just then, she heard Ruth's car door, and thought, 'At last. Help on the way.'

"Oh, my!" Ruth said, out of breath, dashing from the car. "You wouldn't believe that teachers' meeting. I thought those people would never stop wrangling and just make a decision! Useless waste of time if you ask me. At least when that new principal is chairing the meeting."

Frustrated and wound tighter than a drum, Ruth had hung up her coat and put her apron on before she noticed Taylor sitting in the corner.

"What's the matter with him?" she said in a lowered voice, looking at Cassandra and giving her head a slight nod toward the boy.

"Nothing, really. He was late getting here, and I scolded him. I do not have time to worry about him while he dilly-dallies his way around after school instead of getting himself over here. I'm thinking," she continued, "we'll have Ed take him to Dray's when he gets back with the ice."

"Did you call Dray?"

"No, but she should be home."

"Probably. But wouldn't hurt to call. Do you want me to do that before I take the turkeys out of the oven? They are ready, aren't they?"

"Sure. Call her. And yes, I checked them about thirty minutes ago and they were close to being ready. They'll need to rest on the countertop."

Ruth went over to the phone, found Mrs. Dray at home and perfectly willing for Ed to bring Taylor over. "I'll fix him something for his supper and put him to sleep here if you're not back before his bedtime," she said.

"Thank you. I expect this is going to be a long night," Ruth added.

With Ruth having arrived, Cassandra settled herself down. She called to Taylor and told him to wash his hands in the bathroom, then come over to the side table. "You can fold the napkins for us, and then when your Dad gets back, he can take you over to Dray's. She'll fix supper for you while the rest of us take care of this mess."

Ruth took a look in the ovens. Cassandra had cooked two huge turkeys, now ready to take out. 'Good timing,' Ruth thought as she checked the several casseroles of stuffing and sweet potatoes that Cassandra had ready for the heated ovens.

"Guess I'll get the potatoes on the stove and then get these turkeys out."

"Good," Cassandra said. Exactly what she expected.

'Everything seems to be in order,' Ruth thought, seeing Cassandra still washing up the pans in the other sink. "You got the salads all ready and in the refrigerator?"

"Of course!" Cassandra spoke in her irksome voice. "Why would you ask? What do you think I have been doing all day?"

So it went; the familiar rhythms of cooking for a large

crowd at the American Legion Hall, a routine for the three of them that was important for the family budget. And with little attention to the schoolchild dutifully folding the napkins.

Later that evening, while the women worked with the leftovers and cleaned the kitchen, Ed gave the dining hall a quick once-over (he would finish up in the morning). Then he left for Dray's house to pick up Taylor and get him into his own bed. Soon the three adults would fall into their beds, tired but pleased with their efforts. The meal had received high accolades as usual.

Ed and Cassandra each in their own way were glad to be the parents of Taylor, a capable boy who did well in school and caused them little trouble, despite the trio of parental voices: a harried mother, held-at-a-distance, nonemotional father, and Ruth, a strong, second mother who would one day also become his high school teacher.

Earlier, when Taylor reached school age, the first signal of trouble ahead regarding parenting arose as Ed and Cassandra faced the immunization requirement for all youngsters entering their first year in school. Cassandra had not planned to show the official letter to Ed, but he had noticed it on the table before she had put it away in her purse.

"Cassandra," Ed said, a worried look on his face, "you know we must refuse to let our child be vaccinated. It's dangerous. I do not want you to sign that letter regardless of what the school says they require." Rarely was Ed's voice so clear, and direct.

Ed's strong objections to vaccinations were known to Cassandra, but now the two had arrived at a sharp standoff. She said nothing. Trying to slow her emotions, she stepped to the sink and ran a glass of water for herself. She felt parched.

Cassandra knew better than to argue with Ed on this point. She thought his concern irrational and had no intention of wasting energy trying to change his mind. After he left the room, she folded the letter and put it in her purse, mumbling, "I know you object, and you know I disagree."

Later that week, while Ed was at work, Cassandra walked the child over to the school for his shot. However, when they returned, Ed noticed the bandage on Taylor's arm. To Cassandra's horror, Ed grabbed Taylor by his arm, ripping off the bandage as he pulled the child onto his lap, and literally attempted to suck the immunization fluid out of the arm.

It was a traumatic moment, everyone, including the child, caught in a paralyzing shock. Then suddenly Taylor started to howl, his sobs shaking the kitchen as he wiggled out of his father's arms and ran upstairs to his room.

For once, Ed had not walked out of the room filled with anger and his teeth clenched.

The break would resonate for years to come as the parents struggled to raise Taylor from two sides of a fence, the one raised between them that day. From that day forward Taylor's life in his family home would be under Cassandra's unquestioned authority.

In the days before Taylor's schooling, various women had taken care of him; however, once in school, Taylor returned to the Legion Hall following the school day where his mother found small tasks for him to do. "Someone had to sort the silverware," Cassandra would say.

As the years rolled by, with Ruth's teaching, Cassandra's and Ed's day and night work at the American Legion and elsewhere, and Cassandra's catering and party business, the three of them had their hands full. Everyone tried to be sensitive to

Taylor, a youngster who needed his playtime, but many times the adults required him to do more than the child wanted. Seeing Taylor's lack of enthusiasm for helping out, sometimes the women feared he lacked ambition, that if left on his own, he and his neighborhood buddies would idle away their time on afternoons following the school day.

When the women complained, old Mrs. Dray, the neighbor, would say to them, "Leave those youngsters alone. They're just kids, and someday they'll be all grown up and do fine."

Dray, as they referred to her, was right about this, but on some days Cassandra felt she needed Taylor's help.

"Where is Taylor?" Cassandra spoke with growing irritation as Ruth arrived at the Legion kitchen from her day's work at school. "I instructed him to come directly from school."

"He isn't here?"

"No! And those sixth-graders have been out for more than an hour."

Ruth quickly looked around the kitchen. Cassandra, filled with ire, stood over a large pot on the stove getting ready to ladle cooked vegetables into casserole baking dishes. That emptied pot would soon join a stack at the back sink, the cooking pans Cassandra counted on Taylor to wash up. Cassandra had worked all day preparing for a meal that evening in the clubhouse ballroom. She needed help.

"What do you want me to do?"

"Find Taylor!" her first command to Ruth.

Without saying a word, Ruth got back in her car and drove over to their neighborhood. No children playing there. Checked the house; not there either. Then she thought of the golf course, not too far from the Legion building. Recently she had overheard the boys talking about looking for golf balls.

There he stood, along with another kid from the neighborhood, wading through the tall grass at the edge of one of the course fairways, their heads down, looking for golf balls, 'without a care in the world,' Ruth fumed. She got out of her car and walked toward them. When Taylor saw her, a guilty look crossed his face.

"Taylor! You get over to the clubhouse this minute." Ruth shouted. "Your mother expected you more than an hour ago."

"I'm go-ing," he said. 'No enthusiasm in that voice,' Ruth thought. But he did take off across the field to the Legion, and, by the time she arrived, she overheard him saying, "Sorry, Mom. I forgot."

"Well, don't plan on 'forgetting' again," Ruth said, as she put on her apron, while Cassandra kept her focus on her cookstove.

The parents, including Ruth, agreed Taylor did not cause them much worry. However, issues would come up as the three of them tried to walk the fine line between being too permissive and too strict. This effort challenged Cassandra and Ruth in a heightened way, because of their often overextended lives.

For the young child, Grandmother Wright, from Chicago, provided almost the only connection for him to his Thomas family. Alice Thomas, Ed's mother, visited Kansas one summer taking the train from the east coast. Like Alice, most of Ed's family members lived quite a distance from Essex, and, as Cassandra quietly would say, "They're all just different." Grandmother Wright, the exception, became the only one in Ed's family to win Cassandra's and Ruth's approval.

After Taylor got involved in Scouting, the opportunity for some special summer trips came along. Most everyone in the troop had signed up that first summer to attend the

Philmont Scout Ranch in New Mexico. "Everybody's going, Mom! Can't I go?" Taylor desperately wanted to make the trip, and Cassandra wanted very much for him to get his wish. But the expense worried her.

"I don't think we can afford this," she told Taylor.

Later that evening she asked Ruth, "What do you think? Taylor really wants to go. I am worried because I don't think we can afford it."

"What I think, honey, is that you're correct. We really can't afford this in our budget this summer."

However, the next afternoon, as Cassandra worked on the family supper in the kitchen, Ruth arrived home from her teaching day with a smile on her face as she handed an envelope to Cassandra.

"What's this?" Cassandra asked.

"Oh, I made a little side trip on my way home and stopped by the bank."

By this time Cassandra had the envelope open, holding the check made out to the Scout Troop for Taylor's summer trip.

"I decided this is what that rainy-day fund is for, something important we couldn't afford in the everyday budget. So, I still don't think we can afford it, but I also think it will be good for Taylor to go."

Speechless, Cassandra stood looking at the check and then at Ruth.

"Let's send him," Ruth added, still smiling.

"Quick. Call Taylor in. He's out front with Bobby. I'll tell him that we have decided that he can go."

While life together for the two women was not without its difficulties, Ruth had become an indispensable part of the family, making it possible for all of them, including

Taylor, to go places and do things that would not have been possible otherwise.

In the fall of 1956, before they knew it, they were taking Taylor to college. Beside their car in the dorm parking lot, emptied of Taylor's things, Cassandra and Ruth stood together, arm in arm, in disbelief, as they watched Taylor waving to them as he disappeared into the freshman dorm.

"Where did all those years go?" Ruth asked.

"I know what you mean," Cassandra replied.

During the drive home the two recalled memories of Taylor's seventeen years. That two-hour drive felt like a world apart as they headed back home without him.

In the prior week, during days of preparation and packing up Taylor's clothes, Cassandra asked if Ruth thought they should let Taylor do his own laundry. "The information they sent says there are coin-operated washers and dryers in the basement of the dorm."

"I don't think that's a good idea," Ruth offered. "Taylor knows absolutely nothing about taking care of his clothes. We need for them to last, and so they need to be cared for."

Cassandra wasn't sure.

"Look," Ruth suggested, "as long as John comes up here from school each weekend to work with the youth, he can bring Taylor's dirty clothes with him on Friday. I can wash and iron them over the weekend and send them back with him on Monday morning."

That settled it. This meant that, on Saturday, between cooking for parties and getting the week's house cleaning done, Ruth would wash, iron, and repack Taylor's clothes for the return each Monday morning.

By the beginning of his junior year, Taylor had found a sweetheart, Margaret, among the freshman girls, and she could not believe the story about his clothes.

"Are you telling me that you, a perfectly capable twenty-year-old, send your dirty clothes home every week? To have your mother wash and iron and send them back?!"

"Yup. Happens every week just like clockwork," Taylor said with a grin.

"Well, that sounds totally crazy to me," Margaret replied in a bit of a huff. "When are you going to learn to take care of your own clothes? I don't get it."

Whether the women really thought Taylor would not take care of his things like Ruth would, the laundry plan proved workable and lasted all four of Taylor's college years, week after week. Margaret, once she got a good look at his parents, noticed the sheer delight Ruth took in being able to take care of Taylor's clothes. 'Still,' Margaret thought to herself, 'he better not expect all that kind of work from me. I would never think of ironing underwear, pajamas, and handker-chiefs — or pillowcases!'

Each summer between Taylor's college years, the women made arrangements for him to have a job back home. Cassandra's sister-in-law, Florence, owned an ice cream store, and during his first summer, Taylor helped Florence. Among the various jobs Taylor had during his school years, Cassandra always said she thought he enjoyed working in the ice cream shop most of all.

However, in the spring of his sophomore year, Taylor insisted he needed to attend a science camp in Colorado the coming summer. His favorite professor at the college set up the research program in the summers for his best students.

Taylor had high regard for Dr. Jacobs. From Taylor's experience with his professor, he decided to pursue a career in teaching science at the college level.

Cassandra was adamant that Taylor be allowed to go. "Ruth, we must send him. Dr. Jacobs will play an important role when it comes time for Taylor's graduate studies. I'm convinced. He needs to be there this summer."

"Sweetheart, I'm worried. This is a huge expense," Ruth said, while not saying what she was thinking, 'and I've been looking forward to having him at home this summer … we see so little of him.'

But Ruth grudgingly agreed. The women paid the summer tuition and sent him off.

The family needed for him to earn what he could during the summers because paying his tuition and other school expenses had become a troublesome drain on the household income. On many days when a bill came from the college, Ruth would make that increasingly familiar trip to the bank and her rainy-day fund. She was glad to do it, but later grew uneasy when Taylor resisted coming home for weekend and holiday visits, often saying that he had too much work to do. This brought disappointment to the family, especially Ruth.

Later that summer, after Taylor returned from science camp, he told his parents about his new friend, Margaret, from Kansas City. Earlier that spring, before her graduation from high school, Margaret had met Taylor on a blind date during a visit to look over the college. Later that semester, Taylor invited her to return to campus for the big end-of-the-year party, all unbeknownst to Taylor's family.

Now, the women had late August plans to attend a church meeting in Des Moines and would be driving through Kansas

City. Taylor wanted his mother to drop him to off at Margaret's on Friday and pick him up on Sunday as their way back home. Her parents had given their approval, and soon Margaret's mother, Elizabeth, wrote a note to his parents extending the invitation for Taylor's visit.

A few weeks later, as they arrived at Margaret's home and stepped out of the car, there were a few awkward moments among the three women and their two children. Taylor and Margaret, the only ones who knew each other, were obviously glad to see one another.

"Mother," Margaret said with a wide smile, "this is Taylor, and Taylor, this is my mother."

And then Taylor took his turn introducing his family to Margaret and her mother. "This is my mother, Cassandra, and our good friend, Ruth, a teacher who lives with us." Everyone seemed to be pleased to have faces to go with names they each had been hearing about. Except Margaret had never heard about Ruth. 'Interesting,' she thought to herself, 'I wonder why Taylor hasn't mentioned anything about Ruth?'

Elizabeth invited the women to come in, but they insisted they needed to be on their way, saying they were due in Des Moines for an evening gathering. While Ruth got Taylor's suit-case out of the trunk, Cassandra and Elizabeth visited briefly.

"When you come back through on Sunday afternoon, would you like to stop for an early supper before you get back on the road?" Elizabeth asked Cassandra. Cassandra looked at Ruth, who nodded her approval, and then they all agreed to Elizabeth's plan.

It was on that Sunday afternoon that the two families began to get acquainted. Through the years to follow, both Cassandra and Ruth, and eventually Ed as well, came to love

Elizabeth and Alfred, Margaret's parents. The two families mixed well, with the three women taking the lead, as they shared connections to the state-wide women's work in the church and AAUW.

From that first August weekend at the beginning of Taylor's junior and Margaret's freshman year, it appeared the two were committed to one another. But Taylor's family worried: he still had two years to complete and planned to go to graduate school. Ruth made it clear what she thought about their son's new friendship. "Taylor's not in any kind of financial situation to be thinking about a serious relationship," she told Cassandra.

The Essex family did not see much of Taylor that year, as he and Margaret continued to fall in love and make plans for a future together. Cassandra insisted from the beginning they should support Taylor in this relationship. "Margaret is a good match for him, comes from a good family, and she isn't spoiled," she told Ruth and Ed. No one who knew Cassandra would ever think she could have tolerated a spoiled brat for a daughter-in-law. She wanted someone she knew would be strong and not afraid of hard work. For her, Margaret fit that bill.

Taylor did come home for the summer prior to his senior year. The women loved having his feet under their kitchen table once again for a few months. While also home for spring break that year, he had taken it upon himself to find a summer job, working for the county, and had made some good money. Seeing his new effort gratified Ruth. Yet, when the letter arrived from Taylor in the early fall announcing that he had asked Margaret to marry him and had given her a ring, Ruth appeared blindsided and, frankly, speechless, as Cassandra read the letter to her.

"What does Taylor mean he has given her a ring? What ring? Where did he get a ring?"

"He asked me before he went back to school if he could use some of his summer money to purchase a ring for Margaret."

Cassandra's words took the wind out of Ruth. Tired from her long day of teaching and working around the house, she turned angrily to look at Cassandra face to face, hands on her hips. "You mean to tell me you gave Taylor permission to use his salary from the summer, the money he earned to help pay for his tuition — for a ring? I don't believe this," she said, turning back to wiping off the stove with a certain fury. When she thought she could speak, Ruth turned to look at Cassandra again, her look cold as ice. "Why didn't you tell me?"

"I did not tell you, and I am sorry. I should have." Cassandra spoke carefully. "I knew you would not be happy about it, and he so wanted to have a ring to give her this fall. They want to be married next summer."

"I frankly don't care what they want. They are children!" Ruth said. "We can't afford for him to be throwing away his money when we are counting our pennies to send him to college. And what's more, I don't see how Taylor can be thinking about taking on the responsibility of a wife next summer. Margaret will have two more years to finish her college, and Taylor says he is going to graduate school. It doesn't add up any way you look at it."

A deathly silence fell over the kitchen.

"I'll tell you one thing I know for sure," Ruth finally added, obviously not finished with her admonishments. "I am not going to be paying for his graduate school. Let the two of them figure that one out by themselves. This is totally irresponsible."

Ruth was as angry as Cassandra had ever seen her. Angry with Taylor and then with her for letting this happen, and leaving her out of the decision.

Silence.

Holding and rereading the letter, Cassandra finally spoke, tentatively, "In his letter, Taylor says he wants to bring Margaret home for a weekend sometime this month. I think that would be very nice. I'm going to write back and suggest that middle weekend when we don't have a big party to host. Would that be okay with you?"

The awkwardness continued.

Cassandra, hurt and stunned at Ruth's anger, was likely not that surprised.

Ruth continued to fume, as Cassandra left the kitchen and went to her writing desk in the front parlor. Later Ruth saw the note she had written to Taylor. She had left it, unsealed, for Ruth to mail, or look at and then mail.

Ruth chose to read Cassandra's letter before she went to bed.

"Come when you can," she had written. "We'll be glad to have both of you home for a few days. Ruth can fix up the bed in the upstairs hallway for Margaret." In her heart, Ruth knew Cassandra thought she could bring her around, but the deception had cut deep. Neither of them, most likely, looked forward to the cold bed they knew lay ahead for them that night. Cassandra turned out the parlor lights, used the bathroom, and then slowly climbed the steps to their bedroom. Ruth finished up a few last chores in the kitchen … biding her time.

And yet, their lives continued as always. Each day, up early for the work ahead, Cassandra in kitchens, Ruth at school. In and around this often-frenetic activity, Ed would come and go, seemingly oblivious to the current standoff between the women over the engagement ring.

The air continued tight and tense in the house, but if Ed had sensed anything was going on between the two women, he made no mention of it and managed to steer clear of upset.

A few weeks later, on a beautiful fall mid-October afternoon, the family expected Taylor and Margaret to arrive in time for Friday evening supper. As the women worked preparing the meal, Ruth noted Cassandra seemed distracted, keeping her eye out for the kids. When Cassandra saw their car, she uncharacteristically dropped everything and ran out the front door, apron flying, into the cool, early evening to meet them, while Ruth remained at the stove, holding tight to her anger.

"Quickly," Cassandra said to Margaret more or less in a loud whisper while opening the door and almost pulling her out of the car, "Go in and show your ring to Ruth! Go, go!"

Her insistent, frantic words provided a clear, if unspoken, message to Margaret: 'Trouble ahead!'

Puzzled, Margaret, now also on edge, gave a quick glance to Taylor who showed no emotion, then did as asked, got out of the car and, with Cassandra urging her along, a hand on Margaret's back, went all the way into the house, through the dining room and into the kitchen where Ruth stood at the stove, stirring something in a large pot.

"Hello Ruth. It's nice to see you," Margaret said, tiptoeing with uncertainty into the obvious tension. "I don't think you have seen the ring Taylor gave me last month," Margaret said, holding her left hand out for Ruth to see, Cassandra standing close by.

In a most unnatural voice, filled with studied disinterest, Ruth said, "Hmm ... yes ... yes, nice," her seething anger just below the surface, while she focused on the stovetop.

"Oh, it is so beautiful and looks lovely on your hand," declared Cassandra's raised and overly jolly voice as she took Margaret's hand to have a look at the ring herself, pretending she had never seen it, which, of course, she had.

"It is a beautiful ring," Margaret said shyly. All three of them frozen in place, with Margaret wondering what on earth could be wrong with the ring. Feeling she needed to say something, Margaret, in a tentative voice ventured, "I was surprised when Taylor gave it to me … and very happy."

"Ah, yes, well we were all surprised," Ruth, pounced on Margaret's words, in a tone just short of civil.

Hearing her own bitter voice shocked Ruth enough that she began to get hold of herself. "And happy for you, too," she managed with a bit more warmth.

Cassandra smiled. Ruth caught the relief that moved across her sweetheart's body as Cassandra relaxed.

"Now! Where did that son and heir go?" Cassandra almost shouted as she turned and went off looking for Taylor, who had, Margaret noticed, adroitly remained out of the kitchen, off in the living room talking with his father.

But now, Margaret was fuming inside, 'What on earth is going on here? With this crazy family and these feuding women? And where is Taylor? He's going to have some explaining to do.'

Yet, with the help of the good dinner Cassandra and Ruth had prepared, the difficulties, whatever they were, appeared to have been shoved under the table. Finally a lighthearted moment came when Ruth proudly carried in a pie, setting it on the table before her.

"Now, who will have a piece of gooseberry pie?" she asked, with a twinkle in her eye pointed at Taylor.

"What is gooseberry pie?" Margaret innocently ventured, her continuing dis-ease unexpectedly present in her voice.

"You don't know gooseberry pie!" the other four sang out in unison, a celebrative disbelief on their faces as they stared at Margaret.

Now, puzzled again, but this time about something that felt less tense, Margaret smiled while Taylor's family together seemed to enjoy Cassandra recounting the story of the Taylor family's love of this regional pie favorite.

"In fact, giving a piece of gooseberry pie to a newcomer in the family," Cassandra jokingly said with a smile, "has been a family test for many generations back."

'Okay,' Margaret thought, 'I think I can recognize a playful joke when I hear one,' as she worked to remove her concerns and relax.

But seeing the puzzlement on Margaret's face, Cassandra quickly added, "We're just playing with you and you don't need to eat it. However, it is pretty good pie."

More relaxed, Margaret tried to enjoy the pie; however, gooseberry would never become a favorite.

Thus, the crisis appeared to dissipate during the course of the short weekend, and Taylor and his family and Margaret seemed to have a rather pleasant time together in the Essex family home. In particular, Cassandra and Ruth had enjoyed introducing Taylor's fiancée at their Sunday School class that final morning.

It wasn't until after church and Sunday dinner around a perfectly congenial family table, as the visitors got in the car to make their way back to college, that the two lovebirds had the chance for a private moment. The blow up in the kitchen upon their arrival Friday evening still had Margaret stumped.

"What was that all about?" Margaret asked Taylor while still trying to smile and wave goodbye to the three folks standing in the front yard, waving them off. She, after all, had been waiting for almost forty-eight hours.

"What do you mean?" Taylor asked, turning to look at her, seemingly perplexed, as he steered the car away from the curb and away from his family home.

Totally baffled, while taking a good look at him, she wondered, 'How could he have possibly missed the opening fireworks Friday evening?'

"Honey, your mom and Ruth! You saw your mother yank me out of this car seat the minute we arrived."

Seemingly oblivious, he shrugged his shoulders while giving Margaret a puzzled look.

Astonished. Margaret stared at Taylor in disbelief.

"I can't see how you could have missed it!" Margaret continued. "You watched your Mother pull me out of this car and push me into the house!" She paused to catch her breath, then added, "But I guess you conveniently did not see her shove me almost into Ruth who was standing in the kitchen angry as a peacock."

After collecting herself, confused by Taylor's silence, she asked, "Honey, is there something about this ring you haven't told me?"

"Not that I know of," Taylor offered blandly without looking at Margaret, keeping his eyes on the road. He surely could have guessed and said there might have been a fuss about using some of his summer earnings on the ring. But he didn't.

It would be many years before Cassandra recounted the story of the purchase of the ring for Margaret, finally solving an early mystery within Taylor and Margaret's household.

That December, the engaged couple spent the Christmas holiday in Kansas City, sharing their winter break with the Millers and working on plans for the wedding, which had been set for early July. After the New Year, on their way back to their spring semester, they stopped over for two days in Essex to attend an engagement party one of the nieces had organized for the Taylor family to meet Margaret. It was a full-family event, and everyone seemed to enjoy meeting Margaret. By now Cassandra, Ed, and Ruth had all come to think the two made a lovely couple.

In the spring, Cassandra decided to host a shower for Margaret. Elizabeth drove down from Kansas City, and Margaret drove up from the college for the weekend. On a late Saturday morning, Cassandra's and Ruth's women friends arrived bearing gifts for the bride-to-be. The only other out-of-town guest was Elsie Harris, a longtime friend of Elizabeth and Alfred Miller. In fact, for the past few years, she had stayed in the Miller's home on weekdays during the school year. Elizabeth had picked her up in Emporia on her way to the Millers for the Saturday party.

There were many gifts for the bride-to-be. Ruth gave Margaret a rolling pin. Being the pie maker in the family, she wanted Margaret to know how to make a pie and knew the importance of a good rolling pin. There were mixing bowls, cookbooks, and kitchen gadgets galore. And a steam iron from Elsie. However, after the event ended and she and Elizabeth helped Margaret pack the gifts into Elizabeth's car for the trip back to Kansas City, Elsie reached in and grabbed the box holding the iron.

"I'm taking this back to the store!" she announced to Margaret and Elizabeth. "Sitting there watching all afternoon as you opened these gifts, it suddenly occurred to me that every one of them had something to do with all the housework ahead of you. I simply cannot bear it. You will find another gift, something quite different, from me at the house the next time you're home."

The most memorable gift was the one Cassandra had picked out for her soon-to-be daughter-in-law. When Margaret unwrapped the large box, neither she nor her mother recognized the object. Elsie also looked mystified. Cassandra saw the questioning look in their eyes.

"Elizabeth, do not tell me you don't have a Foley Food Mill," Cassandra said, as if speechless.

"I have to admit that I've never seen or heard of one," Elizabeth replied.

Totally nonplussed, Cassandra stated emphatically, "Well! Margaret must have one, and I'm glad I've seen to it. A woman cannot keep house and fix food without a Foley Food Mill."

This little give-and-take also prompted conspiratorial laughter among Elizabeth, Elsie, and Margaret at some point later that spring back home in Kansas City. "People can be so funny," they agreed.

Elsie kept her promise. When Margaret arrived back home at the close of the school year, she found a beautiful silver candy dish, exquisitely wrapped and sitting on her bed. The replacement for the steam iron and all it symbolized, from Elsie, who had already gone home to the farm for the summer.

Ruth remained unconvinced when she heard about the switch. "Margaret's going to need that iron long before she needs a fancy silver dish," she told Cassandra.

The summer wedding, the big affair, took place without a hitch. Taylor walked his mother down the aisle while one of the groomsmen escorted Ruth behind Cassandra, followed by Ed, walking by himself.

The Millers had worked hard to make Cassandra, Ed, and Ruth's stay a pleasant one while in Kansas City for the wedding. Alfred's brother and his wife hosted the Taylor family in their lovely home, a guest room for the two women and another for Ed. Well before that weekend, Elizabeth had worked out every detail with Ruth about the accommodations for the family, as well as who would sit where, both at the rehearsal dinner and at the wedding. She and Alfred wanted Taylor's family to feel welcomed and comfortable with all the arrangements.

The newlyweds left from Kansas City in early August for Florida where they continued their education at the university. Ruth wanted in the worst way for Taylor and Margaret to let her oversee the packing of their clothes and things for the car. She wrote a letter offering to drive to Kansas City to take care of everything.

"What is this with Ruth and your clothes?" Margaret asked after reading Ruth's letter.

Taylor merely shrugged his shoulders. Margaret wanted information.

"Talk to me, Taylor, I need to know."

"Know what?"

"About your family. You never talk with me about these three, your immediate family. Why?"

"Well, I don't know what to say to you, other than maybe Ruth just likes to do up my clothes."

"Taylor, this isn't about your clothes. It's about your family. Do you not want to talk about your family with me?"

"I don't want to talk about them with anyone sweetheart, and, mostly, it's just that I don't know what to say."

Margaret just shook her head, purplexed.

"I would if I could, but I can't," Taylor offered finally.

With a deep sigh, Margaret said, "Okay, honey. Do you want me to answer her letter, say thanks and that things are all organized for our departure?"

"Uh huh," Taylor murmured, adding a weak, "Thank you."

Whether he was thinking it or not, it was obvious that Taylor Thomas was about to make his most significant, and close to permanent, escape from his Essex family.

Margaret wrote the letter.

Friday

Dear Mom, Dad, and Ruth,

We are progressing with our plans to leave here soon. Thanks, Ruth, for your kind offer to come and assist, but we are all organized for the departure. Both Taylor's and my jobs end this next Thursday. We've reserved one of the smallest U Haul trailers so we can take my cedar chest along. Regardless of what we find to rent, this should be a helpful piece of furniture. Taylor will get the trailer on Friday morning. We'll pack up, then say a few farewells around here that afternoon and be on our way early Saturday morning. Will drop you a line from the road. Thanks again for everything.

Love,
Margaret

Back home in Essex, Cassandra read Margaret's letter to Ruth while she was finishing supper preparations. The two women glanced quickly at each other and, without saying the words, both felt another, even bigger shift in their lives lay ahead. Florida suddenly felt far, far away. Cassandra folded up Margaret's letter and left it with Ed's mail on the table by the door. Their son finally out of the nest and out of their reach—a feeling experienced by Cassandra and Ed, yet more profoundly expressed by Ruth throughout the years to come.

The unusual configuration of Taylor's family was never a matter of concern or discussion by Margaret or her parents. However, from time to time, the Millers wondered about this interesting family from small-town Essex, curious about their story. Taylor continued to say little to Margaret about his family throughout the years and professed forgetfulness when asked about his early upbringing.

Taylor had never eagerly rushed back home and this pattern would continue throughout his life. After the marriage, Margaret, and eventually the grandchildren, as well, became the most present links between Taylor and his Essex family. In the family's elder years, when Cassandra died and then some years later Ed passed away, it was Margaret and the children standing by the surviving members in their grief. Taylor, who always lived in the vicinity, would drop by infrequently when driving through the Essex area, stopping for a meal or a rare afternoon visit, always eager to make his escape. However, the three of them, then his dad and Ruth, and finally Ruth alone, with unfailing love, welcomed their now adult son with open arms.

Some of the puzzling riddles that played out between Taylor and his family through the years would one day be unraveled, but only at the last moment. As it happened, Taylor found one final opportunity to draw together some of his untold story.

Ten

The Mistake

eenagers! One would think that teenagers would know better. And of course, teenagers who are guests in someone else's home certainly should." Ruth's thoughts on that early summerlike afternoon as she worked in the kitchen.

"Mi-losz," Ruth called out when she heard the screen door open and close. "Milosz, is that you?"

Ruth had just put down some yeast bread; she would be up early in the morning baking it for their week's toast and sandwiches. Milosz, returning from class, came in the front door dropping his books on the sideboard in the dining room.

"I'm thirsty!" he said, heading to the refrigerator. "Sure is hot out there. I don't remember this kind of heat this early last year."

"Welcome to spring in Kansas," Ruth said. "We could be having winter again by week's end."

Ruth had taken Cassandra down the street to the hairdresser for a new permanent. Ed was still downtown at work in his music store. The house, quiet.

'Breathing room,' thought Ruth, 'especially nice when I get home from school and have things I need to do.'

And now she had the small pleasure of a young man in her kitchen having a quick afternoon snack.

As an aside, and intentionally reaching for a nonchalant tone, Ruth said, "Oh, Milosz, I think you forgot about picking up your clothes. Remember I mentioned that to you last week. I'm the old one around here, the one who is supposed to be forgetful. So before you do anything else, would you gather up your clothes for the laundry, and maybe even organize some of that mess up in your bedroom?"

He did not move or say a word. So Ruth continued, as she punched down the dough again, "If this weather holds, I'm going to do laundry tomorrow when I get home from school. It would help if your clothes got into the hamper today."

He still had not looked up or responded.

"You know," Ruth said, attempting to fold in a chuckle, "some of those clothes you might be able to wear again if you'd hang them up. I don't need any more laundry to do around this place than is necessary."

With Ruth's words still hanging in the air, Milosz finally turned to look at her—a sullen, surprisingly angry look in his eyes. Then, like a robot, he put the water glass down, turned, walked mechanically out of the kitchen, picked up his books, and slowly mounted the stairs. And closed his bedroom door. Hard.

Chilled, Ruth sort of whispered, "Whew."

Shaken by his behavior, a few minutes later she went to the bottom of the stairs to listen. She could hear him in Taylor's old room and the sound of things being thrown around.

Ruth had not intended to make him angry. In fact, when she asked him to get up there and clean up his room, she thought she did it with a bit of humor, trying to lighten the message. From his look and the sounds coming from upstairs now, she thought she might have failed in the light-humor department.

'Maybe it wasn't a good idea to invite Milosz into our home,' her mind flooded with thoughts as she went back to her work in the kitchen. When the idea first came to her almost a year ago now, it seemed to make sense. Overall, Ruth thought it had gone pretty well. But today's encounter had puzzled her. She had a growing feeling of unease.

Milosz, an exchange student from Poland, had arrived in Essex at the beginning of last year's school term. His schooling was already off schedule because he had graduated from secondary school back home and been assigned here as a senior in high school.

As a student, last year he had done quite well. Popular with the students and the teachers, Milosz seemed to make friends easily and do well in his classes. People in the small town came to enjoy him as one of their own, taking him under their wing. His host family belonged to their church and he had been active in the youth group. So Ruth had the opportunity to get to know him at school and at the church. He seemed fine at both places, friendly and outgoing.

Then, toward the end of the school year, instead of going back home to Poland, he had qualified to begin college. Ruth heard that he wanted to remain in Essex another year to attend junior college. So when he stayed after class one day to talk with Ruth about his idea, she encouraged him. Ruth, pleased he wanted to continue his schooling, felt proud of the work he had been doing in her class that year. Now it turned out Milosz had explored the possibility of a one-year extension on his student visa, and his request had been approved.

The situation, however, had changed in his host family. Their son planned to return home and would need his bedroom. Evelyn had told Ruth the experience of having Milosz in their home and family had gone quite well.

Later that week, as Ruth and Cassandra worked together in the kitchen cleaning up the supper dishes, Ruth mentioned Milosz's plan to stay in Essex to attend junior college for a year. And, she told Cassandra, Milosz needed to find a family to host him.

"Well, we could certainly let him have Taylor's old room. It's just sitting there empty," Cassandra offered. "What would you think about that?"

Then, as Ruth thought about what she would say, Cassandra continued, "You know how much I hate thinking about how long it is between the kids' visits. We should fill up that room again with another young man. It would be good for all of us."

After Taylor left for college, they had kept his bedroom as he had left it, hoping he would be coming home on a more or less regular basis, which rarely happened. But their plan did not work at all after the kids had married and moved to Florida. Ruth finally had cleaned the room from top to bottom, covered the mattress pad with an old, clean quilt, pulled down the shades, and closed the door. 'Taylor and Margaret live too far away and will do well to get here for a visit in the summers," Ruth thought with sadness as the door latch clicked behind her.

Back in the kitchen, Cassandra's mind continued tracking the question about Milosz. "So by the summer when we might need to have Taylor's room for the family, Milosz would be gone," she said. "And it certainly would not add much to have one more person at the dinner table, not in this house."

Ruth continued to think it through as she stirred the gravy on the stovetop.

"Of course, we need to talk with Ed," Cassandra offered, continuing to think out loud.

Ruth agreed, a smile spreading across her face that no one could see. She liked the way Cassandra, the take-charge woman, wanted to make sure she consulted Ed. Ruth could, after all these years, chuckle to herself when this happened.

After they talked it over at dinner that evening, Ed said, "Sounds like a fine idea."

'For Ed,' Ruth thought later, as she worked cleaning up the kitchen, it's always the more the merrier,' a thought she kept to herself. Actually Ruth liked the idea.

The next day at school, Ruth asked Milosz to remain after class and extended the family's invitation to him to stay in their home the following school year. Milosz seemed pleased and grateful.

One evening the following week, when Ruth knew they would all be at home, she invited Milosz to come for supper. At the end of the meal, Ruth gave him a tour of the house showing him the downstairs and all the bedrooms upstairs. "Just an old, simple house, with four bedrooms," she explained to Milosz, "but not many closets. However, this room has one," she said as she opened the door to the empty room at the end of the hall.

Taylor's room held only a small chest of drawers and the bed. "I could probably find a desk and chair to put in here for you to use. But when winter arrives, it will be much too cold in here to do anything but sleep. There's no central heat in here; it used to be part of the attic. This small gas burner might take the chill off while dressing, if you stand right in front of it, but not even that if the wind is blowing."

"Ah, it looks fine, Miss Peterson. Thank you for inviting me into your home. I really do appreciate it."

Milosz did not seem to have balked at Ruth's wintery tales, and Ruth felt his words of gratitude to be genuine. 'He's a nice young lad,' she thought. 'How lovely, having a young man in this room again,' she told herself as the two of them went back downstairs to join Cassandra in the kitchen.

Looking back, Ruth remembered the happy times. She recalled her favorite time the past year, when Margaret and the grandchildren unexpectedly arrived in Kansas for an extended stay. Milosz fell in love with the little ones, Patricia, not yet two, and Steven, a baby of about three months. The kids were moving to Cleveland, and Margaret and the children were at her parents in Kansas City while Taylor made the transition. He would drive to Kansas City to collect his family during the December university break.

In late November, not long after Margaret arrived, she and the children came to Essex for a week's stay. Patricia and Milosz became inseparable. Anytime Milosz sat down, Patricia scrambled into his lap, dragging along several books, saying, "Read. Milosz, read." He loved this. When Christmas arrived, Milosz bought a rag doll to give Patricia as a gift. She named it "Milosz's doll" and had it for years.

It is important to underscore how much the four—Cassandra, Ruth, Ed, and Milosz—had become a family across the fall and winter. At least that is how it had seemed to the three elders in the house.

A week or so following the awkward "please-pick-up-your-dirty-clothes" afternoon, Ruth and Cassandra were in the kitchen fixing supper when the phone rang. Ruth ran to the front entryway to answer it. Ida, one of their friends from church, was calling for Ruth on what had been a lovely spring day.

"Do you have a moment to talk?" she asked.

"Yes. Supper's in the oven," Ruth said.

"Well, I don't know how to say this, but I think you need to know. So I'm just going to say it."

"Say what?" Ruth was startled by Ida's strange voice. "Ida, what's the matter? Is Ralph okay?"

"Oh, yes. We're fine. This isn't about us. It's about ... well ... it's about Milosz."

"About Milosz? What on earth do you mean?"

"Well ... Milosz has been ... talking," Ida stammered.

"What do you mean ... talking?"

"Well, yes, I mean he has been talking. Talking about ... well, talking about things there, well, at your place, Ruth. About you and Cassandra ... and Ed."

Ruth felt a cold silence fall over her ... an icy shiver driven by the tone of Ida's voice. 'What on earth could this be,' Ruth thought as she tried to get control of her own voice.

Ruth's frustration finally caught hold, "Ida, what's going on? What have you heard?"

"Ruth. I'm sorry. But I do think you need to know. Milosz's been talking about you and Cassandra living together. You know what I mean ... your bedroom. It's not nice at all for him to do that when you all have been so kind to him. In fact, it seems downright mean."

By now, Ruth's mind and emotions were beginning to catch up with Ida.

"Alright. Thank you, Ida. Thank you for your call. I appreciate it," Ruth said, feeling suddenly very uncomfortable.

"I don't want to upset you or Cassandra. Goodness sake.

We've been friends for all these years. But …"

The thought now occurred to Ruth that maybe Ida had more to tell and now felt she needed to ask again even though she felt uncomfortable for both of them.

"Ida is there more … more you want to say?" Ruth certainly did not need or want to hear anything more.

"No, that's all. I really don't know what he's saying. I've only heard others saying that he's been talking, and they're hearing about it from various corners of the community. You know, some folks at church and elsewhere. You need to know we're all really upset about this. Everyone is mad at him. He has no right to talk about our good friends that way."

Ruth opened her mouth to say thank you again, but all that came out was a tired sigh.

"Ruth. Now I don't want you or Cassandra or Ed to worry about this at all," said Ida. "Not in this community. You do not need to worry. Everyone loves all three of you. You know that. We love and respect you and always will. Please don't worry about us."

"Yes, Ida, thank you for that. And thank you for your call." Ruth paused to think what next to say. "Guess I'd better get back to taking care of supper. Again, I do want to thank you. I really do appreciate your call … and Ida, you truly are a good friend."

And then, still in a daze but trying to get beyond what she had been told, a final practical thought surfaced, and Ruth said, "Oh, Ida, don't forget you're to give the blessing at the Circle meeting tomorrow night. I had you on my list to call this evening."

"Yes, of course. I've got that on my calendar. Looks like we have a good program lined up, thanks to you and Cassandra."

"Okay. Well, I'll see you then," Ruth said as they both hung up the phone.

Ruth stood there. Stunned. Absolutely stunned. Ida's words made no sense to her. And Ida had not really told her anything, nothing about what Milosz said, but her words were bone-chilling nonetheless.

Ruth stood as if nailed to that spot, trying to make sense of this. Grateful for Ida's call? Probably a hard thing for her to do, making that phone call. Ruth knew that, heard it clearly in Ida's voice, deep discomfort in every word she said.

Slowly Ruth realized she probably did need to be grateful, very grateful. 'Friends, thank God for good friends,' her small prayer as she heard Cassandra calling out from the kitchen.

"Ruu-th, are you still on the phone? Did I hear you say it was Ida? Did you remind her about giving the blessing tomorrow night?" Cassandra's voice brought Ruth back from wherever her mind and heart had taken her.

"Yes," Ruth said as she went back into the kitchen, took the potholder, and opened the oven door to check the casserole. Cassandra stood washing the lettuce, getting ready to make the salad. Ed would be home any minute now. And Milosz. He had a late class today but always made it back home in time for supper.

Ruth could feel Cassandra's eyes right through her back.

Cassandra could always read Ruth like one of her books — quickly — even from behind.

Looking over her shoulder, she had her eyes on Ruth and, feeling the pull of Cassandra's look, Ruth turned around and their eyes met, Cassandra's hands in midair holding the head of dripping lettuce, the faucet still running.

"What's wrong?"

When Ruth didn't say anything right away, because she could not think of what on earth to say, Cassandra turned off the water, looked at her, and asked again, "What is wrong?"

Leaning against the stove, Ruth looked at her love's beautiful face and said tenderly with a smile, "You know, honey, I don't think anything is wrong. Not really. It seems our young boarder has been out and about talking about things of which he has no understanding and therefore no business talking."

"What on earth do you mean?"

"Well, I think perhaps I made Milosz mad when I insisted he clean up his room last week," Ruth said.

"What's Ida got to do with that?"

"Well," Ruth sighed, "dear Ida, our good friend, did not want us to be unaware that Milosz has been talking."

"Talking?"

"Yes, talking around town … about us. I don't know, Ida didn't hear him say anything. She's only letting us know what she has heard from others, others who have told her about Milosz making comments."

"Comments? What comments?"

"I don't know. Maybe … well, probably he's saying it is hard to live with me, the old battle-ax from school," Ruth added. "He'll get over it. I'll talk to him."

Ruth could tell by the look in her eyes, that Cassandra knew she had dodged the question. Just as Cassandra started to ask another, the back door opened. Ed, home from work. The women's eyes met silently over the kitchen table between them in the middle of the room. Ed seemed oblivious.

"Good afternoon, ladies," he said with a big smile. "Ruth, that was a great sandwich in the lunchbox today," Ed added as he put it on the sink top with the other pots and pans to be washed up later.

"We'll have supper on in a few minutes," Cassandra said. "I laid your mail on the phone table by the front door." Then she looked back at Ruth, her eyes almost pleading.

At that moment, the women heard Milosz come in the front door.

"Well, good evening to you, Milosz." Ed greeted him in the front entryway. "How were things at school today?"

"Milosz," Ruth called from the kitchen breaking into Ed's welcome to him. "Supper will be ready in a few minutes. Time to wash up."

A few minutes later as they gathered in the kitchen, Ruth dished up the plates from the stovetop and the family sat down to supper. On most evenings at the supper table, Ruth would wish Ed would not tell half the stories he brought home, but on this night she actually said a little prayer of thanks (privately in her heart) when he started in on a story about something from his day.

"A young mother came into the music store with two small children," he began. "I think she might be the daughter of the Lewis family who farm out east by the reservoir. Didn't she marry someone from up toward Emporia a few years back?"

Ruth knew the family and didn't really have the energy to get involved, but on that night she needed a story.

"Yes, she married one of the Hagemans' sons. The younger one, I think."

"Yes, that's the one. He used to be one of the delivery boys at the dairy."

"Yes. What did she want?" Ruth asked.

"The older child has been asking to play in the school band. Don't think the family has much experience with music. She wanted to know if I could show them some instruments."

Ed obviously had enjoyed tooting on all the horns, playing the fiddle and the banjo for them to give them some idea of what kinds of sounds the different instruments made.

"Did they rent or buy something?" Ruth asked, trying to keep alive the sense that they were all having a conversation, even though Cassandra clearly looked worried and not fully present, and Milosz had not raised his eyes to meet Ruth's for even a moment since he walked in the room.

"Well, now, I'm not sure if they will at some later time, but no, they could not make any decisions today," Ed continued. "And I think that's probably best."

"Well! You are in business and do need to sell something sometime," Ruth found anger slipping out when she had not expected it. And aimed at Ed. But, at that moment, what he had said or how he had said it had pulled at that old thread in their life together: frustration about his lack of support for the family.

Ruth's little outburst killed that story and any others that might have emerged. Milosz excused himself, saying he had to study for an exam. They all heard his footsteps on the stairs and the door to his room close. Ed finished his supper in silence, then got up, thanked the women for the good supper, and started for the front room.

"Do you still want to watch the basketball game tonight?" he turned to ask Ruth before he left the kitchen.

"Oh, that's right," Ruth said, grateful for his patience with her at that moment. "Kansas plays tonight. I'd forgotten. Sure, I'll be in soon."

Cassandra and Ruth looked at each other across the table of dirty dishes as the room quieted. In the way of people who know each other well, they did a bit of conversation with their eyes, then got up and got to work. Ruth filled the dishpan with water and set it on the stovetop to heat for rinse water while Cassandra scraped and stacked the dishes. Ruth took out the garbage while Cassandra put the leftovers away. Then Ruth filled the sink with suds and began to wash the dishes. When the water on the stove came to a boil, Cassandra brought it over to the deep side of the sink where Ruth would rinse the dishes and lay them out for her to dry; exactly what they did every evening together. A simple routine, full of pleasure — most of the time. Only tonight they seemed to have nothing to say. Ruth felt weary and concerned.

Soon the two women had things cleaned up and the kitchen put to bed for the night. Only one skillet left on the warm stove to finish drying.

"I'll get that later," Ruth said.

Cassandra said she needed to finish a book she was pre-viewing for a book review scheduled for next month. Ruth had found it for her, a memoir of a pioneer woman from this area, a topic near to Cassandra's heart. Cassandra knew Ruth would go up to talk with Milosz, though the two of them had not actually spoken those words. They would talk later.

Ruth went to the bottom of the stairs, took a deep breath, then climbed the steps, walked down the hallway to Milosz's room, and knocked. He didn't say anything, so she knocked again as she opened the door and went in. She carefully closed the door behind her and turned around to face Milosz. With her back to the door, she stood for a moment, getting ready for whatever she would say.

When she looked at him, her anger began to soften. 'He's so young, even though he is now almost twenty years old, away from his family, his country, his ways of life … testing new waters in his own personhood,' thought Ruth. 'Who knows, he may even be confused about sexuality, maybe his own. We don't really know anything about this young man, about his troubles, his life.'

Ruth's thoughts eased even more.

'All I know, all we can really know is that this young man is a child of God, as we say at church, worthy of our love and care.' That is what it finally came down to for Ruth. Having named this, she found her strength and a way forward.

"Milosz, we need to talk," she began trying to keep her pace slow and easy. "Someone has told me you have been saying things about us, maybe about me, in particular, out in the community."

Her words were met with a cold silence.

'Darn him,' she thought. 'He's not going to face me.'

She could feel her anger on the edge of rising again. 'Milosz's mistake was that he thought he had something to tell,' she thought to herself, 'but his news turned out not to be news. It was as if he thought he could turn our lives into something unseemly or improper.' These thoughts filled her with frustration.

"Milosz, there is nothing here for you to tell others," she said. "There is nothing about our life in this home to tell … no 'news' … because there is nothing hidden here." Then she went on to say, "And your actions, trying to make it so, I believe, have backfired on you. I'm sorry."

Ruth, with her emotions bouncing all over the place, did feel sorry for him.

"Do you have anything you want to say to me? About this? Or about anything else?" she asked.

More silence. Milosz was not going to say anything. Ruth knew that now.

He continued to hang his head, his eyes looking down at the floor. Stoic. Totally stoic.

"Milosz," she said, deciding to take another approach, "I feel you may be angry because of what I said last week about cleaning up your room. Or taking care of your clothes."

Still nothing. He gave no reaction.

"Well, I want you to know I'm sorry if I made you feel this way, made you feel like you needed to get back at me in some way." Then she continued, "But whatever you have been saying to your friends around town is now coming back to haunt you ... and us together."

Now she felt back on edge but did not want to hit him in the face with any anger. She did, however, want to make it clear he'd made a mistake. A big mistake.

"Milosz, when people gossip and talk about things they really know nothing about, and do it behind people's back, it's a hurtful thing. Whatever you have gossiped about has hurt us all, beginning with yourself."

Ruth paused, still wanting to give him a chance, but he did not move, so after a bit, she went on.

"Well, I want you to know our friends who called ... well," she hesitated, hoping to find the right thing to say. "What I want you to know is that they are not worried about us. They are worried about you. And now I'm worried about you. I want you to do well at school this year. I want you to have a good experience to take back home with you to Poland. And, regardless of whatever you have done or said, I want you to know that you are still welcome in our home."

And with that Ruth turned to open the door to leave, and, as she did, added, "I hope you do well on your exam tomorrow," and closed the door behind her.

Ruth paused just outside the door, almost leaning on it for support. She noticed her body was shaking, so she took a moment to breathe and collect herself, while listening for any kind of movement from inside the room.

Not a sound. Ruth took one more deep breath and went back down the hall to the staircase.

Walking down the stairs, Ruth thought how this young man from a faraway place, another culture, had unbeknown to himself probably thought he might rock the boat in this little town and make people feel something, something shameful. But, up there, she had seen shame in him. Only shame.

She took a few deep breaths, quietly hoping Milosz would realize all of them could get past this. She really did not know if they could, but Milosz had to decide. As she went back into the kitchen, her thoughts continued, 'Sometimes that is the way it is with young people. You do what you can and then have to let it go, just let them go. Let them make their own mistakes while finding their way in life.'

In the kitchen, she put away the skillet that had been drying over the pilot light on the stove and hung up her apron. Then she joined Ed in the living room for the basketball game on the TV. In the front room, Cassandra did not appear to even look up from her book as Ruth sat down to watch some of the ball game with Ed, now fully engrossed.

When the game ended, Ruth realized she had fallen asleep in her chair. Ed had turned off the television. Cassandra and Ruth took turns in the bathroom and went upstairs to their room. Later they heard Ed, first in the kitchen, then in the bathroom, and eventually his measured footsteps on the stairs.

Cassandra and Ruth talked in soft voices as they got ready for bed. Knowing little, they guessed Milosz's talking probably came from some anger at Ruth's bossiness around the house. Of course, they did not know and couldn't know. Maybe even Milosz didn't understand what he had done. This they felt pretty confident about.

But as the two women lay in each other's arms on that night, they knew nothing could be improper about the life they shared. Together they understood their lives clearly, lovingly, two people full of deep affection and love for each other and grateful everyday they could live their lives together as they had chosen. They held deep respect for each other and were both filled with gratitude that they had the other close by each day, feeling that together their lives added up to so much more than they would if they were apart. Nothing could take that away from them. This they knew.

Looking back over the years of their lives together and the life of this family, they did belong right there, together in their small town. Cassandra and Ruth grew up nearby. And Ed had been accepted and loved unlike most newcomers before him. In this community, everyone knew almost everyone else, and everyone knew most of everyone else's business, and never before or after Milosz's mistake were these three hurt again in that way.

Among the townspeople, many of whom interacted almost daily, there was a palpable feeling that the town itself was one large, extended family. Most saw themselves as caring about one another and trying to make sure everyone was getting on as best they could. This is how their little town had made it through the Depression, the drought, the wars with all the losses and sorrows, and the other ups and downs all families experience through the years.

Neighbors were known to pool their resources — their eggs, chickens, vegetables from their gardens, the bread they baked, the peaches from their trees, their know-how to fix things, lending their hands to labor for and with one another when needed — and they made it through, together. This town was the place where these two women, and their families before them, had given and received along with their neighbors for decades. And, in that old home of theirs on South Street, Cassandra and Ruth had always been comfortable living their lives as they chose, all the while trusting others were doing the same.

"We know them. And they know us," as Ruth had said to Cassandra when this flare-up happened. "In fact, the people in this town know us very well."

The people of Essex, Kansas, maybe knew this unique family in particular because of their strong leadership and generous spirit shared broadly in the community. They could have spent a lot of time being upset about the household on South Street. But they chose not to do that, regardless of how they might have felt about it or understood it or thought they understood it. They trusted what they knew, and they knew Ruth and Cassandra and Ed. That was enough. When you know people, even if they are different from yourself, fear can't raise its ugly head quite so easily.

Milosz left sometime shortly after his encounter with Ruth. Left without saying a word. No one ever found out where he went. Ruth wondered if he might have had some difficulties at the junior college causing him concern. She could have gone out to the college and probably found someone who would have opened his records for her, but she chose not to. They never heard another thing about or from him. Milosz merely disappeared from their home, from their lives, and from their small town, a mystery to everyone.

Ed quietly asked Ruth one afternoon if she knew anything about what had happened to Milosz.

"No, we don't know," she said. "I think he may have gotten mad at me because I harped on at him a bit too much about taking care of his clothes, but he also may have been having trouble at the college. We don't know. I'm betting he's gone back home. He's young and has been away a long time."

That seemed enough to satisfy Ed. "Yes, he is still a very young man," his only comment.

Cassandra and Ruth, of course, talked some off and on in the evenings after they were in bed about Milosz and what he had done or not done and their concern for him. By and large, the hurt and the sadness of it all slowly ebbed. No one ever spoke to Ed, Cassandra, or Ruth about Milosz again.

Their lives went on as they had for years. The three of them together. Ed and Ruth enjoying all the new things on the TV and Cassandra constantly reading her books and teaching the Sunday School class at church. Ed continued for a few more years to operate the music store. It never made any money, but he seemed to enjoy doing it. By then, "Uncle Ed" was a favorite resident known all over town for making music, fixing instruments, and entertaining the youngsters with his musical saw. And, on the side, Ed continued to teach the men's Bible class at church. And, of course, he continued to pound out something almost every day about his philosophy or thoughts on that old typewriter.

Ed and Ruth remained faithful members of the church choir, while Cassandra read and gave book reviews at the church Circle, for the AAUW group she and Ruth had started together, and other places when asked. And she joined the library board. Eventually, because so many in the community had asked her to do it, she ran for the Essex School Board. Re-elected to the board for several terms, she was also elected president during the final two terms of her tenure.

Eventually, after she retired from teaching, Ruth would follow in Cassandra's footsteps, elected to the school board several times and also elected president of the board in her final term. Naturally Ruth continued to make her rounds to care for the sick and the elderly women, primarily those who lived alone. For many, she made it possible for them to remain in their own homes in their final years because of the food and care she provided.

At the old house on South Street, the three continued to have their familiar squabbles, Ed never far from driving Cassandra and Ruth crazy, or so they said. When asked in her later years, following Ed's death, about their family disagreements, Ruth confessed such feelings were probably mutual, the two of them often driving Ed just as crazy. Cassandra's patience had a shorter tether than Ruth's. She would stomp off in a huff to her desk or the kitchen or out to bring in the laundry off the line whether miffed at Ed or at Ruth. Ed and Ruth often shared a similar role when it came to Cassandra's fury and sometimes would acknowledge this with a brief, surreptitious smile between them.

"I never worried about Cassandra," Ruth was known to say. "For once she had blown her anger or frustration, it was over and she was on to whatever was next on her to do list."

Ruth often tried to reason with Ed, unlike Cassandra, who would never do that, but stomped angrily away mumbling something under her breath. Ruth would sometimes claim she had actually gotten Ed to listen or at least entertain her way of thinking about something. Cassandra doubted this, for she knew Ed, eternally set in his ways and own ideas. Through the years, they had both discovered the best thing to do might be to suggest a task. Ed did like to be helpful around the house.

And, of course, Cassandra always was the one in charge. Ed and Ruth both knew this from the start.

All their lives, even after they had moved a few blocks to the newer one-story house, the three of them continued to enjoy hosting groups from church and their wider community for dinners, celebrations, church meetings, potlucks, and family gatherings of all kinds. Cassandra and Ruth always had everything ready in the kitchen. Ed would vacuum the rugs. And when the doorbell rang, one of them would run to answer, happy to receive their guests, whoever they might be.

"Welcome! Wonderful to see you. Glad you could come. Throw your coats back on Cassandra and Ruth's bed ... ." Or, if one of the women, say Ruth, answered the door, "Just throw your coat back on Cassandra's and my bed, through the family room on the right, and I'll take your hot dish directly to the kitchen."

Only rarely would the name Milosz come up in the family conversations, and then only when the children were visiting and they'd reminisce about Patricia as a toddler lovingly carrying around her favorite "Milosz's doll." They had, at least, one warm memory of Milosz they could all share.

Eleven

The Surviving

uth would never forget that day. A Saturday evening in early spring. Still in the kitchen, she worked to put away the last of the dishes from the day's work. They'd spent the day making jelly out of the sandhill plum juice canned at the end of summer. Since supper, Cassandra had been back in their study, working on her Sunday School lesson for the following morning.

"Rrrruu-th," Cassandra called out from the bedroom, her strong urgent voice carrying over the sound of the TV Ed had turned on in the family room. The move to the new house, on the northside of Central, had taken place eighteen months ago, in the fall of 1968. The family room, in the middle at the rear of the house, had the bedrooms on each side. They made the move to leave the stairs behind and gain a second bathroom. Ed's room, on the south, connected to his small study. Cassandra and Ruth shared a large room on the north separated by a partial partition, their bedroom on one side and a study on the other where each had a desk.

"Com-ing ..." Ruth called out. But as she put down the dish towel and turned, Cassandra came striding into the kitchen in her slip.

"Look at this," she said, lifting her right arm up over her head. "Can you feel that lump?"

The kitchen was still warm from the hot jelly jars sitting in rows on the old newspapers covering the countertop. Ruth had turned off the big overhead lights hoping to cool down the room and herself, the light now soft and low.

"It feels like there's ... something ... right ... right here," Cassandra said as she took Ruth's hand and put it up under her armpit along the edge of her breast.

Frustrated, Ruth said, "Let's go back to the bedroom where the light is better." In their bedroom, they removed Cassandra's slip and her bra so Ruth could explore the areas under both armpits and along the sides of Cassandra's breasts and found another smaller lump under her other armpit.

"Yes, I can feel something there and ... right ... here," Ruth said, her heart speeding. "And," she continued, trying to be as calm as possible as she brought Cassandra's arms back down, "I don't think there is anything we can do about it right now."

"Well, of course not!" Cassandra said, feeling exasperated. She did not like to wait for anything, yet she wanted Ruth to know she knew quite well all by herself that nothing could be done at that moment.

Ruth could hear the strain in Cassandra's voice. She gave Cassandra a kiss and said, "I will call the doctor first thing Monday morning. We'll get you an appointment."

Ruth, never good at sleeping, had a disturbing night. As she lay beside Cassandra who was sound asleep, Ruth tried not to toss and turn, but her mind ran helter-skelter, fueled by fear. Finally she gave up, got up, and went into the kitchen to make the crust for a pie. She had noticed a sack of frozen gooseberries in the back of the freezer earlier that week.

It felt good to get up and get going. 'It's a good time to use these,' she said, talking to herself in the quiet early morning, as the first light, long before sunrise, could be seen through the kitchen window.

She put the pie in the oven around five o'clock. On any other day, Ruth could enjoy the early morning time, with everyone else still asleep. Today Ruth just needed to keep on moving. While the pie baked, she got the roast browned and vegetables ready for slow cooking in the oven during church. The women liked to have Sunday dinner as near ready as possible before leaving the house for church.

Cassandra's Sunday School lesson went fine, as usual. No one in the group of best friends would have had any idea what Cassandra and Ruth were experiencing. In actuality, probably only Ruth carried the fear. Cassandra, no doubt, would have been lost in the topic of the morning.

On this morning, once again Ruth watched as Cassandra created the stage on which this show played itself out over and over again each week, while today feeling a little sorry for herself. Cassandra gave so much to everyone else and with such abandon, enjoying her audience and the audience thrilled with her. But, on this day, Ruth sat there, distracted, working to hold her worries at bay.

Early Monday morning, before Ruth left for school, she telephoned the doctor's office to arrange an appointment for Cassandra. When she hung up, she noticed Ed quietly standing there in the hallway next to the door to his study, a puzzled look on his face.

"Cassandra found a lump under her armpit. Doc Stephens will see her this afternoon, after I get home from school."

"Oh she did, did she?" he said, without emotion.

Ruth hoped that would be all there was to it this time, as Ed turned to go into his study, and then she heard that little sound he often made with his lips before he spoke ... "tsk, tsk, tsk. She may be eating too many fats," Ed said, nodding his head, as if agreeing with himself. Thus, with only his somewhat-veiled disapproval, he stepped further into his study, his shoulders in their familiar droop. Ruth heard him take the plastic cover off his typewriter and pull up his chair.

Ruth continued to sit in the hallway at the little phone desk, feeling worn out already and counting to ten. Soon she heard the peck, peck perfect rhythm of his fingers on the old upright keys.

'Always judgement!' she thought as her blood began to boil.

She really did not have time to worry about Ed, but some days she wanted to ring Ed's neck. 'This day counts as one of those,' Ruth thought as she got up and went to get ready for work.

Later Monday afternoon, Cassandra and Ruth saw Dr. Stephens. He examined her, using his fingers as if they could listen to her flesh, along her armpits, around and across her abdomen and breasts. Doc nodded to Rosy, his nurse, who helped Cassandra sit up and put her office gown back around her as he turned to make his notes. The examination room felt cold and all too quiet.

Finally, he stood, leaning against the examination-room door, sighed and said, "Yes, there are some abnormalities along the lymph nodes. I don't notice anything in the breast tissue itself, but we cannot be sure without further testing. We need to find out about this. I'll make arrangements for a biopsy. Rosy will give you a call when we get things arranged."

In the car on the way home, Cassandra said, "It's cancer; I know it's cancer."

"Why would you say that? Before we have any real information about it? Let's take one step at a time here, okay, honey?"

But Cassandra already felt convinced. It had been some years since she first began to say she had nothing left to live for. Ruth thought back to the last time she talked like that, when the grandchildren were mere tots, which puzzled Ruth even more. Frustrated, she sought to understand what would make Cassandra feel that way. While Ed would think about Cassandra's down times as related to her diet and exercise, Ruth had her own theories. She had decided that life in their small town just never quite added up to enough for Cassandra.

This time, finding the lump created another moment in which Cassandra could simply say, "It's all over." And this time, with the situation being quite different, Ruth could hear finality in her voice.

As Cassandra had expected and Ruth had feared, it was cancer. Lymphoma. And as the test results were complete, the two of them had gone back to Doc's office for a consultation. Cassandra and Ruth had made a list of questions they wanted to talk about.

"Most of all," Ruth said, "we really want to know more about lymphoma. Neither of us can recall anyone we know having such a diagnosis."

"There's a lot that we don't know about this type of cancer but eventually we will learn more." Finally, he said, "There is one thing we do know about lymphoma at this time: it does come back. And we have no idea if it will be in a few months or a few years. Our current understanding is that Cassandra's type of cancer is incurable."

The doctor recommended they begin with surgery, worrisome but not Ruth's major concern. The word that hit her hard was "incurable." "Sometimes," the doctor added, "if the patient is lucky, the disease might be interrupted, but it will come back."

So it began. The surgery went well. Cassandra, not always the best of patients, managed it all with a certain ease, encouraging Ruth.

Then they had the worry with Ed. He could not stand the doctor's recommendations—the surgery, bad enough, but the radiation plan, due to begin next, almost totally undid him. After Cassandra consented to take the treatments, Ed could no longer stand by silently.

"Cassandra, my dear, I've been thinking and praying about all of this ... and I think this isn't a good plan. Instead you could alter your diet, take more walks, and in these ways maybe strengthen some important enzymes. Maybe that way you could get rid of some of the things that are undermining your immune system. I know you don't like to drink water, but right now it could be very important for you ... more water each day will help flush all those poisons out of your system." He paused, but momentarily. "And I'm willing to do whatever I can to assist you in such tasks ... by going on walks with you, in particular. Maybe that would be good and relaxing for you."

Ruth could hardly contain herself. Cassandra, however remained without emotion as she listened to him speak, then took her turn.

"Thank you, Ed, for thinking about this and for your kind offer to help. But you knew all along that we would probably not agree. I have made up my mind to follow my doctor's advice. I'm sorry if my doing so gives you reason for concern."

Ruth followed Ed back to his study to add her two cents' worth, wanting to make clear that he was not to do that again. "You have spoken. We have listened," Ruth insisted. "Do not ever mention it again to anyone. Do you understand? Maybe you do not believe in doctors or in hospitals, but this is Cassandra's life and she is in charge."

Life moved on for the family.

Cassandra had so many radiation treatments that no one, not even Cassandra, who generally counted up everything, could recall how many. Ruth took time off from school to take her to the first few appointments that late spring. She could not do that all the time, but Ruth wanted to be there with Cassandra at the beginning.

Eventually, the two of them got into the rhythm of their new life, organized around Cassandra's trips to the clinic. Cassandra had never driven. She always laughed when she spoke about learning to drive the tractor in her young years on the farm. "I think my older brothers and sisters only let that happen once and then made various kinds of bribes with me to keep me out of the tractor's driver's seat," Cassandra quipped.

As for Ruth, she declared that Cassandra Thomas must never be allowed into the driver's seat of anything that had a gas pedal.

Many friends and family stood by to assist in whatever way they could. Cassandra and Ruth felt fortunate to know that the kids now lived close by. Taylor, Margaret, and the grandkids had arrived at their new home in Hastings during the summer a year ago. When the radiation treatments began, now and then Margaret would drive down in the early morning, take

Cassandra to Wichita for her treatment, and drive back home in the late afternoon. On some days she made plans to stay overnight, to everyone's delight.

Cassandra and Margaret had a good relationship. They shared similar interests, and Cassandra would come alive as she and Margaret talked about all kinds of social problems, often beginning or ending with everything wrong with the church, the church to which they both had been drawn and yet energetically criticized.

In the living room one evening following the trip to the clinic Margaret and Cassandra were enjoying a lively conversation before supper.

"I sure would like to come in there and join the two of you while you're stirring up all that trouble!" Ruth shouted out from the dining room as she set the table. "But someone has to put food on this table, and right now that someone just happens to be me." Everyone was in good spirits enjoying their evening together.

Ed also loved Margaret as his own daughter. They would sit and talk, something Ed always coveted. Having Margaret home again with the family gave everyone a boost they sorely needed.

There was one special time when Margaret came down to take Cassandra to Wichita and then stayed overnight.

"You know, honey, you'll have to make a chocolate cream pie for Margaret. She's staying overnight and will be here for supper," Cassandra reminded Ruth as they were getting ready for bed the night before her arrival.

"Yes indeed. That's my plan. What do you think I should make for supper?"

"Ha! I don't think Margaret cares one iota what you cook for supper, as long as she knows that homemade chocolate pie is waiting on the countertop," Cassandra said with a smile, thinking back to how differently the menu would take shape with Taylor at home. "Now, if it were Taylor, you know exactly what would be on the menu."

"I know," Ruth jumped in playfully, "baked steak ..."

"... and gooseberry pie!" Cassandra finished Ruth's sentence in a flash, grinning from ear to ear.

Margaret arrived, and the trip to Wichita went as usual. Back home they found Ed typing away in his study, and good smells coming from the kitchen. And there on the counter, Ruth's fresh pie, just out of the oven. Margaret could already taste it.

They all enjoyed the evening meal together. The conversation ranged from the grandchildren and their new school in Hastings to how Margaret and the family enjoyed the new house and to Taylor's new beginning as the assistant professor.

Margaret's Hastings stories felt fresh and provided new conversations around the table in Essex that evening, generating good energy for everyone. The next morning, following breakfast, after Ruth and Ed left for work, Cassandra and Margaret lingered in conversation over a second cup of hot tea. By late morning, Margaret headed back to Hastings in order to arrive before the children got home from school.

Later that afternoon, back in Essex, after their family supper, Cassandra helped Ruth with the cleanup and washing the dishes. Then, while Ruth gave the counter and stove top a final wipedown, Cassandra pulled out one of the stools at the counter and began to tell Ruth about her morning with Margaret. Ruth realized immediately Cassandra wanted to talk.

"So what time did Margaret get on the road?" Ruth asked.

"Oh, not too late. By eleven o'clock; maybe a bit earlier. But we had a good chance to visit, and it turned out to be a conversation I realized I needed."

"Conversation?"

"Yes, I was able to talk easily about this cancer and that I might die from it. I needed to say some of the things spinning around in my head."

Ruth didn't speak right away, so Cassandra went on, knowing the topic was one Ruth resisted.

"Honey, you know how my declining strength has also cut into the time we used to have at the end of each day, getting ready and crawling into bed together. Now I'm asleep before you've put the kitchen back together. And I know you're worried, but we do need to talk."

It was true. When Ruth came to bed, she would lie there missing those precious moments when they would talk and giggle and rehash the day in the privacy of their own room. Instead, these days, there she lay, awake and alone, as quiet tears slid from her eyes. Exhausted, Ruth felt sad and afraid, twisted out of shape, into a knot.

"Oh?" Ruth now indicated she would listen.

So, while sitting at the kitchen counter that evening, after Margaret's departure, Cassandra felt her opportunity had come and edged gently into the hard conversation.

"I told Margaret I have been thinking more about my own death, and I don't really understand it, but talking about it, actually speaking the words for someone else to hear, well, ... was comforting." Cassandra paused. "I found myself feeling free and easy, didn't try to tiptoe around words, and peacefulness ... just seemed to fall down over me."

"What did Margaret say?" Ruth asked, after a moment.

"She didn't say much at all, really. She mostly listened and let me talk."

Then, with a twinkle in her eye, Cassandra told Ruth something about one of the pieces of the conversation with Margaret that she had enjoyed the most.

"You've heard me say often that Margaret agrees with me on so much when it comes to traditional Christian beliefs, all that business about salvation, how Jesus died for our sins, and the so-called eternal life. I don't think Margaret's all that interested in them either, which pleases me greatly," she said, as a big smile spread across her face.

Cassandra was on a high from recounting the conversation and seemed to have more energy than Ruth had seen in months. So she did not try to interfere, just let Cassandra spew it all out, but it was clear Cassandra had found a co-conspirator. And Ruth felt grateful, or thought she should, while wondering 'what those two might dream up next about what's wrong with my old time religion!'

"It gave me a great sense of peace," Cassandra continued, beginning to settle down a bit after her recitation. "In the end, I told Margaret when the doctors said I might die from this, it did not make me afraid." And then she looked directly at Ruth, who seemed worried and even somewhat pale, and said, "Honey, I want you to know that I really am not afraid."

And that was it. Cassandra really needed for Ruth to know that she was not afraid, something she hoped would help her dear sweetheart, the one she cared for more than anything else in the world and who had let fear take over her life.

Cassandra got up, and then Ruth, and the two stood there in the kitchen for a long time, their arms intertwined … and then Ruth gave her a kiss and said, with a smile while patting her fanny, "So off to bed with you, my dear! It's past your bedtime."

As Ruth turned to finish up the kitchen work, she was thinking she could actually see the comfort in Cassandra that evening. And during the next weeks and months, as the radiation treatments moved into their final phase, she continued to sense Cassandra's steady confidence hold fast. Finally, later in the fall, the treatments ended, and their lives began to smooth out once again.

Yet, Cassandra's energy had greatly diminished. By the hour, she sat in her chair in the front room in the winter's morning sun with a book in her lap. Ruth would most often find her there, asleep, her head having dropped to her chest. She even lost her interest in helping in the kitchen, which Ruth could hardly bear. Not that Ruth needed her help, but she missed and yearned for their companionship.

However, in the late spring, Cassandra did seem to regain some ground against all that radiation and, Ruth hoped, against the disease as well.

But then, once again, life intervened, in the middle of summer. July first, to be exact.

It was late evening when the phone rang at the Daves' household, Taylor's cousin's who lived nearby in Hastings.

"Hello, is this Donald Daves, the attorney?"

"Yes, it is."

"Mr. Daves, this is Nurse Kohlman calling from the emergency room at the Hastings hospital. We have a family of four here, two young children and their parents, by the name of Thomas. They need some help. All of them were brought in by ambulance some hours ago from an auto wreck out east on the highway, and the two youngsters gave me your name. They say you are part of their family. The parents are both still being worked on in the ER, but the children have been released and need someone to whisk them out of here."

"Oh my goodness! Yes! I'm Taylor's cousin. Do the parents have serious injuries?"

"The man has been admitted; however, he may be released later tonight. The doctors are still working on her in the ER. She has serious injuries and will eventually be taken to intensive care."

"Okay, thank you for calling. My wife and I are on our way, and we'll collect the children."

When Don and Sherry arrived in the ER, after the children jumped into their arms, they found the parents were still being worked on in the ER, so Sherry and Don carried the children to the car and headed home. The two talked a mile a minute about what had happened, but once at the house, they fell sound asleep. With Sherry standing by with the children, Don rushed back to the hospital.

Around midnight they brought Taylor out in a wheelchair, his face covered with stitches. The doctors found no other injuries, other than some cracked ribs, and had released him. Taylor, not able to talk, indicated he wanted to go see Margaret, who had been transferred to the intensive care unit. Don pushed Taylor through the hospital where they found Margaret surrounded by doctors and nurses.

Taylor was desperate to know something about her condition. Finally Don, who was feeling faint himself after a glance at his cousin's wife's crushed face, went to the desk to ask if there was someone who could talk with Mr. Thomas.

Soon the nurse who came out of Margaret's room could see how upset Taylor was. Bending over, she looked directly into his eyes and said, "Let's get you home. We are all here taking care of your wife. She is in good hands with Dr. Wise who has just done a tracheotomy. Your wife is breathing easily now, so, you go get some rest. We will know a lot more in the morning, and if things change for her in any way, I will call you. I will be here with her all night."

"Taylor, the nurse is right," Don added. "Let's go to the house and come back in the morning." Taylor could only hold his head in his hands. Don left his phone number and wheeled Taylor out to the car.

The next morning, Taylor, who had not slept, was up early, eager to get back to the hospital. But he and Don agreed that both his and Margaret's parents should be called. Don rang Essex first.

Ruth had begun to wash up the few things from breakfast while Cassandra sat at the counter reading to Ruth from the newspaper when the phone rang.

Ruth picked up the phone, "Hell-o," her unsuspecting, happy voice rang out.

"Ruth, this is Donald Daves. I'm calling from the house here in Hastings with some really difficult news."

Ruth's expression dropped immediately, not able to fathom Don's words.

"Taylor is here with me, and the two kids are still asleep. They were involved in a bad wreck late yesterday afternoon out east of town on their way home from their camping trip. Taylor and the kids were banged up some but are doing okay. However, Margaret was seriously hurt and is in the hospital here in intensive care. Taylor and I didn't leave there until long after midnight last night, and we are on our way back there now."

Ruth continued to stand there, unable to move, working hard to listen to Don.

"There isn't a lot more that we know at this point, but Taylor wanted me to call you. I haven't talked with Alfred and Elizabeth yet but will call them now, before Taylor and I go to see Margaret." Don did not know what else to say.

"Thank you, Don, for calling," Cassandra heard Ruth say as she put down the receiver and turned to see Cassandra staring at her. Cassandra had guessed it was some kind of bad news and had heard Ruth say, "Don," which suggested her nephew, Donald Daves, and thus Hastings.

"Taylor and Margaret and the children have been in a car wreck."

"Oh no!" Cassandra cried.

"Don doesn't know much about Margaret's condition. She is in intensive care at the hospital, but Taylor and the kids only had some cuts and bruises and are okay and with Don and Sherry at their house." Stunned, she said, "I can't believe this … but Don said he and Taylor are heading back to the hospital, after they call the Millers, and he will call us again later, when they know more."

"But … how did this happen?"

"I don't know. Don really didn't say much, just what I told you. We'll have to wait for his next call."

By this time, Ed had come into the dining room, having heard the obvious concern in the women's voices. Ruth recounted to him what Don had told her. Ed stood there, shock and disbelief on his face, but didn't speak.

In less than two hours, Don called again. There had been no change in Margaret's condition. Cassandra could sense the bad news by watching Ruth on the phone. After Ruth recounted to Cassandra and Ed what Don had said, and paused, not knowing what else to say, Cassandra put down her tea cup, stood up, and simply announced, "I'm going to Hastings."

Cassandra's words, face and entire body appeared set firm. Ruth knew better than to try to talk Cassandra out of any such plan and certainly knew better than to say what she felt—that Cassandra didn't have the strength to be of much help to anyone.

Ruth, Cassandra, and Ed left for Hastings as the sun came up the next morning. Cassandra was now a woman on a mission, with her aprons in her suitcase each washed and ironed by Ruth the night before.

They had driven straight to the hospital hoping to see Margaret and Taylor. It took no time at all to sense the gravity of the situation. They found Taylor, his face swollen and full of stitches, keeping vigil at Margaret bedside, something allowed him for only five minutes every hour. But Margaret. They could hardly bear standing there looking through that window into her intensive-care room. When they had first arrived and looked through the window into Margaret's room, Ruth had whispered to Ed and Cassandra, "That can't be Margaret."

"Yes, it is," Cassandra declared, her pain-filled voice determined to claim her daughter-in-law right through her tears. "Look at those hands. Those are Margaret's beautiful hands."

When Taylor emerged from her room, his few minutes over, they gave him three desperate hugs. None of them could speak.

Taylor couldn't, didn't want to talk. Thus, with nothing for them to do at the hospital, they decided to head to the house and get busy. Finally, Don, who had been standing by, helped them leave and get back to their car, giving them Taylor's keys to the house. Ruth said to Don, "Tell Taylor we will go over and open up the house and prepare for his and the children's return home whenever that time comes."

Once inside the house, Cassandra and Ruth began to get things organized in the kitchen, while Ed took a look around, checking the upstairs, downstairs, and basement. The women took inventory in the kitchen, while Ed carried in his small suitcase and the women's suitcases, putting them in the rooms where they normally slept when there for a visit.

With a list in hand, the women left for the grocery store, and Ed began going through three weeks of mail scattered on the floor in the front entryway, organizing it on the small table in the living room for Taylor. When the women returned, Ed and Ruth carried in groceries. While Cassandra put things away and organized the kitchen, Ruth found how to turn on the air conditioner and checked the windows while Ed swept the garage and closed it up to keep the heat out.

They did not know when they would see the children or Taylor, but they kept doing what they could, all three of them working on automatic pilot. Ruth had been up early back home making sandwiches for their lunch. Soon all three of them were ready to sit down, exhausted by their work but most of all by the emotional strain from worry about Margaret and about Taylor keeping vigil outside the door to her hospital room.

In the late morning, Margaret's parents had arrived from Kansas City. Elizabeth and Alfred, also now in shock after seeing their daughter in the ICU, sat with Taylor, hoping for a chance to talk with some of the doctors, but the nurse told them they didn't know much as yet. Soon, sitting there began to make no sense, and Elizabeth and Alfred began to talk quietly about what they should do.

"There's nothing we can do here," Elizabeth said to Alfred. "We can't help Taylor and certainly can't help Margaret, but we could help the children."

"Yes," Alfred said, rising out of his numbness at finding his daughter in such a state, "I was just thinking about that. We could take them home with us."

"Yes, that seems best. They need all the attention we can give them right now and a place away from all of this where they can feel free to play and talk," Elizabeth added.

When Taylor emerged from Margaret's bedside again, Elizabeth and Alfred told him of their plan, gave him hugs, and, after standing for just a moment at the window into Margaret's room, their arms around each other and tears flowing, they left to collect the grandchildren from the Daves' home.

Back at the house, while Cassandra, Ruth, and Ed sat at the kitchen table trying to eat, they heard a car in the driveway and soon the door opened. Elizabeth and Alfred and the grandchildren had arrived. During their sad greetings of one another, the adults tried to keep from crying as the children circled round them. The children, home again, looked happy and relieved.

"Bet you haven't had lunch," Ruth said. "We've got some sandwiches."

"Grandmother had Granddad take us to McDonalds on the way," Patricia reported. "They are going to take us home with them ... and to the lake, this afternoon."

While the others visited, Elizabeth went upstairs with Patricia and Steven to their rooms to pack a few clothes.

"But Grandmother, my swimming suit is in the car!" Steven suddenly thought, his face full of distress, almost in tears.

"We'll stop on the way home and get you another suit, and also you, Patricia. Everyone needs more than one swimming suit," the grandmother who'd spent her college years as a lifeguard said. "Eventually your dad will get your things from the car, and then you'll have all your other things as well."

As the children left, a huge relief came over the Essex folks. Especially Ruth, for it meant that Cassandra would not have the added responsibility for the children when she had to return home in a couple of weeks to prepare for the coming school year.

Later that afternoon, Don brought everything from the wrecked car back to the house. Between Taylor's times with Margaret, he had asked Don to take him to the salvage lot to find the car. Taylor needed to get his wallet and Margaret's purse, along with everything else.

"What we found," Don told the Essex family, "was a huge mess of clothing covered with dried blood and thrown everywhere. It looked like, once the children had freed themselves, they had grabbed a sack of clothes from the back of the station wagon and thrown clothing to their father to help stop his and their mother's bleeding while they were both pinned in the front seat."

Ed helped Don unload the camping equipment into the garage and found a large garbage bag to put all the clothing into, which Ed took down to the basement laundry area. Now Ruth and Cassandra had a stack of clothes to work on — almost all of them covered with dried blood. This would turn out to be a challenge even for the very best of laundresses.

As the days unfolded, the two women and Ed worked out a routine at the house. Taylor would come and go for lunch and supper, between his five minutes with Margaret, spending most of his time at the hospital where things seemed to be going from bad to worse. With Margaret's head injuries still not well-understood, the doctors feared brain damage. Taylor disagreed. "I know my wife. I can sense what is happening with her. She is right here," and continued his vigil.

No one was getting much rest, especially Taylor.

After a couple weeks, Elizabeth and Alfred drove over with the children one afternoon so they could see their friends in the neighborhood and their dad, while the Millers went to the hospital to see Margaret and talk with doctors, passing along photos of Margaret the doctors had requested.

Back at the house, Cassandra and Ruth put dinner on the bigger table in the dining room. Taylor, who usually offered a prayer at mealtime, bowed his head, as did everyone. They waited. After a long pause, he said, "If this food is going to be prayed over, someone else is going to have to say it."

Slowly, into the stunned silence, Elizabeth's voice began to form a prayer. Frankly, no one around that table knew how she did it. Elizabeth knew deep pain, now reignited; her first born, Charles, had been killed in his Navy plane not all that long ago at age twenty-six.

Later that evening, as Ruth and Cassandra worked together cleaning up in the kitchen, Elizabeth, exhausted, sat pensively on the kitchen stool, waiting for Alfred and Ed to finish a project in the basement they were working on with the children before taking them back to Kansas City again.

Ruth turned to Elizabeth, "How can you stand this, first Charles' death and now Margaret in such a grave condition?"

"I can't stand it," she said, her face fractured by pain.

The three were in tears, totally exhausted, having used up almost all their physical and emotional strength during the past weeks. Each of them in their own way worked to hold their worst fears at bay, unwilling to even think about what the future might bring to this, their young family.

Yet, as the days moved slowly by, Ruth began to think that maybe Cassandra could keep the house going for Taylor and herself. By some miracle, she seemed stronger the last couple weeks. Strongly determined at least. And she would have help. Friends from Taylor and Margaret's local church had arranged for someone to bring a fully prepared meal each day. There could be no dissuading her, and Ruth and Ed would return to assist each weekend.

They all knew Ruth was loath to leave Cassandra at Taylor's when she could no longer put off the need to get back home for the beginning of school. Together, she and Ed put things in order: Ruth did up all the laundry and ironing and scrubbed the bathrooms, and Ed vacuumed the rugs, reorganized and swept the garage, and dug the dandelions out of the yard.

And on that Sunday evening, after Cassandra put together their meal, she and Ruth cleaned up the dishes and kitchen, as Ed loaded the car. Just as the summer sun began to set in the west, Ed and Ruth pulled out of the driveway, headed for Essex, leaving Cassandra standing in the driveway alone, waving them off.

The following Friday evening when Ed and Ruth drove back into the driveway in Hastings, there Cassandra stood, in the middle of that big kitchen, fully in charge. Cassandra had more than survived the week.

Within a week, Elizabeth and Alfred brought the children back home to begin their school year, Patricia in second and Steven in first grade. Elizabeth had obtained the list of what each child needed to begin school, so they arrived back home with new clothes and supplies. School would begin the next day.

Weeks later, in late September, Taylor oversaw Margaret's return home from the hospital by ambulance. He had been fighting for weeks to accomplish this. Margaret, still bedridden and with some mental confusion, could not walk, and only with great difficulty was able to take some liquid nourishment. She needed total, round-the-clock care. No wonder the doctors had been leery about discharging her. However, Taylor finally had convinced them she would get better care and a stable environment if he could provide it day and night, something they would not let him do at the hospital, despite weeks of requests.

A new regime began. Taylor spent his time caring for Margaret. The doctors stopped by the house at the beginning and end of each day, seven days a week. Almost immediately, everyone was impressed with Margaret's progress. Being home was good for her, and Taylor proved to be an excellent nurse, exactly what Margaret needed.

Eventually, however, Taylor also began to feel the pressure to get back to work. He had been away since early June. Finally, after he was convinced Margaret and Cassandra could manage their days without him, he agreed to the change in plans. Now, he would get the children off to school, take care of Margaret's early morning needs, and carry her out to the couch in the family room where Cassandra could watch over her from the kitchen. He returned for lunch, checking in with Margaret for whatever she might need, and be back home in the afternoon early enough to greet the children as they returned from school, "to help keep the children's chaos outside, instead of inside," as he said.

"What have you here?" Taylor asked Steven one day as the child was excited to show him a drawing from school that day.

"A giraffe. I drew a giraffe," offered the first grader.

"Why did you choose to draw a giraffe?" his father asked him.

"Oh! I drew a giraffe because giraffes are very quiet animals … and," shifting to his best whisper, said, "we all need to be very quiet."

The atmosphere continued in a quiet calm so Margaret could sleep and was beneficial also to Cassandra who could catch her breath between preparing the meals for Taylor and the children and the other tasks she took care of around the house.

Eventually, as Margaret grew stronger and was up, or at least awake more, times of quiet frivolity returned to the home.

One day, struggling to communicate, with her face tightly wired together, Margaret had conveyed to Cassandra she was tired of those chalky energy drinks.

"Well, what would you desire, Madame Thomas?" Cassandra asked, only to tease her.

"Chhh-urrrrr-e- pp-p-i-eee!" Margaret responded. They both giggled. Margaret seemed very pleased with herself.

Later that afternoon, from her regular place on the family-room couch, Margaret woke up to whispered snickers in the kitchen. And soon, with a kitchen towel folded royally over his arm, Taylor entered the room, carrying Margaret's glass with a straw and handed it to her.

"Your wish is our command," he said, as he bowed, his mother hardly able to contain herself peeking around from behind him. "Your evening meal is ready," he managed, beginning to lose his composure.

Cautiously, Margaret did her best to get a sip of the liquid into her mouth.

"Wahh-aa on uu-rrrr-th s thh-s?" she tried to say. The other two were giggling themselves crazy by now.

"Cherry pie!" Cassandra called out.

The friend who brought dinner that evening had made a cherry pie for dessert. Cassandra could not believe it! She and Taylor had taken a small slice and put it through the blender with some milk. It wasn't great, but it wasn't awful either, and Margaret enjoyed her few sips as much as Cassandra had enjoyed making it. Later that week, someone brought, among other items, turkey, dressing, and gravy, and, knowing how much Margaret enjoyed dressing and gravy, Cassandra took on a second experiment. The bits of turkey, stuffing and gravy together with milk in the blender did not make nearly as big a hit, and Margaret settled back in with her prescribed daily beers and power drinks.

During the fall and early winter, Ed and Ruth made the drive to Hastings every Friday at the end of their workweek to do the work that Cassandra really could not do. The week of Christmas found everyone there, Margaret stronger even after having been back in the hospital for additional facial surgery in early December.

By the end of January, Taylor and Margaret decided they could manage on their own. Margaret, though still weak, was up more every day, and, with the women from church still bringing in a hot meal each day, the necessary daily tasks became manageable for Margaret and Taylor. The time had come for the kids to have their life back to normal as much as possible.

Both families felt ready. "Truth be told," Ruth ventured, "with things improving, we three needed to return to our own life and routines. It had been a strenuous time for us."

Cassandra had grown strong, healed in several ways by her almost seven months in Hastings. She overcame her debilitation from the radiation. It was as if Cassandra needed a reason to live. Seeing her family's critical need for her, her bout with cancer slipped into the far reaches of their lives, and Cassandra's strength and verve returned.

Watching the renewal of Cassandra's life by those who knew her was nothing short of spectacular. Cassandra, never again bothered by her cancer, lived well into her nineties to die of old age, as people often say, although that cancer worried Ruth until the end.

"It is such a terrible disease," fearful words spoken often by Ruth, "and even if she was not afraid to die, I never could bring myself to think about my life without her."

Twelve

The Melancholy

assandra relished counting things. She counted the number of stone fences in Kansas as she and Ruth drove around the state, counted—and recorded—the number of souls in her Sunday class at church each week, and now, after her recovery from cancer and her retirement, she was counting up various aspects of her life, making notes for a memoir. In this exercise, while she prized her own version of the life she had experienced, a deep unsettledness remained evident in her writings. It is likely that Cassandra told these particular pieces of her life story wanting to convince others, along with herself, of the truth in things that mattered to her.

When I think back through my life, she began, *I like to think of the things I have loved doing and the things I have hated to do, the difficult times and the moments of which I am most proud.*

This sorting and counting allowed her, in the end, to reaffirm the pride she took in having lived her life the way she had, given the circumstances she had faced. *I think my life turned out pretty much the way I wanted it to, at least once I came to terms with the woman that I am.* Cassandra wrote this without apology.

Once she fully understood her yearning to be with a woman, her life did come together in a somewhat satisfying manner and over a long span of time. However, deep regrets haunted her from time to time, often confounding Ruth and others who cared about her.

Many contradictions existed between the absolute strength of the young, and then mature, Cassandra and the person who could fall rapidly into despair. For while she began to feel and exercise a sense of her own empowerment early on as a young woman and demonstrated great strength in her ability to work hard, she could easily crumble into a cavernous sense of hopelessness. In her later years when she began to record her life story on paper, she began by adding these up, especially what she had experienced as the most painful moments — what she viewed as failures — in her life.

Either it came to me naturally as a bright daughter of a domineering, take-charge father whom I adored, or somewhere along the road in my early schooling I picked up, perhaps naively, the idea that I could decide what I wanted to do and be.

Early on, Cassandra had been drawn to the model she observed in her female teachers, the determined, independent women who were creating a life for themselves and happily so, as it appeared to her. Later she would assert she did not see herself as a teacher; however, a few of those early, self-reliant women lived in the back of Cassandra's mind and continued to exert a significant influence on her life.

In describing her young years, Cassandra wrote, *There are those who have said I was bratty, a high-minded, bookish child who would rather read and go to school than do anything others needed or wanted me to do. It is true. I never liked being told what to do. I only wanted to read. Nothing else ever interested me very much.*

Cassandra learned to read at an early age, and reading was one of her greatest pleasures throughout her life. Known to assert she had read almost every book in the school libraries where she studied, it was a story she proudly repeated over and over. Often it worked its magic on those in her audience, that is until people learned she had studied at the University of Chicago. Then she would add, with a knowing smile, "… well, at least until I arrived at the university."

Seen as generally incorrigible in her young years, Cassandra made daily life at the farm a challenge for her mother and especially for her older sisters, who were put in charge of her from the time she was born.

"No!" the young girl could be overheard saying to her sister Edith, "I will not wear that dress, no matter how much you like it because you made it. It is silly with all its frills and ruffles. I would be the laughingstock at school, and already no one likes me except the teachers."

And, "No! I do not want to bring in the cows. Let George do it. I'm busy."

Also, "Pauline, I have told you before. I don't like it when you reorganize my stuff just because you are my older sister and think you know how things should look. I know where everything is because I put it where I want it to be. Stop bothering me!"

Cassandra, throughout her life, wanted things to be in order, the way she, not anyone else, had in mind or thought was appropriate. Some few in her family, circle of friends, and colleagues dealt with this tendency in Cassandra a bit better than others. Ruth, of course, became the expert.

One evening as Cassandra and Ruth were cleaning up from supper, Ruth asked, "Did you get back to your writing today? Yesterday you were having trouble getting started once again." Ruth wanted to encourage Cassandra as they were making the transition from the caregiving for Margaret and Taylor and the children to being back home in Essex.

"Yes, I did," she replied energetically.

"Good. So how or where did you begin?"

"I began by making a list about what has happened in my life. You know how I love to count things and make lists."

"Yes, I know," Ruth said as she stood at the kitchen sink, her hands in soapy dishwashing water, smiling to herself.

"I actually began by making some notes about the pride I have in my pioneer heritage," Cassandra said. "It's something about me that is truer than a lot of things I might say. I wrote about my strong-willed and highly principled father as the one who sired our large Taylor clan, and how I am proud of all the generations of Taylors that have come along during my lifetime."

Again, Ruth smiled, glad Cassandra was getting back to her new project. And Ruth understood better than most that there was no end to Cassandra Taylor's pride in her family, including her own son, Taylor, to whom she had given her beloved Taylor family name.

Yet, even with her pride in Taylor and his life, often Cassandra, when mentioning her son, would also speak with frankness about having had a child even when she had not wanted to be a mother.

Those in my family remember ... she declared easily as she wrote about Taylor as an infant. *I am proud to have had a son, a child I didn't participate all that much in raising. Nonetheless, he is an accomplished professor today, making his mark as one of our Taylor descendents.* This was an honest statement, Cassandra suggesting her pride in their clan — maybe even more than love for her son — a sentiment familiar to those who knew her.

It was one thing for Cassandra to list her Taylor clan as the primary part of her successful life story, but when she listed what she considered her other most successful moment, she wrote it was when, as a young adult, she took herself to Chicago. *Once I arrived in Chicago, I thrived! I fell in love with the university, my beautiful women friends, but most of all with the city that captured my imagination as the kind of place in which, ever since, I've wanted to live.*

And it was also true that, after leaving her beloved city to return home to Kansas, she could never get Chicago fully out of her heart and mind. Cassandra's memoir list of her two most highly regarded successes document this lifelong tension between the reality of her long life in rural Kansas amid her family and her primarily fantasy-driven dream of life in Chicago.

Given this tension, throughout the rest of her life in the moments of despondency that would come to her, she suffered from memories of what she referred to as *the most wrenching moment in my life.* For Cassandra, leaving Chicago to return home became the turning point of her life story, a fought-against leave-taking in which she felt powerless.

Yes, Cassandra missed Chicago, but more than that, Cassandra felt she had been torn out of Chicago against her wishes, hopes, and dreams. She resented it then. And she continued to resent it, after all the years, even when she stated — and now was calmly writing down — that her life had turned out *pretty much the way I wanted it to.* There was a deep paradox hidden from Cassandra in such words.

Why did that have to happen? Why wasn't it possible to live the life she wanted? These were two questions Cassandra asked herself over and over again, as if what happened to her in Chicago simply did not seem fair. As she made notes for her story, she wrote about this moment that became the central predicament of her life.

My heart was broken open when I was pulled out of Chicago and brought back here. And I know, absolutely I know, I will never get over all of that. She appeared determined to never make peace with this loss in her life, not even to her very last breath, as Ruth learned the night Cassandra died.

Never able to get past this tension between her actual life and her dream, it could have been that part of Cassandra craved both the dream of life in Chicago as well as the life she had. For, as family and friends watched her yearn for all she experienced back in Chicago, they also observed her appreciating the life she was living among them in rural Kansas. There, upheld and honored by her family with its long history on the prairies — once free and open themselves — perhaps Cassandra came to understand that some freedoms do not last forever. While wonders amid big-city life continued to call out to her, she celebrated and honored how rural folks knew how to do with less, gathering themselves into caring and sharing communities, enabling simple pleasures of life to unfold. Cassandra knew and understood and even valued this, when life rolled out smoothly within and around her.

However, for her, at the moments when the reality of what she had settled for fell harshly upon her, she could physically break apart, claiming that the disparities were just too strong: *Back there, in Chicago, I had the freedom to come and go as I wished. With women, of course, but also with men, especially friendships with a few older men of great minds like Dr. Ames. And the nightlife, how I loved it ... the city culture and the glamour of the downtown, including the tea room.*

Cassandra finally felt forced to make a terrible choice — and for reasons she felt were beyond her control. Caught between what felt like the promise of a real job back home in Kansas with a place to live and what she currently had, her two part-time, low-paying jobs and a tiny room-share apartment she could not afford, she felt forced to choose against her own heart. Struggling, she made a concession — a rude compromise — with herself for something she did not desire. She chose the job in Kansas and the marriage that made it possible while trying to convince herself she could make it work.

Oh, I knew she confessed years later in her writings, *none of what I loved about Chicago could in any way be matched in Halton or Essex, Kansas. I did celebrate the idea of having a tea room in Halton for a while, but down deep I always knew it wouldn't approach the tea room of my dreams.*

However, the longing never left her for something more glamorous, richer in ideas and luxuries, and with greater freedom. More. Cassandra Taylor — from her youth — always wanted more.

Yes, she admitted, *my family, and even friends, have seen it. I can pout and whine, as Ruth would say. Or be stubborn and even hot-tempered or quick with a sharp tongue — which I always recognized in myself — again, just like my father. However, my lifelong challenge has been facing the melancholy, the feeling of despondency over the futility I feel of life itself.*

Circumspect when reflecting on her down times, Cassandra acknowledged such bouts as part of what she called her "Chicago legacy." Still wanting, in vain, what she continued to think of as her carefree and expansive life back there, she could plummet emotionally, unable to see or acknowledge the real twists and turns of that Chicago life, difficulties that found her struggling to create even a semblance of a life on her own.

Now, writing for her memoir, Cassandra had placed "Leaving Chicago" at the top of her list of failures. *I had loved my time in Hyde Park and found it almost impossible to leave behind what living there had come to mean to me. But I really did fear coming back home* she confessed. Perhaps the memories of her youth lay heavy on her, especially after having been away from home as a young adult, living in a new, novel-like world that much better met her own early fantasies for how her life might be lived.

Cassandra had another notion about her on-again, off-again feelings of meaninglessness, another part of her Chicago legacy—that set of issues that comprise what she understood as her greatest failure in life.

I sometimes wonder if these feelings of being lost came from my interest in life's questions, the big questions, for which others tell me no real answers exist. During my university days, I thrived on such conversations. I continue to be unsettled about all the mysteries of life and nevertheless want answers because I cannot bear what so often can feel like the uselessness of my life. I still, even today, want those answers, perhaps foolishly, as if there could be an obvious and quick fix to any of life's contradictions, especially those I know lie deep within me.

Cassandra said it best when she wrote, *Yes, I want these answers now! I have never been a patient woman. Just ask Ruth.* For years those in her family had heard her say this, usually accompanied by a grin.

But the questions about God, death, life, and the meaning of it all, Cassandra claimed, brought her constant struggles. Yet, her years of wrestling appeared not to gain her any real satisfaction or merit, unless it was the grappling with the questions itself for which she yearned.

While rejecting traditional Christian beliefs, Cassandra still longed for something to take their place. *I need to understand to know with some kind of certainty, something I can rely on in the troubled days of my life, a struggle that totally exhausts me.*

Cassandra feared being caught in the ruts of her own life with something important missing. Her lifelong burden of not knowing all the things she felt she needed to know became at times an unforgiving load for her to carry, a dilemma perhaps giving reason enough to understand her times of melancholy.

Then Cassandra turned to what she viewed as her second great failure—her inability to create a financially stable life for herself. Many, if not most, seek the good life of financial success and meaningful work and those things that make for a happy life. Regardless of the education Cassandra had, she did not feel herself successful enough to create this for herself, thus leaving the life she desperately desired beyond her reach.

Then she wrote in a side note, as if making a confession, *I married a man who did not have that in him either, something I did in desperation, having been deserted in Chicago and needing a way to earn a living. But why? Why did I do that?*

If, in her nights of grief over this decision, she did know why she did this, certainly others did not understand. Even Mrs. Wright, Ed's grandmother in Chicago, who did not know Cassandra and did not understand why she was marrying her grandson, had taken Cassandra aside at the wedding back in 1936.

"You need to know, Cassandra, that Edward will never be a husband who will bring financial well-being into his household. He is too much of a dreamer and has no sense of practicality."

At the time of the marriage, Cassandra already was the primary breadwinner, even with her low wages. And Ed was working part-time on her staff, making far less. At some level, Cassandra probably knew this was how her life with Ed would unfold and had decided she did not care. What she cared about was being in charge of her own life, and she probably had guessed this desire driving her decision to marry would have its consequences. Whatever she thought she had given up by marrying, she did not plan to relinquish what she had lusted for from the beginning — control of her own life and thus a way to make a living and grasp the life she wanted.

Ed worked hard alongside her in those early days, an able helper. However, it was because of Cassandra's far greater energy, planning, and strong determination that they even approached making the dining room a meager financial success. The reality was that neither Cassandra, nor Cassandra and Ed together, would prove able to make enough to live on in the late 1930s and 1940's, managing a small hotel dining room — or the larger Legion Hall — in rural Kansas.

Cassandra and Ed lived at the margins of poverty until Ruth joined the household. Once finally together under the same roof in the postwar era, with Cassandra's income and Ruth's teacher's salary, along with meager assistance from Ed, they were able to provide a comfortable home and some measure of financial security for the family. Cassandra, for the first time, came to enjoy some of the things she had always longed for—better quality clothes, the chance to travel, and to primarily do as she pleased with whom she pleased. But even being fulfilled in these ways did not always suffice.

One contradiction of Cassandra's long life was that, while desiring financial well-being and luxury, she often declared she thrived on hard work.

I was always determined and proud of my abilities to get things done, and I didn't let much of anything stand in my way of accomplishing what I set out to do. Such words were frequently heard from Cassandra during her lifetime.

I did not mind standing for hours over hot stoves and pans of boiling water for the cleaning up because my accomplishments removed any thought of drudgery.

For someone who as a young woman spurned kitchen work, both the cooking and the cleanup, Cassandra's transformation was almost total. She came to love everything involved in creating and serving a good meal.

When the table was in her home, for her family or groups of their friends, Cassandra always sat at the head of the table, feeling it her right. She liked being in charge in this way and put Ruth at the corner beside her to be the runner, keeping the serving dishes replenished.

Sometimes around her Taylor family tables, some of the younger ones would ask her questions about her life, seeking stories they had heard tidbits about as they were growing up.

"Aunt Cass, do you still think about those hard struggles at that small college up north, when you needed to keep the students from starving?"

"Yes, I remember. I've always hoped that no one ever went away hungry from one of my dining room tables," Cassandra replied, her face immediately clouded over with the memories, "at least not back here in Kansas." Obviously she was still haunted by the effort it took to ensure none under her charge would go without nourishment years earlier in northern Michigan. "Thank goodness, at my tables here, I have always been able to be sure that there is more, much more than people can eat ... even today."

Cassandra's penchant of counting things up and making lists about her life easily succumbed to a list of what she thought of as failures—things in her life that did not turn out the way she wanted. It is easy to notice that the ways in which Cassandra actually succeeded—being a good teacher, her hundreds of book-review performances, the planning, preparation and serving of good meals for decades—the things that played the central roles in her public life, were not seen as important to her. However, what she considered to be her failures, each lay wrapped or hidden within her hunger and private longings for something she did not have—things that continued to be important to her, even into her elder years.

"Living and working in Collingwood, Michigan," came next on Cassandra's list of failures. Many knew that Cassandra's time in Collingwood had not worked out for her, despite a couple of important successes—in the campus dining hall and in the classroom. Indeed, it was at that small college she found she could teach and enjoy it. For Cassandra, whether in a dining room or in front of a class, was learning she liked having an audience. *Eventually I came to understand what I loved about teaching, in particular, had to do with having an audience* Cassandra wrote down with a hidden grin, feeling pleased with herself.

And yet, she listed her time in isolated, rural, northern Michigan, at Collingwood, as a distinct failure. She did not write much about her time there — or about her departure after those three terribly challenging years — even though, now, those years she counted as proof of what she knew to be true for her, that she could not succeed.

Cassandra also placed "Being a mother" on her list as one of her major life failures. Never shy about this, she presented her failing at motherhood by publicly stating here and there that she never wanted a child and, when she had one, largely passed him over into the care of others.

I was known to boast about this, saying things like "I've never been good with babies or toddlers and small children" and "I do not know what to do for or with them" — and was never interested in finding out.

Now Cassandra was boldly writing these statements down on paper.

As the son grew up, she found herself somewhat more interested. However, once he became a professor, she adored feeling her own success through him. She would never forget the pride she felt standing beside her son, Professor Thomas, the day he addressed the graduating class at the Essex high school. There they were, standing together in their academic regalia — he to give the commencement address and she on the stage to hand out diplomas, as the chair of the local school board. But again, it was primarily pride, rather than the personal joy of a mother's love for her grown son that she felt.

The final entry in Cassandra's list of failures she put in the form of a question, *Does hating to get old make one a failure at this business of living?*

Cassandra dreaded getting old. Never hesitant to mention this, she often talked about hating what old age had brought to her and how she had thrived on *feeling as strong as a bull* adding something about how long it had been since she felt that way.

Being weakened physically has weakened me emotionally, she wrote, with trembling fingers, *and I dislike that even more. I don't like the feeling of wallowing in my own despair. I don't know what I would do without Ruth, she takes care of all my needs. I could not live without her and would not want to. But, yes, I yearn—and there's my needy word again—I yearn for the days when I could work, could stand for hours with the best of them, be in charge, and make things happen.*

When looking back, as the aging process began to take hold of her, it became evident that Cassandra's feelings of not being needed—especially in her own kitchen—caused her great pain. She was able to continue with her book reviews for their church circle and sometimes for the local library readers group, but the pleasures of her work, the work that had sustained her for decades, no longer held for her, as her physical abilities lessened and life ebbed toward her passing.

Early in the spring, before Cassandra's final illness, she had called to ask her daughter-in-law to give the eulogy at her memorial service on behalf of the family, saying, "Margaret, I think you understand me better than most, especially regarding my thoughts about religion."

Cassandra, the student of theology, did not want insipid comments made at her funeral. She wanted assurance nothing would be said that might contradict her lifelong beliefs, beliefs she viewed as contrary to the thinking of most in the church.

"I am not the least bit interested in being told—or having others be told—that Jesus died for my sins, thank you!" Cassandra told Margaret, "and especially not at my funeral in an effort to assure others that I am safely 'off in heaven!'"

Margaret felt honored by Cassandra's invitation. Regardless of how Cassandra might have counted up her own successes and failures, Margaret loved her mother-in-law and understood her as a wonderfully complex woman. "Cassandra was a woman who was alive in a time of testing and openings that were new for women, a particularly unique woman who lived out her life as best she could against many forces, which often took courage," Margaret claimed, "even when others might have only seen a contrary, self-centered, and stubborn woman—all of which could be true, of course!"

At work on the east coast when Cassandra died and unable to make it back to Essex soon enough, Margaret had stayed up through the night and written a eulogy for Cassandra at a small desk in her hotel room. The next morning she wired her comments to Essex to be read by the local pastor during the following day's service. The evening of the day on which Cassandra's service took place back in Kansas, Margaret stood at a podium in Boston, ready to give a talk to a group of graduate students.

After being introduced, feeling sad and a bit tearful as she stood at the front of the room, she paused, looked out over the gathering, and realized she wanted her audience to know something personal about her life at that moment.

"Before I begin this evening, I'm going to take a moment of personal privilege and tell you a brief story. My former mother-in-law, born in 1903, today at the age of 92 was buried in her small Midwestern hometown. She was a unique and gutsy woman who dared to live out her life as best she could, given that she could not live it as she really wanted. She did, however, pull off something totally amazing. Though she had, under the urgencies of the Depression, married a man in order to have a way to gain a job and support herself, and even gave birth to a son early in that marriage, for the rest of her life she chose to be with the woman she loved.

"Her name is Cassandra, her husband is Ed, and her woman lover, Ruth. And here is what is so amazing: the women lovers and Ed shared a home, openly, in their small town for more than fifty years where they each became respected pillars of the community.

"This family is important to me, and I'm grateful for what the three have brought into my life. From the beginning, I was enthralled by their story. I'm feeling a lot of love for each of them today and wanted you to know a bit of their story—and mine—before I begin what it is I came here to say to you this evening. However, it is important for all of us, including graduate students like those of you in this room, to understand that having the courage to live the life you passionately desire is worth your ongoing attention … and that to deny doing so, you do at your own peril."

"That was one lecture," Margaret said to some of the students following her talk, "at which the audience clapped before I even got started."

Cassandra, who always liked to have the final word, summed up her life in the closing paragraph of her memoir …

In the end, my neighbors say I have been a good neighbor. I hope so. That they say that means a lot to me. And the members of my family, my wonderful extended Taylor family, they have always seemed to appreciate me. I continue to be grateful for all the ways across the years they have added to my life. If I were to point to any other final great accomplishment, other than having had a son to be part of this family, it would be to point to the pride I take in being the matriarch of the Taylor clan. I never intended to marry and certainly never intended to have a child, but I am ever so pleased that I have become the leading elder of the large, extended Taylor family—maybe accomplishing something that I did intend to do, following in the footsteps of my father.

Thirteen

The Leaving

n the years following Cassandra's recovery from cancer and Ruth's retirement, the women enjoyed their travels in the summers to attend national meetings of teachers or church women, trips often organized around visits with Margaret as her work moved her around the country, first in Minnesota, then in New York City, and eventually in California. Margaret's mother, Elizabeth, had passed away unexpectedly early in 1976, and her dad had moved to Florida. Until Margaret and the children moved to Minnesota in 1979, the three Essex folks continued their visits to Hastings, primarily around the holidays. The last holiday visit there took place in 1978, the winter Taylor and Margaret separated before the divorce the following spring.

Taylor had left the family home Thanksgiving weekend, but only after his family had departed. Ruth had perceived tension in Taylor on Thanksgiving Day, surprised he hadn't eaten much at the holiday dinner table, something highly unusual.

"All's not right at the kids' house," Ruth remarked to Cassandra and Ed as she turned the car onto the Turnpike, headed home that Saturday morning. Cassandra thought Ruth might be making things up, but Ruth's intuitions proved correct.

Back on Thanksgiving evening, the three women had finished cleaning up the kitchen, and Margaret, with her book, had settled into her favorite reading chair in the living room when Taylor sauntered in to ask if she would like to go to a movie.

"The kids, Dad, and Ruth are all deep into their Monopoly game, which is going to keep them busy all evening, and Mom is happily reading her book, with one eye on the antics going on around the board game. Let's go see a movie."

"Right now?"

"Yes."

"Wow, that would be an unusual treat," Margaret said as she got up out of her chair. "Have you any idea what might be playing?"

"No, but we'll find something interesting," Taylor added. "I'll tell the folks while you get ready."

As Taylor backed the car out of the driveway, he suggested an alternative plan. "Maybe just finding a quiet corner where we can talk and have a cup of tea is a better idea. Things have been pretty hectic around the house these last few days."

"Okay, that's fine; the evening is giving off a bit of early winter chill."

Yes. Taylor wanted to talk, or at least he had something he wanted to say, as the two settled themselves into the corner booth at a small restaurant downtown. They ordered hot tea, as Margaret smiled and said, "Well, this is very sweet, doesn't happen often these days, the two of us busy with work."

But then, at that moment, Margaret noticed a change in Taylor's face and suddenly felt a tiny stab of fear.

"I want you to know that, when I got up this morning," Taylor began, "I suddenly realized I'm not very happy. All day long, I've been trying to decide what to do about that, and what I've decided is that I'm going to leave. I want to start a new life."

Without a pause, certainly not long enough for the shock of his words to reach Margaret, he continued, "Tomorrow, I'm going to tell the folks I need to go to work and instead I'll find an apartment. I'll move out Saturday morning after they leave."

Taylor's words stung like arrows. She was stunned to disbelief, as he continued. "And, in the meantime, I do not want you to say one word to the folks. After I am settled, we can tell them, maybe write a letter together."

Margaret just sat there, muted by Taylor's words, her tea totally forgotten. Eventually she would talk, would ask clear questions and demand answers, would cry, would worry, would sink into all of this frightening mess. But that would come later, once she gained a foothold in the shocking, new reality brought on by Taylor's words to her that Thanksgiving evening.

The next day went exactly as Taylor expected while giving off a thin veneer of normalcy. Friday morning, Taylor made his excuses and went "off to work" and located an apartment. Gone most of the day, he returned home as if from work in time for supper, having left Margaret in a daze while surrounded by and responsible for their company, his family. The kids, now in high school, had gone off with their friends, and Margaret managed to survive a shopping trip in downtown Hastings with Ruth and Cassandra.

That evening, the three women put together a traditional Thanksgiving leftover Friday-night supper. The folks and children cheerily made their way through turkey, potatoes, dressing and gravy, plus leftover pies, as Taylor and Margaret sat at the table, both off in some other world, while attempting to act their parts amid the family circle.

Saturday morning came. The children said their goodbyes to the grandparents and dashed off to school, eager to prepare for a big high school band performance that afternoon. Ruth packed the car, and the folks departed with Taylor and Margaret standing together, his arm around her, in the driveway waving them off.

Then, without a moment's hesitation, Taylor turned to his plan, carrying things out to the car. Margaret realized that, while she had fixed breakfast for the children and his folks, Taylor, back in their bedroom with the door closed, had filled grocery bags with his clothes and personal things he wanted to take. Within minutes, with the car filled, he gave Margaret a big hug and drove off ... while out on the highway, after having left their family behind, Ruth, Cassandra, and Ed puzzled together over Ruth's comment, "All is not well with the kids."

Later that week, Taylor's heartbroken family received his letter, startled, but not as much given Ruth's premonition. Life for the family began in a new configuration under a cloud of confusion and loss. Without Taylor in the home, Margaret and the children moved ahead with uncertainty, learning to make adjustments as needed. Taylor's new life proved to be difficult for everyone, including the Essex family.

Somehow Thanksgiving turned into Christmas, and, as it did, the children and Margaret found their lives not all that changed, except Taylor did not come home for supper. The Essex family returned to Hastings for Christmas, racked with sadness but eager to be with their family. Margaret, working hard to provide a secure home for the children and manage her dismay at Taylor's departure, received the folks with open arms and tears. The Hastings and Essex remnant, determined to not miss Christmas, planned their holiday morning amid the sharing of gifts and the traditional meal, fully aware of, but not focusing on, the one missing around the dining room table.

Margaret's dad called from Florida on Christmas Day afternoon. With children off enjoying their neighborhood friends, the adults got on the various extension phones around the big house, Cassandra in the family room, Ed in the study, Ruth in the basement, and Margaret on the phone in the kitchen.

"What on earth has happened, Margaret? What did you do to cause Taylor to leave?" Alfred more or less shouted into the phone at his daughter. Margaret hesitated, wondering how to respond to her father's quick and startling words, when her dad added, "Well … maybe I was not as good a father to you as I could have been. Maybe I shouldn't blame you."

Margaret again found herself speechless, but, before she could open her mouth, Ed quickly spoke up.

"Alfred, I've been thinking the same thing. Maybe if I had been more what Taylor needed in a father, this would not have happened."

And then …

"No, Alfred, you're wrong," Cassandra chimed in. "This is about Taylor's family, our family, and somehow we have failed him. I believe I neglected Taylor. I never was really a mother to him during all those years when a child and young adult needs his mother."

Margaret, in the kitchen stood reeling, trying to get a word in edgewise …

"Cassandra, you know that is not correct!" Ruth, determined to have her say, began. "I've been thinking a lot about this myself, Alfred. Maybe my presence in the family home might not have been all that good for Taylor ... in the long run."

Shocking words tumbling out from all of them, one after the other.

"Stop! Stop this! Listen to me — all of you!" Margaret shouted. "What has happened here to this marriage can only be attributed to the two of us, to Taylor and to me. Together we have proven to be more than sufficient to undermine our marriage, and it is something that has been underway for some time, even if we did not totally grasp or see it. Please, you all must stop such thoughts and self-blame. Leave it to Taylor and me. We'll sort this out."

Soon after Christmas, Taylor called Margaret, asking her to get a lawyer, saying, "I want a divorce because I'm going to get married again."

Margaret stood there, where she had just hung up the phone, Taylor's words ringing in her ears, 'I want a divorce.' She was immediately startled by a memory. She recalled an event earlier that fall. The local radio station had arranged to interview her, the only woman campus minister at the college, now widely known for her work there and in the community during the last seven years. The topic of the radio show focused on social movements of the times. It had startled her then, and did again at this particular moment, as she remembered that the interviewer had introduced her, in an offhanded way, as "the angry Hastings housewife."

'Of course, Taylor and I have drifted apart,' she thought, sadly.

Yes, Margaret could see it more clearly. The late 1960s and 1970s — the women's movement, the anti-war movement, and the continuing struggle for civil rights for African-Americans had swept across the country, changing lives everywhere, including in Hastings, Kansas, and the Thomas household where Margaret's work had become a regular part of their family life.

In the New Year, finding she had no other choice, Margaret filed for divorce. In the later weeks of January, she and the children shared late afternoons sitting on the floor of the family room, warmed by the fireplace burning slowly beside them. They talked, sorted, and resorted various ways forward. Margaret felt it now more imperative that she complete her graduate work, which meant relocating. The children supported her in this and together began to put together a list of priorities.

Margaret applied to graduate programs. Accepted by several, she chose the University of Minnesota in order to keep the children within a day's drive of their father in Hastings. Then she sold the house and in April made a trip to St. Paul and bought a small house with three tiny bedrooms. She and the children moved there in June once the school year ended and the divorce finalized. Taylor remarried in July. Life continued for everyone, only radically reorganized, at least for Margaret, the children, and the Essex family.

The next Christmas found Cassandra, Ruth, and Ed with Margaret and the children in St Paul, Minnesota. It was a fun-filled time as Margaret and Ruth prepared the holiday meal in Margaret's small kitchen. Together they enjoyed the energy of new lives, new surroundings, and looking ahead, surprised by how the children had grown and aware that, before the adults knew it, their young ones would soon embark on their own college journeys.

The changes continued to hold some pain for all of them. Taylor's parents and Ruth still could not understand their son, who seemed more distant than ever, regardless of their continued love and reaching out to him. They felt somewhat helpless and could only hope things would eventually get sorted out.

From that point onward, many of the family Christmas celebrations took place in Essex, with everyone gathered around Cassandra's table, much to her delight. Taylor and Nell, the new wife, would arrive, enjoy the day, and then return to Hastings. Margaret and the grandchildren, driving together from Minnesota, would arrive just before Christmas and stay for a couple of days. The Essex holidays with the kids—Margaret, Taylor, and Nell—and grandkids continued through the years with only a few exceptions.

One exception took place the Christmas of 1985, the year Margaret and Patricia graduated and moved from Minnesota to New York City, living together in Margaret's large faculty apartment in Manhattan. Steven, who had also finished college that May and was living and working in Minnesota, had flown in for the holiday as had the Essex family. Cassandra and Ruth, since their first trip to New York City years ago, had loved the big city and had a great time finding Margaret and Patricia happily at home there.

"We all loved visiting," Ruth later said as she reminisced with family and friends, "all the homes that Margaret had through the years, that wonderful apartment in New York City and, of course, her lovely home in California. Proud of our daughter-in-law, we were pleased that she continued to love and care for her Essex family, regardless of where her work took her."

However, the family gathered less in Essex, other than for Christmas.

The Christmas following Cassandra's death in the spring of 1995, everyone came together again in Essex around the family table. Cassandra, while still a strong presence in their lives, was the only one missing. Margaret flew in, the grandkids drove together from Minnesota where the two lived and worked, and Taylor and Nell came from nearby Hastings to be with everyone for the day, returning to their home that evening.

As always, Margaret and Ruth pulled out the big dining room table to full length and fixed a turkey dinner with all the trimmings. Ruth had been up early making everyone's favorite pie. Ed and Ruth were overjoyed, thrilled to have the family "back home," until they all departed.

"It is so hard to let them go!" Ruth exclaimed to Ed.

"Yes, I know," he said. "But we sure are lucky to have our family drop in for Christmas, aren't we? Especially when they come from all over the country."

Ruth agreed. She and Ed continued their life together in the family home, enjoying their familiar routines. Out and about with their friends and family, especially at church, they continued to teach their different Sunday School classes and sing in the choir. Ruth cooked for the two of them, always with an eye on what she knew Ed thought he needed as well as what she knew he really wanted, smiling to herself as she made mashed potatoes and rich gravies plus pies. TV sports continued to fill their evenings together, to their great delight—even if their favorite teams did not always win.

"Maybe they can do better tomorrow night!" Ruth would say, as she got up and headed for the kitchen to put it together for the night.

"I sure hope you are right! It's fun to watch, but even more fun when they win," Ed added with a bit of a chuckle.

As Ruth put the kitchen to bed, Ed made sure the front door was securly locked and the porch light off, the same jobs the two had had for all the years they were a family of three — as if Cassandra were still there.

Fourteen

The Ending

In the closing months of 1999, only a few years after Cassandra's death, life intruded into Ed and Ruth's comfortable life together. In the early fall, Ed suffered a stroke. Not totally debilitated by it, he soon began to do his exercises as best as he could working to regain some of his former strength. Yet, by December, the two of them, along with the rest of the family, knew that their life together in the old home place faced a radical change.

Perhaps the saddest Christmas holiday in Essex took place that December.

At the time of Ed's stroke, Ruth had already begun to acknowledge, reluctantly and only to herself, her own decreasing strength. While Ed seemed to improve in small ways week by week, Ruth, after a full day on her feet, found she had accomplished less and less. She tried not to complain, knowing that she had to continue working her way through each day as she always had.

"The day I would let myself merely sit down and quit was not a day I was ready to face," she confessed.

However, now Ruth watched the life she and Ed shared slipping away from them and experienced a gnawing uncertainty as time flew by without relief. "Seems like I had just gotten the jelly made up from the fruit juice I canned last summer and suddenly the holidays were upon us again."

Ruth, feeling a little blue, faced new fears as the holidays loomed. It appeared none of the family, now spread across the country and busy with their own lives and work, would be home for Christmas.

"Ed, I have an idea about Christmas. It looks like none of the family will be here, so let's invite some of our widow friends to join us, the ones without family, including Florence and Lillian, of course. How does that sound?" Ruth asked.

"Well, now, I think that is a fine idea, but I'm worried about the strain on you, Ruth. I'm afraid I can't be of much help."

"I know, but we have to have Christmas!" Ruth had always promised herself it would never be only the two of them sitting at the table for turkey and trimmings. "I'll figure something out," Ruth added.

But first, she felt she and Ed had to figure out some things together about their future. With Ed's unsteadiness and her feet giving her such fits, she thought it necessary for the two of them to make some assessments.

In truth, on many days Ruth was making it through on sheer stubbornness. After Ed's stroke, sleeplessness haunted Ruth constantly, helped along by her fear and dread.

When the phone rang, Ruth hollered to Ed, "I'll ... get it," as she wiped her hands on the kitchen towel and picked up the phone.

"Hello Ruth," Margaret said from across the miles. "Just thought I'd check in and see how things are this week with the two of you."

"Well, it sure is good to hear your voice," Ruth said, with a smile on her face. "Guess we are doing okay. Ed knows I continue to worry about him but says he's coming along, maybe just a bit slower with everything," and knowing that Ed perhaps could hear her, she added, "and that's probably a good description of both of us these days."

Yet, Ruth did not say anything about her fear, an agonizing fear of the future she felt as a shadow hanging over the two of them. In her head, she understood that everyone faces difficulties as they age, especially physical diminishment that can bring on all sorts of losses in one's life. But this moment felt so personal. She knew she faced some kind of an "ending," while in her heart she could only resist and worry.

Margaret had watched this coming for months. She also knew Ruth well enough to know she would hesitate to talk about these things.

"Be sure to call me if I can help. I'll do what I can."

"Yes," Ruth responded, with tears in her eyes, "I know that, my dear. Just stay in touch. That means a lot to me, to both of us. We look forward to your calls."

And with that, the call was over.

For one of the few times in her life, Ruth felt out of control.

Some years ago now, at the time of Cassandra's passing, Margaret was in Boston and unable to join the family for the memorial service but had flown in from the east coast as soon as she could. She planned to stay for a while to help soften the transition after Cassandra's death and memorial service.

"I'm so glad," Ruth said to Margaret, "that we're not suddenly all alone here. How long can you stay?"

"I have a flight on Saturday, which should give us a nice long visit. Maybe there is something I can help you with here at the house."

"What I really want to do and don't think I could face alone is to go through Cassandra's things, her clothes, jewelry, her desk, all those personal kinds of things. Do you think we could do some of that while you are here? I don't want to wear you out."

"I think that would be perfect for us to do together, as long as you feel you're ready."

"Yes. That's exactly what I'm ready for."

"Well, then let's get started," Margaret offered.

Those days flew by, and to Ruth's surprise, they got through everything and enjoyed sharing the task. They relived many memories, telling stories about things they found.

Ed would wander into the room from time to time, stand there shaking his head, smiling at finding the two of them knee deep in stacks of books and a box full of bras, girdles, and panties.

"My, my! You two are digging deep in here. It's amazing all the stuff that can get collected throughout the years," he said. "Do you know what you are going to do with all this?"

"Yes," Margaret said. "So far we have these books for the public library and a lot of clothes for the downtown thrift store."

"Well it's good you have some things that can be given away to help others," Ed said. "That seems mighty fine."

"It is fine, Dad," Margaret added. "Some women will get a lot of use and pleasure out of these clothes."

All too soon, Ed and Ruth sadly said goodbye to Margaret but were glad for her visit.

"I don't know how I would have gotten all that done by myself," Ruth said, as she and Ed had their lunch later that day. "It had to be faced, Cassandra's clothes, everything in her desk, and her books. A task I dreaded but knew I'd have to do. With Margaret's help, we just took care of it, and we also got the bedroom, closets, and study reorganized for my use."

"And now she has flown away, back to her own work," Ed said with a bit of unusual melancholy in his voice.

So then it was just the two of them at home together, their home. Ed and Ruth keeping house as they had for years. Ruth doing the laundry and cooking, he the vacuuming and picking up, sweeping the front porch and garage, and, in season, digging the dandelions in the yard. Each day they had their lunch while watching their TV soap opera.

"My goodness, this story really keeps us on pins and needles!" Ruth said to Ed as he stood to turn off the TV as their program finished.

"There always seems to be some kind of terrible trouble for one of those folks to be getting into. I really never knew anyone like that cast of characters, always stepping into difficulties one right after the other!" Ed said.

At night, Ruth and Ed had their supper on their trays again, watching first the news and then most likely some sporting event. On Thursday evenings, they went to choir practice, and on Sundays to church. But, primarily, these days they stayed home, tending to their own tasks then enjoying the end of their busy days, sitting in the family room together as they had for decades.

That was more than four years ago, and now things had become stark. 'Until now, I don't think I ever gave a thought to

how Ed's and my life together might end,' Ruth would ruminate in her heart. 'Probably thought I'd take care of him until
he died here at home. That would be my choice, and probably
what Cassandra expected, maybe even what Ed expects now.
I just don't know.'

Ruth, trying to distract herself from these troubles, put
down some yeast bread for rising and baking later that afternoon but found it hard to relieve her mind. 'Will I really be
able to take care of Ed?' Ruth's thinking now pushed toward
new and uneasy questions.

'Maybe Ed could live at Elnora. Cassandra and I always
said we were grateful it was there should we need it. I could
easily drive over there and continue to take care of things
for him,' Ruth thought. But she could not stop hearing
her sweetheart's words, "Take care of Ed," a commitment
now growing more difficult to fulfill.

One morning, after Ed had improved enough to make his
breakfast again, he was working slowly to put together what
Ruth and Cassandra had always referred to as "that horrid
breakfast mix," which consisted of raw grains, nuts, and honey,
topped off with wheat germ and, in Cassandra's words, "God
forbid, a tablespoon of vinegar!"

As Ed put away the vinegar, Ruth stood there, shaking her
head and smiling at herself even with all the tension reeling
within her. She poured herself a bowl of Special K and a cup
of coffee and sat down with Ed at the kitchen counter.

They ate, slowly, in silence for a while.

"Ruth, I know you're worried. Probably about me."

"Yes, I am. Sorry to be so obvious."

"Well, that's no problem. I'm actually grateful for your
thoughtful concern. I know that we have a lot to manage here

in this house, mostly you have a lot to manage, and maybe it is too much for you now that I can't really help."

Thus, the two began to talk about their situation. Ed wasn't naïve. He understood things had changed in ways he regretted every bit as much as Ruth.

"What do you think, Ed? Could you see yourself moving to Elnora, to the Elnora Christian Home?"

Quiet for a moment, Ed then said, "Well … I suppose I could go there," his voice as flat as Ruth had ever heard it. "I think we have talked about that in the past when we were over there visiting friends … how we might eventually do that."

"I don't like to even mention it now as a real possibility. I would hate to see you go."

"Yes … yes, it would mean a big change for you, also, I guess."

"Well, a huge change for you; however, you might be able to get the kind of support you need, and you would not be all that far away. I could drive over easily to see you, help you in ways I could."

"I know how hard you work every day," Ed responded. "I don't want to be an added burden to you. So we probably should think about this."

"Well, we don't have to decide anything today. Let's sleep on it."

Everything about his tone of voice and the way he sat in his chair told Ruth his true feelings, 'Of course, I'd rather stay right here.' But he never said that; Ed was not one to assert himself in that way.

That night, after they had shared supper and the evening and Ruth was finally in bed, she could not stop thinking, rehashing her worries.

'This is too hard! I feel Ed is my responsibility, a responsibility I was willing to assume. But what can I do when he can no longer do for himself?'

The only things Ruth could acknowledge that she continued to do for Ed included taking care of his laundry, his lunch and supper, and a little housecleaning with which he still wanted to help. All of Ed's other needs, his breakfast, getting dressed, and all the rest, Ed continued to do for himself, even if more slowly since the stroke. With the weakness on his one side, he had merely stopped wearing shoes that needed to be tied and found ways to keep himself together as much as possible.

'Our lives are really quite simple these days,' Ruth's thoughts continued. 'Ed rarely leaves the house now, and even I don't get out and about like I used to.'

However, Ruth found it more difficult to acknowledge all that Ed did for her. Only yesterday he had noticed the stack of pans she needed to put in the bottom cabinet and offered to hand them to her one at a time, which helped her greatly. She thought of how they enjoyed watching TV together, and visiting about things in the community, at church, and within the family. Ed provided a lot more company for Ruth than she had ever let herself acknowledge, plus she had always thrived on having someone to take care of, especially to cook for.

'I love cooking for Ed. He is so appreciative. What would I ever do in the kitchen, cooking for myself?' she wondered. 'Oh, how I dread what life has brought to us!'

The next morning over breakfast, Ruth having not slept, the two of them decided Ruth should call and find out if they had a room for Ed. They did.

"Thank you. I'll call you back sometime today. I understand

you need to know. Yes, put my name on the room for the moment," Ruth told the admissions director at the Home.

"So there is a room … one that looks out over that central courtyard, which is nice," Ruth said, her voice quivering with emotion.

"Well, I think we need to do this. Let's take the room for me. I can make this work, and I know you'll be a big help," Ed said with resignation as well as some energy, which Ruth noted with gratitude.

So Ruth got out the calendar, and together they decided to wait until after Christmas, to plan the move that last week of December. Ruth called back and reserved the room.

"Ed seemed settled. But this was his way," Ruth later confessed to Margaret. "He met whatever came stoically, at least in appearance."

Ruth did not feel settled at all about the decision, but the two of them continued to move forward. She sent the room deposit in that day's mail.

Ruth called and talked with both the kids, Taylor and then Margaret.

"Ruth, you are not to feel guilty about this," Taylor said. "Would you like for me to come down to help Dad make some choices about what to take?"

Ruth thought that would be a big help, and the two of them would enjoy seeing him.

Then she called Margaret.

"Not a single one of us wants you to jeopardize your own health trying to take care of Dad, and that includes Dad himself," Margaret stated clearly. "He would never want you to do that, and neither do I."

Ruth remained unconvinced. And concerned.

The next day, Margaret called again. "Do you need me to come to help you and Dad get organized for this? You say the word and I will be there."

"No, but thank you for offering. Taylor said he would drive down to help his dad sort what he wanted to take to Elnora. That should be all the help we need, I guess."

But, in truth, Ruth had no idea how she could manage getting Ed ready, let alone over there. They would have furniture to take and many other things. Now the sorting of clothes appeared a minor issue; the move felt ominous, as if dark clouds were gathering over her.

One day soon after Ruth's conversation with the kids, Taylor drove down to spend an afternoon with his dad. After lunch, they went into Ed's room and talked and talked, but nothing actually got sorted, let alone packed up. However, both Ruth and Ed enjoyed Taylor's visit.

The next day, Margaret called back to say she had made plans to come for Christmas and would stay long enough to help get Ed moved.

"Ruth, I've been thinking about what all this move is going to entail and think you need some help for a few days. And since I'm coming, I might as well get myself there for Christmas. We'll enjoy being together for the holiday."

Ruth felt overwhelmed with relief.

"Ed, that was Margaret on the phone. She's coming for Christmas!"

"Oh, she is, is she," Ed almost sang out. "Well now, that just seems to be mighty fine to me. Aren't we the lucky ones!"

Margaret and Ed had a special relationship. She had realized she wanted to be there with him and Ruth at this moment. However, Ruth had guessed Margaret had another topic of conversation on her mind she wanted to talk about, face to face, with Ruth herself.

"I was right, of course," Ruth later admitted to Margaret, "about what you had in mind, that I should be thinking of moving to Elnora along with Ed. You were thinking like I should have been thinking back then, but at the time, I was having none of it."

But now, Ruth's heart sang out when Margaret arrived the day before Christmas, 'Here we are, happy again! What joy to have her here. It will be a family Christmas after all … even in the midst of my sorrows.'

And Margaret went to work. She gathered a few Christmas decorations from the attic, put the wreath on the front door, set bowls of Christmas balls around, pulled out the dining room table, laid out a Christmas tablecloth, and created a centerpiece with holly she cut from the bush in the yard. She also found the little Christmas manger set she had made for them years ago and set it on the TV like Cassandra had always done.

"Margaret has lifted all our spirits." Ruth admitted to Lillian with tear-filled eyes.

Together, Margaret and Ruth fixed a marvelous holiday dinner, and having Florence and Lillian with them made a very nice family table. Ruth planned to have all of Ed's favorite dishes, including homemade rolls and gooseberry pie with homemade ice cream for dessert. When Ed poured the leftover turkey gravy over his ice cream, Ruth and Margaret and everyone at the table almost died laughing, with Ruth having forgotten the years of complaining she and Cassandra had made of Ed "ruining her homemade ice cream."

"Ed, you have to really, really love gravy to put it on your ice cream," Lillian exclaimed through her laughter, while Ed just sat and smiled broadly at them all.

"I was in tears almost around the clock, hiding them from everyone, of course," Ruth confessed weeks later to Lillian. "But it was a wonderful family day. Having you and Florence there made it special and, with Margaret's help, we all survived that week."

During the next few days, Margaret worked some with Ruth on meal preparations, but she focused on time with Ed. Hand in hand into his bedroom they went. She had fixed a comfortable chair in there for him and laid out a few empty boxes along the side of the room. Margaret moved easily, letting Ed think things through as she posed questions.

"Which of these shoes do you actually wear, Dad?" she asked, as she laid them in pairs between the two of them.

"Well, now, that is a good question. Some of them I have not worn for a while, like that brown pair over there. They're for working in the shed on instrument repair, comfortable for standing, but too worn to wear to church."

"Which pair would you put on to go to church?"

"Oh, I don't think I'll need any of those shoes really, not any more. I'll not be going to church. I'll not be going outside to go anywhere."

"What do you mean, you will not be going outside?"

"Well, I'm thinking that in the nursing home I won't need anything but my bedroom slippers."

"Dad, you're going there to live, not to wear your slippers. Of course you'll walk outside. Remember there's a lovely courtyard with a pathway through the gardens. You will be out there every day the sun is shining to get some exercise and good

Vitamin D. I know you, Dad," she said with a smile. "Let's put these good leather shoes in the 'to go' box. Okay?"

"Well, if you think I should," Ruth heard Ed say, from beyond the hallway door where she stood eavesdropping, now having to tiptoe quickly back down the hall and into the bathroom while trying to stifle her giggles and not give herself away.

'Oh, that Ed Thomas!' she thought, once she caught her breath. 'He has such a way of always being so like himself!'

Together, an hour or so at a time, Margaret and Ed went through every item in that room, a process that took a couple of days. Margaret was trying to help Ed make his own decisions about what he wanted to take with him and what he no longer needed. Ruth tried to stay out of it but couldn't totally. So, they would work for a while, and, when they took a rest, she would surreptitiously sneak in and look through what they had packed to make sure Ed would have what Ruth knew he needed.

'After all, I know more about when he wears which kind of underwear during each season of the year than he does,' she thought to herself as she continued to watch the packing in Ed's room. 'No one else knows what kinds of blankets he'll need for his bed. He easily gets cold at night if he doesn't have the right blankets!'

After Margaret went to bed that evening, Ruth stepped into Ed's bedroom. Sitting in his chair, he worked slowly to remove his slippers and socks, always the first step in his lifelong, well-honed bedtime routine. She sat on the edge of his bed. As the day of sorting and boxing up his things had progressed, Ruth had become more and more distressed.

"Ed, how are you feeling about all of this? I am worried that you might be feeling railroaded into this decision, this move.

I hope you don't think or feel like I am pushing you out. I couldn't bear it if you felt like I was the one making you do this," Ruth, on the brink of tears, struggled to control herself.

"No-o. I do not feel you pushing me. It's true, I don't want to go, but then I know I need some extra help now. I can't put such a burden on you anymore. You already have too much to do taking care of the house and yourself."

"Well, I'm concerned. I hope you feel like you really had a choice and were able to make it yourself."

"I don't think either of us has any choice in this matter," Ed said, looking directly at Ruth. "We have to do what we think is best."

Ruth had suffered all day as the packing continued, concerned that Ed would feel she did not want him in the house anymore. And, at the same time, she now carried another concern. Margaret had quietly asked her again if she didn't think it would be a good idea for her to move to Elnora as well.

"I have a longtime woman friend," Margaret told Ruth, "about your age, who lives quite happily in one of those lovely independent-living apartments. She's surrounded by wonderful women friends, some of whom I am sure you already know. I'm wondering if that might not be a good idea for you, Ruth. At least I hope you will think about it."

Ruth realized she did not want to push Ed because, in fact, she did not want anyone pushing her into such a move. When Margaret had taken Ruth aside asking her to think about it earlier that day, she told Margaret she would, but she merely told a fib. She had no intention to entertain such a thought.

'I've lived in Essex all my life and see no earthly reason to leave because Ed is going,' Ruth had told herself as she sat there with Ed, working to shake off those feelings and return to her concerns about Ed.

"No-o. I don't feel you are pushing me out," he said again in his older, now weakened, gentle voice. "I'm sorry to leave you with all the work, leave you to do it on your own. This house takes a lot of work to keep it going."

"That's not a concern, Ed. My concern is about this decision."

Their rambling, many layered conversation was frightfully awkward for these two, who, having lived together for over fifty years, had very little experience talking with each other about personal things and feelings. However, they persisted, both wanting to help the other at such a difficult moment in their life together.

"I'd like to be able to be here to help you," Ed said, "but I will be fine over there."

Ruth, feeling lost, could not think of anything else to say.

"Things change," he said. "I guess people, each of us, have to learn to make adjustments."

"Yes, we do. But that doesn't mean we have to like it," Ruth added. "You will not be all that far away. I will come over every week to help you … and we can catch up."

"Well now, that will be mighty nice of you," he offered, then added, "I do hope they will let me make my own bed. I've always made my own bed and don't want to stop doing it now."

"Ed! You will not have to make your bed. They will do that for you."

"That is what I am saying. I don't want them to make my bed."

"Well, we don't need to worry about that now," Ruth said, suddenly disgusted, as she got up and left the room.

'That man can be so aggravating!' Ruth thought as she stomped across the family room to her own bedroom. 'No one has ever been allowed to touch that bed of his. Had to have it made exactly according to his plan. Talk about old maids!'

The family's longtime Essex friends, Jim and Judy, had offered to help with the move, also providing their pickup. With Judy, Jim, Margaret, and one of the their younger cousins, they managed to get Ed's small dresser, recliner, typewriter, desk, and swivel chair into the truck, along with the boxes of clothes, shoes, and books. Plus those blankets Ruth knew he had to have for his bed, wrapped up in a big plastic bag.

The next morning, on a very wintry day, with the pickup loaded and on its way, the three of them got bundled up and into the car for the drive to Elnora. Margaret would drive. Ruth had not slept a moment all night and was up early to make sausage gravy and biscuits — Ed's favorite — for their breakfast.

While Ed was off in his room getting ready, Margaret helped Ruth do up the dishes from breakfast. Ruth, reaching for a smile while guarding her tears, said, "Did you see the amount of pepper he put on that gravy? I sure hope they serve gravies at the Home ... and have a large pepper shaker on his table!"

The family knew whenever Ruth was at her wits end what she usually did was cook. The kitchen was a saving grace for her once again that anxious-filled morning.

Ruth noticed the tears in Margaret's eyes once or twice that late December morning. However, Ruth had declared no one would ever find her crying, as she determined to get through that day, even with her weary mind running, spinning almost out of control.

Once at Elnora, it all seemed to happen so fast. They went from standing in that small, empty room to suddenly having all of Ed's things in there and comfortably arranged. Margaret had thought to bring a hammer and wall hooks to hang a few family pictures she had taken off his study wall, while Ruth took satisfaction in seeing Ed's typewriter table and chair fit in nicely.

"Oh, look here," Ed had said, with a tired delight in his voice, "you thought to bring the floor lamp to set beside my typewriter so I can have that good light. That is very nice."

Late in the previous day, Margaret had placed the small items for the move in the living room. Ed noticed she put his small typewriter desk and chair along with the typewriter there near the front door.

"I don't really think I'll need my typewriter," he said to Ruth, standing with him early that morning.

"Ed, when did you ever not need your typewriter?" she replied. "I told Margaret to put it out here. It goes in the truck; we'll find a place for it in your new room."

Now Ruth stifled a giggle, thinking, but not saying, 'Just because you aren't living back home doesn't mean you're going to stop typing away at that old upright!' And now there it was in Ed's new "home," and he seemed pleased. 'Good,' she thought.

Their friends with the truck left to return to Essex, bidding Ed goodbye and telling him they would be over to see him soon. Then the administrator at the Home invited the family to remain for lunch with Ed. Somehow that gave them a bit of breathing room before the inevitable hour arrived: the ending none of them wanted to face.

After lunch, as the clouds gathered outside, looking every bit like another winter storm, Margaret gave Ed a big hug, as Ruth heard him thank her for coming so far to help him get settled so nicely. Margaret kissed him and moved toward the door.

"Then it was time for me to say goodbye as well," Ruth recalled, with tears again in her eyes. "I was not sure I could. This was another moment I had not prepared for at all, it seemed."

Suddenly there they stood, in the middle of Ed's room, their arms wrapped around each other and tears streaming down both their faces. As they held each other and cried and cried, it was as if each of them was trying to say all the things they had never said to each other through all the years.

"I have loved living with you," Ed said through his tears. "You have been the best house partner I could have ever had."

Ruth's tears freely flowed at last. "Yes, we've been good together, haven't we?" Ruth cried, still holding on to him, "I am going to miss you so much!" She already felt bereft without him. 'Oh, my goodness,' Ruth cried, asking herself how she ever thought she could live without this man to take care of ... as their tears continued to fall. Then Ruth added, "I've loved the way you introduce me as your adopted sister. That always meant a lot to me."

"The way we've shared almost every day together ... for years ... of course you are like a sister to me, and now I can't imagine my life without you, right there in the kitchen," Ed said sweetly.

Ed's words helped Ruth get hold of herself, "I'm still going to worry about you when I am not here to be sure you get your chopped salad every night. I talked with the folks in the kitchen. They know you need a salad every evening and have assured me you will get it," Ruth said, as she pulled her head back a bit from their embrace so she could look right into his eyes. "Now if they don't bring you that salad, will you please ask for it? I mean it—ask, Okay?"

"Okay, I'll try to remember."

And then Ed said, "You know, it's not really about the salad, though I have loved that you were so faithful and made all those wonderful salads every night all these years. It's ... well ... it's you're the best friend I've ever had."

They continued to stand there for what seemed like a very long time, letting the tears flow, neither of them wanting to let go of the other. Not wanting to let go of the past. Ruth knew, once she let go of Ed, he would stay, tomorrow would come, Margaret would leave, and she would be all alone in their big, old house.

Eventually, the two of them decided to look for Kleenex and realized that Margaret had left the room, giving them their privacy. They each blew their nose, gave each other one more hug, and Ruth turned and walked out the door and down the hall to where Margaret put her arm around her. They walked out to the car for the drive back home, tears streaming down their faces. They did not talk, the moment too full for words.

As Margaret drove into Essex, they decided to stop and get something to eat. Ruth did not think she had the strength to face putting together a meal, even with Margaret there doing most of the work. Not tonight. They stopped at Ed and Ruth's favorite buffet restaurant, on Main, not far from the house.

After filling their plates in the cafeteria line, they chose to sit near a window at the side of the large room, seeking a bit of privacy, grateful for the almost empty room. Not feeling all that hungry, they ate lightly and talked quietly about the day.

"Looks like we're both about through here with our plates," Margaret said. "Do you want dessert or some of that ice cream?"

Ruth suddenly burst into tears, saying, "Oh, my! I'm going to miss Ed so much! He hardly could wait for that bowl of soft ice cream every time we ate here."

Margaret shook her head remembering back to other days when she had been there with Ed, Cassandra, and Ruth. How could anyone forget watching Ed's bright smile as he returned to the table with his soft ice cream piled high with spoonfuls of every sort of sweet topping they had.

"What a mess that man could make of a very good dish of vanilla ice cream!" Ruth said, as her tears turned into a soft giggle ... "and no, I don't think I could face having ice cream here tonight ... not without Ed."

Fifteen

The Departure

n that cold winter night following their excruciating day taking Ed to Elnora, Margaret and Ruth went into the kitchen to put things away for the night. Ruth appeared in the mood to talk. Margaret suggested they have a cup of hot tea. The two settled down at the kitchen counter.

Margaret listened as Ruth spilled out whatever was going through her head. Eventually, as Ruth might have suspected she would, Margaret brought up the issue Ruth had hoped to avoid.

"Ruth, although during these next few months I know your focus will be on helping Dad get settled in at Elnora, you could begin to sort out in your own mind the idea of perhaps making the move there yourself."

At some point during the day, Margaret had slipped off to ask the woman in the admissions office if any of the independent apartments were available and had been told they knew of one coming up in the next couple of months. Without telling Ruth, Margaret asked her to put Ruth's name on the list for the apartment, hoping to give Ruth time to think about it first.

"You aren't the only one who has suggested this to me. I will at least think about it. But I have a lot of trouble seeing myself leaving Essex."

"I know," Margaret said easily. "You have been here all your life. But in these next few weeks, I do hope you will give some real thought to the idea."

"And I will," Ruth replied. "When I say, 'How could I leave Essex?' what I really mean is there is way too much I would have to leave behind. How could I leave my church? Or my doctor? Or Bev, who is the only one who knows how I like to have my hair done? Or the folks at the bank?"

All these people, the bank owner and bank tellers, her doctor, her dentist, most of the people at church — including the minister — had all gone to school to Ruth. Essex, her home. These, her people.

"I wouldn't know how to begin thinking of leaving this place," Ruth said freely, her voice filled with sadness, her body sagging under the weight of what lay ahead for her.

"I know ... I know," Margaret said again, as she, and Ruth, stood for a goodnight hug.

Ruth put their teacups into the kitchen sink. Margaret went to the front door, made sure of the lock, and turned out the porch light. The women had one final hug and headed for their beds after their physically and emotionally grueling day.

Yet, already in that very minute, Ruth felt sure and admitted to herself, 'I can't leave Essex.'

Until the next morning.

After Margaret pulled out of the driveway headed for the airport, Ruth went back inside the house. She stood there by the front window for a while, then turned around and just stood in the middle of the front room. Quiet … eerily quiet. Not a sound to be heard. Everything in its place. Margaret and she had even done up the breakfast dishes before she left. Margaret had put the big dining room table back in the corner where Ruth and Ed kept it and had packed up the Christmas box and put it back in the attic … and now, no one at home, never going to be anyone at home ever again.

'Just me … all by myself … for the rest of my life,' Ruth gasped.

As Ruth walked from room to room, her thoughts tumbled out. 'There is nothing, absolutely nothing, to do. The laundry is done. The kitchen cleaned up. No one to cook for and more jam and jelly and pickles out in that cupboard than I could possibly ever eat — even if I live more than a hundred years.'

And then, thinking she could call Ed to see how the night had gone for him, she realized, 'Darn! I can't even call Ed.' The two of them had decided he could probably get along without a phone. Immediately, Ruth found herself questioning that decision … and maybe others as well.

"What a silly decision that was!" she said out loud, berating herself, while feeling overwhelmed by a growing number of questions, including the crazy notion to let Ed move to Elnora. Ruth sat down on a kitchen stool, crumpled onto the counter, and wept as hard as she had ever wept in her entire life.

Ruth could not recall much about how she got through those next days and weeks. She did remember the loneliness she felt night and day. Friends did call to check up on her, but, once they called, most did not call back. After all, she didn't really "need" anything.

She showed up at church to teach the Sunday School class and sit in the pew for worship. She had stopped singing in the choir when Ed could no longer sing because she didn't want to go alone.

But two things were undeniable to Ruth: coming and going from Elnora was an easy drive, and Ed seemed happy. In fact, he appeared to thrive surrounded by all kinds of new friends. He had always been more gregarious than Ruth and far more so than Cassandra, and his new home seemed to satisfy this natural tendency in him. In addition, the staff was terrific and obviously enjoyed working with him. Given his great interest in doing as much as he could for himself—including wanting to make his bed—they celebrated his good, uplifting spirit. Ruth enjoyed being at the Home, as Ed introduced her to friends there, some new and others from Essex, including many who had been to school to Ruth.

"The days of my visits to ECH to see Ed and other friends were turning out to be my very best days," Ruth later told her family. "I was by that time never as happy as when I was over there with Ed and our friends. And the staff, they're wonderful people."

And back home? A far-too-quiet place. Ruth could hardly stand it. Without Ed at home, there was less for Ruth to do to fill the hours. She found she didn't even like to watch their story on the TV without Ed to talk with about the most recent scandal. Eventually, she realized she had given it up. There never seemed to be anything on TV that interested her anymore.

'Lord a mercy, what I need to do to eat and do the laundry for myself seems like nothing and not many friends left to do for either,' she lamented. Ruth noticed how many of their friends were gone, moved away or just plain up and died.

Somewhere along there, maybe without realizing it, Ruth began to think about selling their big house and moving to a smaller place. "I did go look at some apartments, but they all looked dark, old, and rundown," Ruth finally confided in Margaret during a phone call, "but I don't like rattling around all by myself in this big house. I'll figure it out."

"Yes, I'm sure you will," Margaret said, wanting merely to listen, let Ruth talk it out.

Soon members of the extended family, making regular visits to see Ed in Elnora, expressed concern for Ruth alone back in Essex and began to ask her why she hadn't moved there along with him. "You don't want to sit around in that old, empty house. Get yourself over to one of those great apartments in ECH where we can visit you when we visit Uncle Ed."

'They all sound just like Margaret,' Ruth thought to herself.

In late January, their granddaughter Patricia arrived for an after-the-holiday visit. The two of them drove over to have lunch with Ed in Elnora. As they ate in the dining room, the admissions director saw Ruth and stepped over to speak to her. "Ruth, there is an apartment available now, if you are still interested. Your name is at the top of our waiting list," she added, to Ruth's surprise. "I was going to call you today to let you know, but here you are. If you would like to take a look at it before you leave, stop by my office and pick up a set of keys."

"Thank you. I'll think about it," Ruth offered.

Then she turned to Patricia, "This is you and your mother's doing," Ruth said questioning with a grin.

Ruth relented. She and Patricia went to look at the vacant apartment. 'My, this looks rather nice,' Ruth thought as she entered the large, open living room. 'It's certainly clean and feels new … and look at those wonderful windows.'

"Look at this, Ruth," Patricia called out, cutting into Ruth's thoughts, "an attached garage and just outside the kitchen door."

"Ah … yes, interesting," Ruth said, putting on her not-too-enthusiastic voice. But in her mind, she was thinking, 'I hadn't expected a garage … assumed these folks would have to park on the street and lug groceries through rain, sleet, and snow, like the apartment buildings I've looked at in Essex.'

"Also," Patricia added, "without a step."

"Really? No steps from the garage?" Ruth responded as she stepped into the kitchen area looking past Patricia into the garage, thinking, 'I do hate those steps getting from the garage into the kitchen back at the house,' and then said, "Well, the kitchen is small but like you say, perhaps convenient. I'd have to have room for my pots and pans. I can't live without those!"

But then Ruth went into the bedroom and discovered the large, fully equipped bathroom, 'That's a gorgeous shower,' Ruth said to herself, 'no old bathtub to climb in and out of to take a shower… and it's all right here, part of this spacious bedroom.'

Ruth disliked that long walk out of her bedroom, across the family room, dining room, and front hallway to get to the bathroom. 'I've never complained all these years, but at night, that trek from the my bed to the bathroom seems twice as far as it does in the daytime … and, even though Ed isn't there, I don't seem to be able to use "his" bathroom that's only a few steps from my bedroom door. Silly old me!' she thought.

At the apartment, she liked how the front door opened into an indoor walkway connected to the main building. "This hallway would make my place accessible to Ed's room, regardless of our crazy Kansas weather," Ruth remarked, as she and Patricia walked along it on that cold, wind-blown January day to say goodbye to Ed.

She and Ed had loved Patricia's visit, and the next day, as Ruth waved her goodbye, she continued to think about Elnora. 'Maybe, if I were to move there, it would be the best way for me to continue to take care of Ed as I promised Cassandra.'

The more Ruth let herself entertain the idea, the more she began to accept the thought that she really could move there—that leaving Essex and moving there might not actually kill her. Things were going well with Ed, but Ruth insisted she could see a few little things not exactly right for him. And she came to think, if she lived there, just down that hallway, she could continue to make sure Ed had what he needed when he needed it.

"I would still have a nice kitchen," she said, "and could make Ed some of his favorite dishes. He could come for supper from time to time. And we could watch the basketball games together as we have done for decades." Ruth found she was talking to herself again, a practice she had recently taken up almost full time.

It no longer looked like Ed might be dying. In fact, by every measure, he had improved, actually gaining strength with the support of the staff working with him on his walking. 'Maybe,' she thought, 'maybe I would also do better living there,' certainly a tenuous thought, but at least she could think with new eyes now.

But then she would walk around that old, big house and almost sag onto the floor, feeling the weight of everything in it on her shoulders. 'What about all this stuff? This house full of stuff! So many beds, dressers, chairs, lamps, tables, books, art on the walls, family pictures, knickknacks, and the kitchen, oh my.' She found such thoughts paralyzing.

For her to even think about selling this house, she would have to find something to do with all that stuff. At that point, she stopped herself. "I can't face it," she moaned, with her head in her hands. But then reminded herself, 'Cassandra was never very good at getting rid of things,' and then a new idea popped into her mind, '—maybe this is the answer, maybe the only time I could face getting rid of all this stuff was after I was alone.'

Cassandra had been impossible. Frankly unable to let anything go, especially family things, especially her family things. Cassandra had always said, "I do not ever want any of my family things to be put out in the yard for a sale! The family is to be called in and things passed along." How many times had Ruth heard her say exactly that?

But circumstances change. Right then Ruth, felt sure no family members would want any of the stuff in that old house. Any memory or tender meaning formerly attached to various items was certainly now long ago forgotten.

Standing that afternoon in the family room, Ruth said, "Who even knows these awful-looking, uncomfortable green couches that we have had forever came from Grandmother Wright's house in Chicago a century ago," challenging herself out loud. "And the kids, Taylor and Margaret both have everything they need. In fact, they are at the stage in their lives when they are beginning to downsize and get rid of things themselves."

However, even if Ruth could say to herself, 'Cassandra is gone, and I'm the one left, and if I have to have an estate sale, so be it,' it still felt impossible. To Ruth the stuff felt like another huge barrier, a terrific amount of work sorting and getting ready. She did not know if she could face it, even with help, did not know if she had it in her.

Ruth took on a self-assigned task of making an assessment. 'Okay, yes,' she thought, 'we know Ed has everything he wants or needs in his place in Elnora. That's important.'

Ruth walked through the house. She tried to think of what she might take to that nice apartment. It didn't take her long to realize she would need very little of what was there. "I never did like wall-to-wall furniture in a room or house," she said to herself.

Many older folks she had visited in their small apartments lived buried, surrounded by every piece of furniture they had ever had back in their old, big, family houses. Cramming things into a living space would not work for Ruth. She needed her bed, her desk, her chair, an end table, the TV and a table to set it on, a couple of chairs for guests, a small table for the dining area, and a couple of straight-back chairs, a lamp or two, the laundry hamper, and the kitchen stool. Period. Well, and, of course, a few dishes, cooking utensils, and her pots and pans.

But this was the moment it got hard. When it all came down to it, she knew this stuff actually did not matter. She could find a way somehow to manage that. It was the move itself, the move away from her hometown, she couldn't face. One by one, Ruth had whittled down her defenses surrounding the idea of such a move. Now she had reached the bedrock of her resistance: 'I cannot face anything that would take me away from my hometown and everything I have always known.' And when such thoughts overwhelmed her, her hesitation grew, and she admitted what she knew to be true, 'I don't think I can do this ... even if it seems to make a lot of sense.' Even in her disappointment Ruth felt she knew herself pretty well and understood the consequences. "I can't do this. The price is just too high," she said with finality.

Feeling a clear and total resignation, she walked back into the kitchen, looked in the refrigerator, found a cold leftover from a few days ago, poured herself a cup of hot water, and sat down at the counter for supper.

The luxury of indecision, however, was not to be hers. That next afternoon, the admissions director called to let Ruth know they now had another person interested in the apartment she had looked at the week before. If she wanted it, she needed to make a deposit to hold the space. The administrator had to know by the next morning.

So, now Ruth had been caught. She would have to tell others what she decided yesterday evening, that she did not want the apartment.

After Ruth put down the phone, she stood there in the kitchen, absolutely torn apart. But then suddenly, surprisingly, she felt a surge of something, perhaps her own strong "will" pulling her forward.

"Something clicked in me. I didn't even bother to call the kids. I knew what they would say. Instead I picked up my checkbook, put it in my purse, found the car keys, got in the car, and drove out to the highway. I did not cry. I did not let my sadness overwhelm me. Not now. I let myself feel resolved, not defeated."

As Ruth drove along those miles between Essex and the Elnora, she felt stronger and stronger, her mind clear and maybe even her heart. She would do this. She could do this. It would be okay, even if not the way she had envisioned her life ever before. But Ed had led the way, and she now determined to follow and make it work for both of them.

That afternoon, Ruth signed a contract for the apartment and gave them a check—before she lost her nerve. Fortunately, they would be doing some interior painting and putting in a new carpet, a beautiful blue color she had chosen while there. The apartment would not be ready for her to move into for a couple months (or begin paying rent). This would give her precious time for the work ahead.

That done, she stopped to find Ed and give him the news.

Ed smiled and, even in the face of her heightened excitement, said in his understated, simple way, "Well, now, that sounds mighty nice," reminding Ruth of how she had come to care for this man who could be so predictable. And then with some concern, Ed added, "That's going to be an awful lot of work emptying that big house all by yourself."

"I can't do it by myself. But I think Patricia will come to help me do an estate sale. I've decided that is the only way to manage it," Ruth told him.

"Well, now … that's probably a good plan," he said, followed by, "Maybe there are some in the family who could use the furniture, as Cassandra used to say."

"Ed, we just need to sell the house and everything in it. All of it, whatever we can. With both of us paying rent here, we are going to need all the funds we can generate to support us."

Ruth, moving ahead, said, "I told them I'd be ready to move in here by March first."

With the decision made and Ed told, Ruth got in the car to drive back to Essex. Time to get to work. Neighbors down the street had said to her sometime in the last year or so that, if she ever wanted to sell the house, they might be interested. They were getting older and looking for a good-sized place all on one floor, exactly like she and Cassandra had been when they bought it years ago.

"I drove the car into the garage, opened the door, and went to the phone and dialed."

She had not even bothered to take her coat off.

"Bud, this is Ruth Peterson up the street. We have decided to sell the house, and I wanted to see if you're still interested."

Bud and his wife came right down to have a look and talk with Ruth. Ruth did not even think about not having dusted for weeks now. She showed them the entire house. They said they would think about it.

In less than an hour, the phone rang. It was Bud. They wanted to buy the house. He and Ruth agreed on a price, and Ruth called Don, the family lawyer, in Hastings and asked him to make up the contract.

In one day, Ruth decided to move to the Elnora Christian Home, drove to Elnora, signed a contract to rent the apartment, found and told Ed, drove back home, and sold the house.

That turned out to be the easy part.

"That evening, standing in the middle of our living room," Ruth recalled later, "I was a woman with a plan, not merely a lonely old woman without anything to do. There was, in fact, a lot to do. I had the list already forming in my head." Ruth was back on track.

First she called Taylor and Margaret with her news. They were astounded at how quickly things had fallen into place once the decision was made; Ruth felt their obvious relief.

"You did all this ... this afternoon?" Taylor asked, disbelief in his voice.

Then Ruth called Patricia, who offered to come for a week and help prepare for a sale. Everyone patted Ruth on the back for what they all saw as a wise decision. Yet, while one minute Ruth was beginning to feel her energy for her plan, in the next she could be overwhelmed with grief.

'So many more losses coming my way!' she cried out to herself in anguish.

On day two, she began by calling a man she knew who did estate sales in the area. He gave her some possible dates and made an appointment to stop by to make a first assessment. He described, in general, what Ruth needed to do to get ready.

'Thank goodness.' Ruth thought, when he said he would bring some papers describing in detail how to prepare for sale day. "I've helped others," she admitted to him, "but it sure feels different when it's your own."

She called Patricia back. They got out their calendars and made some plans, and decided on a date for the sale. Patricia made some suggestions about things that Ruth could do before she arrived, such as sort the things in her desk and bookshelf and closet. Things that only Ruth could do. Then, when Patricia arrived, they could take on everything else together.

"Closing up the house almost killed me, physically and emotionally. It felt so final," Ruth reflected long after the move.

A few weeks later when Patricia arrived to work with Ruth for a few days, they arranged tables around the house and began to empty closets and drawers, one by one. Patricia reorganized Ruth's study and bedroom suite to hold the few things she would take with her to Elnora. They removed everything from that room except her bed, dresser, and desk.

Patricia put tags on every piece of furniture, marking things "for sale" and "Elnora." Patricia also called her dad and mom and brother, at Ruth's request, to see if they thought of any particular item or items they would like to have. Everyone named something. Margaret said she would like to have the cut-glass bowl she had given to Cassandra on her eightieth birthday.

"Good," Ruth said. "I want the kids each to have something. It's fun to see what they are interested in."

Patricia wanted a few small things, but most of all she wanted the old-fashioned, beat-up salt shaker that had decades of Cassandra's and Ruth's handprints all over it.

Ruth said, "What I want is that last photo of Cassandra and me taken not many years before she died. I can put that on my desk. Other than that, I only want what I need to make my simple life work in the new apartment. The kitchen things are what's important. Not the fancy china, just a few everyday dishes will do me fine. But I want the pots and pans ... things to cook with!"

They decided to leave packing up the kitchen to just before the day of the sale.

After Patricia left to get back to her work for a while, Ruth continued to sort and stack things here and there. And she finally got some rest. The work was physically hard. But she kept at it a little bit at a time.

"Often in the middle of the night," she told Patricia in a phone call, "I'm sitting at my desk and sorting through papers. I've thrown tons away. Makes me wonder why I kept all that stuff for decades."

Patricia returned the week of the sale, and together they made the final push toward sale day. When that morning began, before the crack of dawn, an entire crew of friends and neighbors arrived to help move everything out of the house and into the front yard. It was quite a mess! People started standing around the edges of the driveway and the lawn at about that same time. Ruth had heard that the eager ones arrived early, but this seemed ridiculous to her, standing there for hours waiting and watching stuff being carried out.

When the sale finally began, Ruth wilted. Patricia and she sat down in the family room in the rear of the house and tried to stay out of the fray.

"I was not all that interested in watching," Ruth told Margaret on the phone. "Every once in a while, Patricia wandered out to see how it was coming along and would bring back some stories. The two of us played cards most of the day on the old card table I decided at the last minute to keep, and I am sure glad I did."

Ruth would, in the years to come, use that old card table as the centering pole for her life in the new apartment. Right next to her chair and always within her reach, it had the most important items on it ... her address book, her calendar, the bills she needed to pay, her checkbook, her planning book for her past and current projects, the newspaper, and telephone.

At the end of the day, the auctioneer pronounced it a success. Ruth was almost in disbelief but grateful there would be new, important money for their bank account and was greatly relieved everything had been hauled away.

The women from the church sold food out on the street all day. Patricia had gone out to fetch a small plate for each of them, but they had merely nibbled, not feeling very hungry. But now it felt very good to lock the door, get in the car, and drive over to their friends' lovely home. Feeling at home with Jim and Judy, they took off their shoes, had a bowl of good homemade soup, and fell into their beds early. They had been up, dressed, and packed for this departure well before five o'clock that morning, prior to the arrival of the auction team.

The next morning, Jim and Judy went back to the house with Patricia and Ruth, and, along with some other friends, they loaded Ruth's car and Jim's pickup once again, this time with

Ruth's things, and headed for Elnora. Jim drove the truck and Judy drove Ruth's car. Patricia and Ruth followed in Patricia's car, but Ruth wanted to make one final walk-through to make sure they had everything.

"It looks so huge," Ruth said to Patricia, as she began to reminisce, 'What a wonderful home this house has been for all of these years.' And then to Patricia, standing there watching, Ruth said, "My goodness. What a lot of living went on in this house ... if only these walls could talk."

Patricia smiled.

Ruth ran her hand over the kitchen countertops, stretching her mind and heart back, not wanting to forget any of it.

"I loved this house even more perhaps than Cassandra loved that old house on South Street," she exclaimed to Patricia, who had far fewer memories of the older house except the photographs her mother had taken of her and Steven as small tots on the back porch in their little summer wading pool.

"Just imagine all the meals we cooked here, in this kitchen ... all the summer canning Cassandra and I did together right here," Ruth's voice kept recording the pictures running gently through her mind.

Then she walked through the big rooms, thinking of all the family gatherings and all the church and Women's Circle meetings, the gatherings of their "Us Girls" small group of single professional women. 'Oh! How we gals played together here and there, took trips together, fixed picnics right on that countertop to take out to the lake on summer afternoons. We did have years and years of fun together.' Ruth smiling as her thoughts rolled out, almost unendingly ... . 'So much life, so much living ... oh, yes ... so much living.'

Gratitude filled Ruth's heart.

But now, now they needed to be on their way. "Well, it's totally empty," Ruth said to Patricia, who had been standing by, "and I hope my stuff has not been carried off by some happy buyer at the auction!"

Ruth was glad she had made arrangements for a neighbor to do the final cleaning because she could see it was badly needed. "I'm not pleased to see that dust behind the places where furniture had been," Ruth said as Patricia stepped out into the garage, Ruth behind her.

Ruth closed and locked the door for the last time, then checked the cupboards she had had built along the side of the garage after they moved in. Amazingly empty. The memory of all the years of canned goods that sat on those shelves washed over her, she felt faint ... until she found a little chuckle coming up at the thought of how much Cassandra loved to get into those cupboards and count the jars of canned pears, peaches, tomatoes, pickles, and the different kinds of jams and jellies.

"Oh, how that woman did love to can and then count and recount all those jars," Ruth couldn't resist saying as they walked out of the garage, Patricia closing the door behind them.

In the car, Ruth did not say it but was quietly thinking that Cassandra would not have appreciated all that had just taken place. 'The auction. The sale. All of her things out in the front yard.' Ruth found herself again very glad she had not gone out there.

'Better not to have that image in my mind to carry forward into my new life,' she thought sadly.

And in her heart, she found herself saying to her dear Cassandra, 'Honey, you were not there ... you are not here ... so the pain is not yours ... the pain is totally mine, yes, all mine.'

Ruth was determined not to dwell on it any more. She had sold and closed up the house, and she had had to do it by herself ... and now she would have a new home where she could continue to take care of Ed, as she had promised Cassandra.

Sixteen

The Home

ove-in day at The Home. It all happened so quickly as Ruth sat in her favorite chair to oversee the setting up of her new home. Exhausted but happy, once the furniture and boxes found their place in each room, they all, including Ed, piled into cars. Ruth, ready to celebrate, took everyone out to lunch at the Chinese restaurant in downtown Elnora.

That afternoon, Ruth watched another miracle unfold around her as her small troupe of workers unpacked all those boxes and put things in their place.

After the others left and time for supper had come, Patricia and Ruth walked over to Ed's room and the three of them had supper together in the ECH dining room. Ruth enjoyed greeting all their old Essex friends, those from church or school, some she'd spent years driving over there to visit.

'With Ed and so many of our friends here,' Ruth said to herself, 'maybe thinking of this as my home will come easier. I've been uprooted but not entirely.'

For a body that rarely slept, that night Ruth sank into her own good bed and slept. In the morning, feeling renewed, Ruth and Patricia shared a quick breakfast before putting the final touches on things. By midmorning, Ruth sent Patricia off with a big hug and heartfelt gratitude. "You, my wonderful granddaughter, managed to get me out of that old house. I could never have done this without you!" she told her.

After Patricia drove away, Ruth walked through her new, small apartment, touching this and that, admiring how the wonderful light came through the large, clean windows into her two rooms.

'Oh, the light is wonderful,' she thought, 'and now I realize just how dark our old house was in every room.'

She admired the new carpet and how wonderfully her furniture fit just as she had imagined. Thrilled with the sense of openness, Ruth liked her unencumbered plan, nothing felt crowded, leaving her rooms flooded with space and light. And she was pleased with her new hide-a-bed couch. "Finally, I'm rid of those darn couches. I don't sit all that much; however, I put in way too much time sitting on those old, miserable couches. I hope the people who bought them at the auction find some redeeming quality to them. I certainly never did!"

Grandmother Wright's art deco, green sectional couches were among the prized possessions of Cassandra, who would never put up with anyone saying anything untoward about them. Ruth had wanted to complain for years. Finally, today her tongue had been loosened by her joy in having left them—along with a whole lot of other stuff—behind.

'Now,' Ruth thought to herself, 'there is work to do here. I have to make sure everything is in its proper place. I'm sure the dresser drawers are in a mess.'

But as she looked out the front windows, she hesitated. 'What a beautiful day!' Ruth thought, as she stepped out the door and felt the day's early warmth on her covered patio. 'Indeed, a lovely Kansas spring morning.' she said to herself. And right there, calling out to her, sat their old patio table and chairs, which Patricia had cleaned yesterday.

Ruth changed her mind, went inside, made herself a cup of midmorning coffee—just like Cassandra always insisted they do—and went outside to sit and listen to the birdsong.

Within moments she heard someone calling out to her.

"Hello, Ruth!" the unfamiliar voice shouted across the lawn. "I'm Hattie, your new neighbor."

"Well hello," Ruth called back to the heavy-set woman moving gracefully toward Ruth's patio.

"We heard you were coming. Friends told us we were about to get the best-ever neighbor!"

Ruth felt a bit embarrassed until she experienced Hattie's warm welcome.

"Glad to meet you, Hattie. I'm Ruth Peterson from Essex."

"Thank you," Hattie said, now out of breath, as she sat down in one of Ruth's patio chairs. "But we know who you are, as your reputation precedes you. My sister Pat and I went to the store and saw you on your patio as we came back home. She'll come over after putting the groceries away. We picked up this box of our favorite cookies for you as a welcome gift."

"Well, thank you. If I put on the coffee pot, would you and your sister join me for a cup of coffee—and one of your favorite cookies?" Ruth asked.

"You bet," Hattie said.

While Ruth was in the kitchen getting the coffee made, the doorbell rang, and when she opened the door to the inside hallway, there stood another woman Ruth had never seen before.

"Hello there, Ruth. I'm Pat, Hattie's sister. We're glad to have you here."

The younger, vivacious sister had a wonderful big smile. Ruth almost immediately saw something in Pat that made her sense that she had found a new friend.

After a quick tour of the apartment, Pat and Ruth—plate of cookies and coffee pot in hand—stepped out on the patio and joined Hattie. In that moment around Ruth's old front-porch table (where, by the way, Cassandra and Ruth had rarely if ever sat while always saying that it would be a nice thing to do), right there began one of the best friendships Ruth would ever have.

The two sisters lived across from each other just down the hall from Ruth. Filled with gumption, these two women loved to laugh and make a practical joke, all of which thrilled Ruth. She would soon learn that she'd never really known anyone who could be as naughty (and nice) and as much fun as her new neighbors, Hattie and Pat.

After the coffee time on the patio, Ruth walked through the hallway to see Ed. He reported that Patricia had stopped in to give him another farewell hug as she departed earlier that morning.

"I sure hate to see her go," Ruth said, as she sat to visit with Ed. "She was so helpful getting everything organized ... and did it with such ease."

"Well, I can surely say knowing Patricia was there helping you made me feel grateful also," Ed said, shaking his head. "I just could not imagine how you were going to get everything out of that house. But here you are, so you managed somehow."

"Yes, we did. It's still kind of a blur in my mind, but I can tell you that last night I slept like I've never slept before. I'm exhausted. It wasn't only yesterday that wore me out but everything that it took to get to yesterday."

"I hope you'll take the time to get some rest now and not take on too much, Ruth."

"I'm fine. You don't need to worry. I have a few things yet to get organized at the apartment but wanted to check on you this morning before I dig in."

"Well, I'm mighty glad you stopped by. Oh," Ed continued with an afterthought, "I just had a note from Joyce saying that the boys are all coming up to Wichita next weekend to go to the ballpark and looking forward to seeing the two of us."

"That's good news. I've been thinking it was about time for that annual trek from Dallas. Be good to see them. They're somewhat crazy about that baseball team, but I do enjoy their visits."

Ed smiled, recognizing Ruth's characterization of the Taylor nephews.

"Maybe I'll walk over later this afternoon to see how your new place is coming along. I take a walk every day, you know."

"Good. When you saw the place yesterday, it was a huge jumble. You need to see the results of the afternoon miracle we pulled off. I'll look for you after your lunch and nap."

On that happy note, Ruth got up and headed back to her apartment, continuing to think about what Ed had said, that it was fun to have Patricia here "with us" and the Dallas nephews coming "to see us." She liked the sound of that.

It was as if Ruth's body got lighter and lighter, as burdens and worries over their lives began to lift from her shoulders.

Mid-morning coffee on Ruth's patio with Hattie and Pat became a frequent ritual on those lovely warm days. Ruth's new hallway buddies proved to be the best of friends and a great tonic for her moments when she felt the losses, whether for Cassandra or merely for the "way it had always been," back home.

Sometime later, Ruth finally admitted to Margaret, during one of her visits, that from her first day in Elnora, she began to see things a lot more clearly. "I was just totally unwilling and unable to see how I could leave Essex."

"Yes, but yesterday," Margaret said, "I heard you say that living here has turned out to be life-giving for you."

"Yes. It's true. I got some of my strength back and I don't recall really ever feeling lonely again—at least not until Ed passed away," Ruth confessed as the two women sat on the patio one beautiful September day when Margaret was in Kansas for the month.

But on that day, as Ed arrived to see Ruth's new apartment all put together, he seemed pleased, especially pleased to have Ruth close by within an easy walk.

"My goodness, this all looks just fine," Ed said. "How smart of you to keep that table to set the TV on," he added, as his eyes moved around the room and finally to the kitchen area. "And how is the kitchen? Do you think it's going to work okay for you?"

"Well, I haven't attempted much more than cold cereal yet, but eventually ..."

'Aha!' Ruth thought, as she watched Ed's face light up, 'I bet Ed is thinking about a pie.' And if Ed wasn't, now Ruth was. At that moment, she got the idea to get in her car, go and bring in some real groceries, and fix a first good meal for the two of them. She had thought, of course, that she would continue to drive back to Essex to get her groceries at all her old familiar places, but at that moment that seemed ridiculous.

Coming out of her reverie, Ruth turned to Ed.

"How about some baked steak, potatoes and gravy, followed by gooseberry pie on Saturday night?" Ruth asked with a broad smile. "Maybe we could even watch the ball game together after supper." Nothing Ruth could have said would have put a bigger smile on Ed Thomas' face.

"Well, now! That sounds mighty nice."

The next day Ruth asked Pat about the local grocery stores.

"Are you going this morning?" Pat asked.

"Yes, I've decided I really need to get acquainted with the grocery stores around here and get some things to put on the shelves and in the refrigerator."

"Let's go together," Pat offered. "I need one thing I forgot earlier this week, but it will be fun to show you around. We'll find everything you need." And then, as Ruth turned to go back to her place, Pat called out, "Make a list! And try to remember to bring it with you!" ... as the two of them enjoyed a good laugh. 'That woman is such a wonderful tease,' Ruth thought to herself.

Later that morning, the grocery shopping in Elnora turned into a happy surprise for Ruth. She found everything she wanted and never gave another thought to her and Cassandra's old grocery haunts back in Essex.

Once back in her kitchen, Ruth enjoyed putting her groceries away, a task that suggested some reorganizing of cabinets, the results of which pleased her greatly, until she began to make Saturday's supper.

"Oh, you should have seen me!" Ruth reported to Patricia

on the phone on Sunday afternoon following Ruth's first meal prepared in the new kitchen the evening before.

"What do you mean? Doesn't the space in the kitchen work for you?" Her granddaughter's asked in a puzzled voice.

"No, no. It's fine. Only I'm not used to where things are yet, so as I got started, every time I needed something—like the pepper, or a particular pan—I couldn't find it. And, of course, I needed my baked steak pan that day. You know me. I would never try to make my baked steak in any other pan."

"Yes, I do know you, Ruth."

"I knew it was down there someplace and ended up standing on my head, dragging out all the pans you and I had put in the bottom cabinets. Suddenly I had this terrible mess, pots and pans everywhere covering every inch of the countertops and the kitchen floor."

It was clear to Patricia on the other end of the phone call that Ruth had had a good week, totally in her element, enjoying every moment even though she had couched this conversation in the frame of a complaint.

"And that's when I thought about those still empty shelves in the garage," Ruth revealed. "So now, everything is in perfect shape. I moved my large pans out on those shelves where I can see every single one of them without moving a thing."

"Sounds like a good plan," Patricia offered.

"Yes, it's perfect. So back here in the kitchen, I have my more everyday pots and pans and all of them sitting right at the front of the bottom cabinets, so I can see exactly what is there when I open the cabinet doors. Of course, there is all that unused space behind them, but it's too difficult to put anything in the back of those bottom cabinets. I don't want to have to work that hard ever again."

"Good. I know how you don't like to have things in stacks," Patricia agreed.

"Exactly. All my life I have lived with Cassandra's views on storing things in the kitchen: stack it up, don't waste a square inch! But no more. Cassandra couldn't get rid of anything, even an old rusty can. She'd say, 'Ruth, don't throw that away. Someday we might need it to melt canning wax.' Then I would say, 'Honey, we have a can we melt our canning wax in.' And then she would reply, 'But it may not always last …' when in truth that old can was probably one her mother had used when she was a young bride 150 years ago! In Cassandra's kitchen nothing could ever be thrown away!"

Finally, for the first time in her life, Ruth would have a kitchen exactly as she wanted it.

Back on that Saturday night, Ruth put her first meal together. Ed, who used his walker to walk over to her new home, was overjoyed by the good smells when he arrived at Ruth's door.

"Hello, there," Ed said as he opened the door and stepped in. "Is that a pie I see over there?" he asked, almost swooning from all the aromas arising from Ruth's kitchen.

"Yes, it is …" she sang out, "gooseberry!"

"Oh, boy!"

"I thought we'd use our old TV trays, if that's okay with you. We could sit at the table, but this is a lot easier I think."

"This is just fine. I'll sit myself down in this lovely old chair …"

"… and I'll dish up our plates," Ruth said.

Ruth felt rather proud of herself and pleased with her new home; at that moment, she especially loved her new kitchen.

Together, they enjoyed their evening meal on their old TV trays, from their old familiar chairs, sitting in front of their old TV, watching one of their favorite sports teams on the basketball court. Ruth felt content and happy, grateful to see Ed doing so well at "The Home," as the two of them came to call their beloved Elnora Christian Home.

'And, now that I am also here,' Ruth told herself, 'I can help take even better care of him in my own way, as I promised.'

But Ruth wasn't finished with Essex and wouldn't be for some time. That Monday found Ruth needing to drive over there again to take care of some business at the bank. While there, she stopped by the church to drop off some things for the upcoming Foundation meeting she would chair later that week, things she had forgotten to bring with her the day before when she came over to teach her Sunday School class and go to church.

After taking care of her business, Ruth stopped in to see Florence. She had not been very well. Her children and grandchildren, who lived in Dallas, pressured her at every opportunity to move there.

"Well, hello, Ruth," Florence called out from her chair, as Ruth knocked and opened the front door. "What are you doing back here so soon? Didn't I see you yesterday at church?"

"Yes, I was here yesterday. Sorry, I didn't get a chance to visit with you but thought I'd drop by on my way home this morning. Came over to take care of a few things at the bank and to leave some things in the church office for a meeting coming up later this week."

"Well, it's good to see you. Lillian and I were saying only yesterday that we really miss having you and Ed around here these days."

"Yes, not many of the old family left anymore, are there?"

"No there aren't. And I'm just too stubborn to move, even when I'll soon be the only one left."

"Oh, that's right. Someone told me yesterday at church that Lillian has decided to go live with her son down in Houston. I'm not surprised," Ruth said.

"Yes, but I'm not moving to Texas even though the kids keep insisting, 'Mother, almost the entire family lives here.' But I know who lives there. Do they think I've lost my marbles?"

"Why are you being so stubborn, Florence?" Ruth asked. "It sounds like an excellent idea for you, and, frankly, I worry about you myself, since I'm no longer right here to make sure you're okay."

"Why, Ruth Peterson—you of all people! You know how I feel about the thought of leaving Essex. Like you, I've lived right here all my life and don't want to leave. I wouldn't know how to act, or even think straight, if I lived someplace else."

Ruth tried to listen. What she wanted to say but didn't was, "Go now! While you are able to make decisions yourself." But Florence had Ruth on thin ice. Not only had Ruth resisted for a long time but had continued some of her long-held resistance, to which her presence in Essex that very day (and the day before) gave strong evidence. Ruth had in no way moved her life out of Essex, only some of her furniture and her pots and pans.

As Ruth left that morning, Florence uncharacteristically got out of her chair to wave Ruth off at the front door, as if her departure signaled a thousand-mile journey. To anyone who might have seen this, it would have been obvious that Florence missed having Ruth right there, down the street and around the corner, like always.

Once in her car, Ruth paused as she put the key in the ignition. 'Will I drive by the old home place to see what it looks like today? Or go on over to Main and out to the highway ... head back to Elnora?'

An important pause, for Ruth was just beginning to find her way in rearranging her long life in this small town. Ruth would now meet challenges daily about how to take, or not take, steps toward composing a new life — over there. This time "change" won out. Ruth decided to get on the highway and head back "home."

Ruth kept her car going and coming from Essex every week, often two or three times, even while finding herself feeling more and more "at home" in Elnora. But she was beginning to realize how few of her Essex friends were left there. 'I have taken care of so many old friends and neighbors,' she thought, 'but now there's hardly anyone to "do" for.' With no one left to take care of in Essex, Ruth had lost something important for her life.

Ruth, the youngest in their cohort of friends — hers and Cassandra's — had overseen not only Cassandra's decline and death but also the decline and death of almost all their best women friends. Soon after Ruth moved to Elnora, the last of them, Mabel, the young widow in their group, died suddenly. Years before, Mabel had asked Ruth to be the executor of her estate, a task that now kept Ruth even more often on the road to Essex.

Overseeing the memorial service and burial for Mabel, and then getting the house organized for a large auction and eventually being sold, meant months of work for Ruth.

At least once a week while she worked on Mabel's estate, Ruth would stop in to see Florence, sit a spell, and catch up with news.

"Hell-oo-o," Ruth would call out as she knocked and opened Florence's front door.

"Oh, there you are! Good to see you, Ruth," Florence called out from the kitchen. "Just fixing myself a glass of ice tea. Want some?"

"Sure," Ruth said, as she wandered into the kitchen. "It's hot out there. Summer is putting its best face forward this week."

"Yes, it certainly is," Florence agreed. "Have you been over to Mabel's?"

"Oh my, yes. What a houseful," Ruth exclaimed. "I thought Cassandra and I had a houseful of furniture. Whew!"

"Don't you have help? I thought Lillian was working with you."

"Oh, yes. Lillian has been helping a lot. I'm glad her move isn't until later this fall. But you know Lillian; she is not willing to make any decisions about what to do with things. She has been helpful boxing up stuff I sort into piles and also pulling everything out of the closets so I can go through it faster." Then, Ruth lowered her voice, and her eyes, and said, "You know with Mabel's death all of Cassandra's and my single women friends, our "Us Girls," are all gone now. Those women would have been glad to give me a hand … but … well, that's the way things are now," Ruth's voice trailed off as she fished for a Kleenex in her pocket.

After a bit, Florence said, "Well, sure wish I could help you but I'm just no good anymore — can hardly walk, can't stand, can't lift. I'm at my best right here in this chair." Florence admitted.

Florence's comment had brought Ruth back to the current moment.

"I sure wish you would think about the kids' offer to bring you down to Dallas with them, but don't get me started! I know you'll figure it out one of these days," Ruth said. "Maybe sometime this fall after all this estate work is over, you and I can drive down there to see all the kids—and maybe even Lillian if she's settled by then. I'd really like to do that."

"You tell me when to pack my toothbrush and I'll be on the curb waiting for you to pick me up. But only for a short visit, remember. I do not want to move there!"

"I know, I know. Well," Ruth said with a deep sigh as she got up. "I guess it's back to work for me. Thanks for the iced tea," she said as she opened the door. "I'll see you again soon."

Some weeks, you wouldn't have known Ruth had left Essex. She enjoyed the work, or perhaps better to say that she thrived on having a major responsibility once again at the age of ninety-one when, for many, such tasks would have been left to others. Ruth managed it all, and in the end it proved quite a boon for her. As the executor, she received a percentage of the total estate. That money became a most welcome financial cushion for Ruth. From that point forward, she fretted a lot less about how she would pay the monthly expenses at The Home for Ed and herself. In fact, Ruth's money turned out to be sufficient through Ed's and her own death. And no one ever had to help Ruth take care of her finances. She paid her own bills and kept her checkbook up to date, correctly, to the very end.

Ed continued to improve in small but significant ways—he could now tie his shoelaces. The results of his stroke almost two years ago became less and less evident. One day, during a special party the staff put on for the residents, the music got some folks to dancing. Ed, the lover of women and never shy about holding a woman close, began asking the younger staff women to dance. To his delight, some of them revealed they did not know how to dance. Thus began Ed's short tenure as the dancing instructor at The Home.

Members of the staff had grown fond of Ed. They liked his independent ways and good humor and how he enjoyed his life. He lifted their spirits amid their days of heavy and often challenging work. Certainly not your "average" resident—even though one of the oldest, Ed's dancing lessons were a big hit with everyone, beginning with Ed.

And then Ruth, often away in Essex doing her work, heard about Ed's new occupation. She was horrified.

"What if you fall and break your back, or your neck? Then we'll be in a fine pickle. Act your age, and stop this silliness!"

Ed acquiesced to Ruth's demand, as he always had, but those few days teaching the women to dance had thrilled his heart. And he greatly enjoyed telling the story to folks who dropped in to see him, while easily acknowledging to them that it perhaps had been "foolishness" on his part (taking Ruth's reprimand to heart).

For the younger members of the Taylor clan, who continued to be Ed's greatest admirers, this story thrilled them. In it, they recognized their beloved "Uncle Ed" whom they knew as a real charmer.

"Hey, Paul," his Aunt Joyce, Florence's Texas daughter, asked him on the phone one day, "Did you hear that your Uncle Ed has been giving dancing lessons to the young women on the staff at The Home!"

"No way!" Paul replied. "Isn't he a hundred years old by now?"

"Very close," she managed to get out amid her laughter.

As children, they had been intrigued early on by the one and only "outsider" in the family, a man from Chicago, no less—their Great Aunt Cass's husband. To their delight, he proved to be someone who enjoyed them while their parents appeared to be somewhat puzzled by him. But the children easily loved their Uncle Ed and still did. When they were together, especially after they learned about his dancing lessons at The Home, they spoke about him with love and giggles.

"Our crazy Uncle Ed! Yes, he's one for the books. How could anyone describe him?"

"Well, I think that's easy," one of the great nieces said. "He grew bald early, was not bad-looking, and worked to wear the correct clothing so as not to embarrass the two women he lived with, so wasn't flashy in any matter ... well, maybe except for his ever-present hand-tied colorful bow ties."

"Uncle Ed's greatest talent," another offered, "might be his love for everyone he met, especially children. He has such a welcoming heart and great smile."

"But don't forget his musical saw! I remember when he came to my grade school and entertained us all. I was so proud to say he was my Uncle Ed!" another niece added.

"Seems like he's always noticing what others might need," Cousin Marilyn said thoughtfully. "To bring a chair, footstool, repair things for others, especially any kind of musical instrument, or greet the neighbors, greet and speak to everyone. He never met a stranger."

"Yes. That's exactly right," another of the cousins said. "Uncle Ed knew everyone and always seemed to notice who was ill, who had died, had lost a job, or needed some kind of help."

"And then there is all that typing out his thoughts," Marilyn added. "How many times did I hear Aunt Ruth or Aunt Cass ask, 'What in God's name is that man typing about all the time?'"

At this, they all shared a good laugh together. Everyone knew about their Uncle Ed's typing habits.

However, Ed's long life was now drawing toward a close. He continued to live a happy, easy, purposeful, and caring life, always young at heart, making his own bed, having fun doing for himself—and others. Many had to be reminded of his age, for he did not show it.

Whatever else was true, at this time in his life, Ed, a resident in the nursing-home in Elnora, Kansas, someone who lovingly spent his days doing real things for real people, whoever they happened to be, had managed to create a life filled with abundance … and was typing far less.

It happened while Ruth was in Essex one day. After stopping at a stop sign at a busy highway intersection, Ruth had pulled out in front of an oncoming car she apparently had not seen. Her car was totaled, and Ruth taken to the hospital, badly shaken. Sore and bruised from head to foot, but without any broken bones or life-threatening injuries, Ruth was lucky once again. A friend on the hospital staff had, as she requested, called Elnora and asked the staff to make sure Ed knew he need not worry.

"Please," Ruth pleaded, "make sure that Ed understands that I am not in any physical danger and that I will be back home soon."

The news shook Ed. Frustrated because he could not call her, Ed insisted he needed to talk to Ruth. Finally the staff helped make a phone connection to Ruth's hospital room so they could visit.

"Ruth, my goodness, I'm worried about you!" Ed began. "They say you are in the hospital, but they also keep telling me that you're alright. I really wanted to hear your voice myself …

be assured that you're okay ... and ... and I want you to know I hope you will be better and back home soon."

"Now, Ed," Ruth struggled to talk, "please don't worry. I told them to be sure you knew that I'm okay. Nothing broken, and, yes, I'll be home soon. Now, don't you worry about me. Just take care of yourself like you always do. I'll see you soon. Thanks for calling."

"Okay. Get a good night's sleep if you can." Ed closed off the conversation, clearly filled with concern.

Ruth, weak and in pain and without the ability to hold her voice firmly in control, might have unintentionally conveyed to Ed what appeared to be a more tenuous situation. Her repeated assurances had not comforted him.

'If the car was totaled, how could Ruth be okay?' he kept trying to think it through.

With deep concern, a broken heart, and prayers on his lips for Ruth, Ed went to sleep that night.

Ed Thomas died, on his knees, early the next morning. He had been saying his morning prayers on his knees by his chair, as he was known by the staff to do early each day. One of them found him there, hands folded, head bowed over them. But on this morning, his head rested on his hands.

No one ever knew exactly what he died from, but it could easily be said that his concern for Ruth and her situation played a part and, in such worry and love for her, his heart just gave out. Maybe he realized he would not be able to help her at the very moment she needed him. Maybe his heart gave out because life had finally overtaken him.

A few weeks short of his ninety-eighth birthday, after having lived in Elnora for three years, though obviously worried about Ruth's well-being, Ed died a happy man. Perhaps the happiest he had ever been—his household filled with so much more than he had ever experienced. Content and feeling, at moments, really in charge of his life, Ed had continued to honor the debt he owed to others, beginning with his best friend Ruth.

Ruth, shaken by the car wreck, was now totally undone by Ed's death. Brought down the aisle in a hospital wheelchair at the Essex church a few days later, her badly bruised face and arms were obvious to all. She sat in her wheelchair next to Margaret in the front row with Taylor, Nell, and the children for Ed's memorial service. Taylor had asked Margaret to give the family eulogy. Ruth, probably for the first time in her life, wept openly and constantly during the service and throughout the day. She was bereft.

'Oh, I feel so guilty!' she said over and over to herself, through her tears. 'How could I not have seen that car? But now, look what I have done … I caused him such a shock … and it killed him.'

After all the family had departed, Margaret remained to help clear out Ed's room and take care of all his belongings and other matters resulting from his death. Together, she and Ruth revisited old stories—the good ones and the puzzling ones—about Ed, a man that both of them had loved deeply, and, after all these years, were able to take in his quirks and gifts in equal measure.

Ed and Ruth had experienced a real love, one that comes along through years and years of shared life experiences. None of the close relationships within this family—Cassandra with Ed, Cassandra with Ruth, and, finally Ruth and Ed—in their family home, conformed to their neighbor's expectations.

In Essex, Kansas, at this time, intimate relationships were about carrying one's given family forward through having children. Ed and Cassandra, by default, accidentally fell into this pattern, but only briefly. However, what Cassandra and Ruth sought and found, went far deeper than that. And what Ed and Ruth unknowingly stumbled into had nothing to do with what people thought of as intimacy. Yet, these relationships were each rooted in love. Maybe Cassandra had never really sought love, or when she thought she had found it, it was just never enough. But she did seek and find an intimate relationship with Ruth. Ed sought both sex and love and missed most of the former, while becoming rich in the latter. However, Ruth, the orphan, always hoped to find love and was fortunate because it continued to find her.

Ruth's weary grief bore down hard upon her. Shaking her head and wiping her tears, she said over and over again, "I cannot let go of this man who has been so important in my life."

Following the memorial service, Ruth returned home to her apartment at ECH. And once Margaret left for home, Ruth's wonderful women neighbors, with loving care, helped her to heal from her injuries and her loss. Slowly, Ruth regained her strength.

Eventually, Ruth would be elected by the residents at The Home to be their representative to the Elnora Christian Home Board of Directors, a board that carried the legal and fiduciary responsibility for the well-being of the institution that every day became dearer to her. Ruth relished her new role, for she thrived on holding a position with the responsibility to get things done. Ruth Peterson flourished on being handed responsibilities.

Ruth decided on her own not to replace her car. And to give up her driver's license. "They're going to take my license away from me, I know that," Ruth said. "I'm just going to tear it up, put it in the trash, and not be a driver any more. This is my decision to make, not others."

Without a car, Ruth faced another new day and began to make choices that would cut most of her lingering ties to Essex. She had discovered months earlier that she needed a more accessible dentist, and, when her doctor retired, she reluctantly agreed to take on a new, local doctor in Elnora.

Now, she had reason to test out the Sunday morning "church" gathering at The Home and also a local hairdresser. A beautician came regularly to wash and set women's hair, and Ruth found she did fine. Some around her may have wanted to ask, sarcastically, "How could this be, Ruth? Someone else can fix your hair?"

Fully at home in Elnora, Ruth's life continued as she cared for her neighbors, gathered to eat, laugh, and play with her women hallway gang, and came to enjoy her "new" church.

"We don't know if she offered or was asked," Patricia reported, "but before anyone knew it, Ruth was giving a brief Bible study at the weekly Sunday morning gathering of the residents at ECH." Ruth had found her stride once again, now at age ninety-six.

As a woman teacher who never married and was thought of by some of the townspeople as a nosy, bossy, old spinster, Ruth continued to love her life amid former students who populated Essex, Elnora, the surrounding counties, and beyond, now professionals and farmers alike. Known as a tough teacher, she was loved by most, if not eventually all, her former students.

"I know I really didn't appreciate Miss Peterson when I was in her classes. But that all changed when she was teaching my children. Then I understood what a great teacher she was, even for me," Tommy, one of her former students, told Margaret when she was at Ruth's and he came calling, "just to say hello" to his favorite teacher.

Margaret noticed when she visited that the phone or doorbell rang frequently at Ruth's Elnora apartment, bringing a former student from somewhere—near and far—back into her present-day life, checking in with their teacher.

"I was there one day when a tall, lean, handsome, middle-aged man in a beautiful silk suit knocked on Ruth's door," Margaret told the story. "Standing there with a box of Ghirardelli chocolate, he had arrived with a huge smile and something he knew Ruth loved, a special gift for his special high school teacher. Then I found out that Tim, the out-gay, highly successful San Francisco lawyer, was making his annual trek to Ruth's door to visit, find out how she was doing, and bring her up to date on his life."

Tim came for decades, first to Essex and now Elnora, to say once again how much she had meant to him as a young, confused, and closeted gay high school student. Tim was only one of many who continued to find their way to Ruth's door, bearing similar expressions of appreciation and respect.

For the rest of her life, Ruth continued to be meticulous about her appearance, had her hair "done," and always wore her wind bonnet when going outside, even to the grocery store. And her family, Cassandra's family, her only family, continued to pour out their love for this woman.

As for Ruth, she continued to miss Cassandra, her great love, and now also missed Ed, her special friend. They were always with her in her heart, each day, along with her wonderful friend, Pat, who had such a playful way of being a friend, bringing joy to Ruth's days. Thus Ruth continued to live at The Home amid the glow of family and friends … and her dearest loves, past and present.

Seventeen

The Unriddling

When the phone rang, Ruth smiled at hearing Margaret say hello.

"Oh, it's so good to hear your voice again"

"Yours, also," Margaret replied.

"Guess you got back home from your Christmas holiday up the California coast with your friends."

"Yes, back home after a lovely time away, settling in for the coming New Year ... and my birthday!" Margaret added. "Your lovely card was here when I returned home, and the check."

"Glad to know the Pony Express is still working out there in the West," Ruth chuckled.

For years, Margaret's Essex family had sent a box of chocolates for her birthday, always insisting that their Kansas daughter should have her favorite Kansas specialty, Russell Stover chocolates, for her birthday. In the last few years, Ruth had sent a check instead, but with explicit instructions: "For your R.S. chocolates only."

"I want you to know that the Pony Express not only is working but that I have complied with your instructions and have a new box of my favorite chocolates sitting right here."

"Oh, you have," Ruth said, pleasure easily heard in her voice. "Well, I trust you won't eat them all in one sitting!"

"No, not me." Margaret said. "But if Dad were here, I'd have to hide the box."

"Yes, Ed sure did have a sweet tooth and, like you, loved those chocolates."

"Patricia called the other day," Margaret reported to Ruth, "to tell me how much she'd enjoyed a few days with you last week."

"Yes, it was wonderful to have her here. Did she tell you we were invited over to Jim and Judy's in Essex for a fancy holiday meal?"

"Yes, she did. What wonderful friends they are for you."

"Yes ... they are. And speaking of friends, Pat has stopped by to pick me up. We're going to take a little drive. It's such a beautiful winter day here, but I'm sure glad you called. And enjoy every one of those chocolates and have a fine birthday."

"I will, and thank you, Ruth, for the lovely gift. My love to you ... and tell Pat I said hello!"

The 2009 New Year had arrived in sunny Southern California. Life was moving forward at a fast pace for Margaret. In a few days her community was putting on a play about Eleanor Roosevelt with Margaret in the role of Mrs. Roosevelt. Margaret, who had met Mrs. Roosevelt and knew her distinctive voice, was now working to get it right.

'I'm not close to capturing that voice,' Margaret sighed, as she paced in her small apartment one morning, script in hand, practicing her lines ... when the phone rang.

"Mom," her daughter Patricia said, with an urgency in her voice, "I just had a call from Elnora. Ruth was taken to the hospital in the night and is not doing well."

"Oh dear. Did they give you any information about what had happened? Why they took her to the hospital?"

"No, not really, only that those on the staff felt she might have had another small stroke, like she did last fall."

"Oh, poor dear. I know how she hates to be taken to the hospital."

"I can't go, Mom. I just got back from there. But someone needs to go. Can you?"

"Does your father know?"

"Maybe they called him. I called you first. I knew you would want to know. But I'll call him now. I'll let you know what I find out."

When Patricia called back, Margaret relaxed a bit. Patricia had reached Nell in Hastings and found that her dad had already left for Elnora. The folks at ECH had called him. Nell said since he hadn't seen Ruth for a while he decided to drive down.

"He's probably already there by now," she said.

"This is good. Ruth will be so glad to see him, and he'll let us know what he finds out."

Margaret had spent several weeks that fall in Kansas with Ruth. In fact, now retired, she had been in Kansas for the month of September for each of the last three years as artist-in-residence at a historic artist studio. This gave Margaret special time with Ruth. The studio was only a few miles from Elnora, and Margaret could visit at least once a week. Ruth loved having her nearby for the entire month.

But this past fall, Margaret found Ruth's health had greatly declined, especially her ability to stand and walk. Her doctors said she'd had one or more small strokes and Margaret changed her plans to stay until she could rearrange Ruth's living situation. Her first step had to be convincing Ruth she needed to move to the nursing wing.

Margaret worked with the admissions director sorting options; both expected Ruth to resist. And soon a bed did become available but wasn't a great option.

"Ruth, those of us who care about you feel you need to get yourself settled over in the nursing wing," Margaret said, "and we know what you want is to stay right here, in your own home. But being alone, especially at night, concerns me and everyone else in the family, plus your friends on the staff here. They are worried."

"I know you love me and have what is best in mind for me, but I really do think I can still manage here." Ruth, with all her being, wanted to remain in her own place.

Sitting close, Margaret leaned toward her, looked directly into her eyes, and said, "Yes, Ruth, this is where we began this conversation a month ago when I arrived. And from what I've seen, I don't see you managing as well as you may think. You eat very little because you can't stand to fix food. You've lost so much weight your clothes are about to fall right off you, and you aren't getting exercise because of the difficulty you have with walking."

During a long pause, Ruth looked down at her folded hands in her lap.

"Let's get you over there where you can have all kinds of good help," Margaret continued. "I think you would feel stronger with better nourishment and with some exercise they would help you with," Margaret said, again.

Ruth had not looked up, did not want to see the concern she knew was on Margaret's face.

"Sandra says there is an opening you could have today. It's not the best option … it's a bed in a three-person suite. But getting you over there, even in this room as a temporary step, would help you to assess how it might be for you to live over there, once a single room becomes available."

Eventually, Margaret convinced Ruth to think about it, as a "temporary move," as she had suggested.

"Once I got Ruth to agree to look at the room," Margaret told her daughter that evening on the phone, "I took her over to the nursing wing in a wheelchair."

They found the room barely acceptable; however, the open bed was positioned, fortunately, next to a spacious window, looking out on the sunny courtyard filled with fall flowers. Privacy curtains separated what would be Ruth's bed from the two on the opposite side of the room, each with a comatose patient. The bathroom would be Ruth's private bathroom; the room was generally quiet.

What Margaret knew was that, once there, Ruth would have all her meals provided and have round-the-clock care, for whatever her needs might be — and, Margaret also knew she was not going back to her apartment. But she would face that with Ruth later.

Margaret had to rely on the promise from the admissions people that Ruth would be first in line for the next available single room and trust it would come along soon.

Ruth reluctantly agreed with Margaret's temporary plan, and, under Ruth's careful supervision, back at the apartment, together they packed a few things they knew Ruth needed for a short while. "This isn't what I want to do," she told Margaret, "but I've trusted you before and I guess that is what I need to keep doing."

Margaret wheeled Ruth, with a small bag of her things on her lap, back down the hallway to the attached nursing wing and began to help her settle in, as they had said, "for just a short while." Margaret had asked the staff to bring Ruth's favorite chair, a comfortable recliner, which they brought in and placed beside the bed.

"Oh! Wonderful. I didn't think they would bring my chair over, and I'll be very glad to have it right here. You know me. I'm certainly not one to stay in bed ... even if I am old and somewhat crippled up," Ruth said with a smile and a wink.

'Thank God. There is that wonderful smile. This is going to work,' Margaret said to herself. She felt she could almost always count on Ruth's spirit to shine through whatever difficulties she faced. Margaret remained hopeful and grateful.

Ruth, after being at home in Elnora for almost nine years, knew every square inch of the nursing wing, and, in fact, she knew the entire many-acre campus there as well as she had known every part of the old farm place where she had grown up outside of Essex. She was well known in every part of the ECH as she had taken everyone who lived and worked at The Home under her wing at some time as a friend, counselor, helpmate, colleague, and even their pastor, the various roles she relished throughout her now almost one hundred years.

Margaret had cajoled Ruth into accepting a "temporary" move by suggesting that from there she would be far more able to visit with all her friends in the nursing wing, for whom she felt a particular calling: "You will be right there, close by your good friends who enjoying having you call on them every day." Ruth could actually "walk" herself, using her feet, around the entire nursing wing in a wheelchair.

With Ruth settled into her recliner in the new room, Margaret went back to the apartment and collected a few more things, especially Ruth's lap throw and her Sunday School lesson-planning book. Ruth's preparation for her three-minute Bible lesson each Sunday morning most certainly was not going to be interfered with because of this move.

"Thank you, Margaret, for bringing my lesson book. I do plan carefully to make sure my words are lively and relevant," Ruth said with a telling smile; she knew many in her captive audience could easily nod off for a quick nap if she wasn't well-prepared.

After Margaret had everything set up for Ruth, the dinner hour arrived. "I'll push you over to the dining room in your wheelchair," Margaret offered innocently.

"No, thank you. I'm not going in there to eat with all those old folks who have lost their minds and are drooling into their soup!" she announced.

"Well … o-kay," Margaret hesitated, surprised by Ruth's comment and not knowing what to say, but she really wanted this temporary arrangement to go well. "Then I'll go and ask the kitchen staff to bring you a supper plate. Would that be alright?"

Ruth agreed, and Margaret headed for the kitchen. While waiting for them to prepare a plate for Ruth, Margaret shared with the director of the staff what Ruth had said. She agreed to give Ruth a chance to settle in and eat in her room for a while, but eventually they would want Ruth in the dining room along with everyone else. "Yes, I understand," Margaret agreed.

After Ruth ate a bit of her supper, she said, "Enough of that … it's time for our evening card game." Ruth got out her deck of cards, and they began to play, as they did every evening, but on this evening, tiredness won out. Soon Margaret helped Ruth figure out where to put her bathroom things and her slippers where she could find them. She made sure Ruth knew how to use the call button before she left, hoping she would be fine and sleep well. It had been a big, emotional day.

When Margaret arrived at Ruth's door the next morning, she wasn't there.

"If you're looking for Ruth," one of the nurses walking down the hall offered, "she's over in the dining room having breakfast."

"Okay. I don't think I'll disturb that," Margaret happily said and went back to Ruth's where she had begun to go through some things in preparation for closing up the apartment.

Later that day, Margaret spent some more time with Ruth, but Ruth knew Margaret had her own work and did not expect her to stay with her every minute. Besides, Ruth had plans to "walk herself" in her wheelchair around the main hall to visit her friends who always looked forward to her visits and welcomed her warmly.

"We can have our game of cards this evening, can't we?" Ruth asked.

"Of course. I'll be over after I have a bite of supper myself."

That evening, Ruth and Margaret repeated their after-supper card game. Margaret did not say a word or ask where Ruth had eaten her supper, however, she was curious. The two laughed their way through another card game, enjoying time together.

The following late morning, Margaret went over to check in with Ruth, but soon, after checking her watch, Ruth said she needed to use the bathroom and get ready for lunch. This sounded good to Margaret.

"Lunch in the dining room?" Margaret asked timidly.

"Oh, yes. I'm sitting next to Jessie every meal now. She refused to eat when she moved here last week, but when I am sitting next to her, I'm able to get her to eat. So, yes, I have to go to the dining room. Jessie won't eat if I'm not there."

Margaret's heart soared. Once again, she thought, 'there she goes, my soon to be ninety-nine-year-old, sweet, dear friend having created a new calling for herself, one pulling her forward on a mission in life — this time with another new friend named Jessie.'

Margaret's inklings were now fully confirmed: Ruth was going to do fine in her new setting. That afternoon, Margaret went back to her artist studio up the road, coming and going every few days to check in.

Within a few weeks, a single room became available. Now they faced the challenge of asking Ruth to think about taking that room, signaling a move beyond a temporary arrangement. Margaret had looked at the room and knew it would be excellent with its wall of windows looking out to the east over the courtyard. Ruth always wanted to "get up with the sun."

Margaret told her about it. Ruth knew the room and also said she was not interested in going to see it.

Patricia arrived that late morning. She decided to make the trip down to see her mother, and Ruth, before Margaret returned home to California. She had been on the phone with her mother regularly, and Patricia wanted to help her clean out Ruth's apartment. Together, they went over to see Ruth and talk with her about the need for her to make a decision. Ruth welcomed Patricia with open arms.

"I've been thrilled ever since your mother told me you would be coming down for a bit of a visit with the two of us," said Ruth, as Patricia gave her a warm hug.

"Ruth," Margaret broke into the welcoming moment, "that room I told you about ... why don't we take Patricia down and show it to her?"

Ruth reluctantly agreed. Patricia rolled her down the hall in her wheelchair. Once in the room, the three of them sat there for a while without speaking, Ruth in the wheelchair, Patricia and her mother on the unmade bed. The view out the east-facing windows sang with the beauty of fall flowers and colors and a tall tree, now beginning to lose its leaves, whose bare limbs would provide sculptural beauty in the coming winter, right outside that window.

Into the quiet, after what seemed like a very long time, Ruth finally spoke.

"You both know I do not want to do this," Ruth said in a conversational tone, soft and easy, her emotions hidden beneath caring words. "I love my little apartment and think I would be fine there. But I love the two of you, and I know you think I would be better off if I moved here."

She paused, her eyes out the window, as if watching clouds move across the sky. Finally, she spoke again.

"I also know you are wise women and have what you think is best for me in your hearts. I'm also grateful that you are asking me to make this decision. And I guess that is one reason I need to think carefully. I don't want to put the two of you—or anyone else—in a situation where you have to make decisions for me."

It was a long, thoughtful word from Ruth ... followed by another long pause ...

"So-o … I guess I will … do this. Even if I don't want to. No one ever wants to give up their home, and yet no one always gets to do exactly what they want either."

With barely enough time to feel the poignancy of the moment, Ruth sat up straight, took a deep breath and continued.

"So, Margaret, go tell Debbie I'll take the room and find out when I can move in. Then, when you get back, we can begin to think about what to bring from the apartment. I don't want a lot of stuff, but I will need a few things." Ruth, her voice strong and clear, if somewhat strained, had decided to move ahead.

Debbie came right back with Margaret and gave Ruth a hug. Ruth's eyes glazed over, as did Debbie's, just a bit, but Ruth did not shed a tear.

Clearing her throat, Ruth looked at them and said, "Well, it's time for lunch and I'm needed in the lunchroom. I have to be there so Jessie will eat her meal. She needs her nourishment."

So that was it. Ruth could move in that day.

Ruth did not know of Margaret's work back in the apartment organizing for this move. She had started going through all the paperwork, and soon Patricia would begin working her way through closets, drawers, and the kitchen. But first, they needed to collect a few things for Ruth's new room. They knew Ruth and her apartment well, so easily gathered together the few things they knew she would need and want.

Together, that afternoon, the three of them re-established a new home for Ruth. They managed to fix the room to suit her with very little fuss. She had everything she would need but not more than that. Some of her favorite things made the room both beautiful and homelike. Margaret hung family pictures on the walls and stood the beautiful photograph of Cassandra and Ruth on the top shelf next to Ruth's chair.

Later that evening, Patricia and her mother worked into the night back in Ruth's apartment sorting things into piles to give away, throw away, or keep.

"We're all managing fine," Margaret told her son who had called to see how things were going with the move. "Ruth is doing good work visiting her friends over there during the day and in the early evenings, your sister and I play cards with her in her room, laughing and telling stories. She is easing into her new space quite well."

During the days, the women would come and go to visit with Ruth for a bit—that is, if they could find her at home.

Ruth's old hallway girlfriends, primarily Pat, came regularly to visit, and Ruth continued to make her daily rounds, "walking" herself in her wheelchair to visit the folks in the nursing wing as well as the staff.

Soon Patricia needed to get back home. She and her mother had sorted and disposed of furniture, pots and pans, clothing, and almost everything else during their work between visits with Ruth in her new home. That evening, while playing cards, Patricia told Ruth she needed to get back to work and would leave in the morning but return during the holidays. "Wonderful ... and I'm grateful," she added, "that at least the two of you are not leaving at the same time."

During these days, not once did Ruth ask a question about the apartment, never once express any interest in what Margaret and Patricia did with any of her things. Ruth had moved on with the basics, only what she needed for her present-day life, which she expected to continue to enjoy. Once she decided to be at home in the nursing wing, she had graciously let go.

Finishing up the paperwork took the most time; Margaret had to look at everything carefully and make decisions about what to toss, what to shred, what to save. As she finished, she put together a small box of legal and financial papers she wanted Ruth to have.

"Ruth, see this box?" Margaret took it over to show her. "It has your name and address on it, and 'Personal Papers' written across the top. Everything you might need regarding legal issues, taxes, whatever, is right in this box. And I want you to see where I'm going to put it," Margaret said as she walked over to the small closet, opened the door, and put the box in the bottom, beneath Ruth's few slacks and shirts hanging there. "See, it would be very easy for Don Daves to get it if he needed it, or Taylor, or yourself. It's not sealed, so you can open it if you want to have a look at what's in it."

"Thank you, my dear," Ruth said as she turned around in her chair to watch Margaret place the small box in the closet. "Thank you so much for taking care of my papers and leaving things where I could get to them if I need them." Again, Ruth asked no questions, merely showed her trust and not a bit of concern.

The day finally came when Margaret was ready to leave, the apartment completely empty and clean and the keys turned back over to the admissions staff.

Ruth and Margaret enjoyed the evening together and had such a sweet talk. Her gratefulness for her family—all of her family—was palpable, as she told Margaret a story she'd never heard.

Patricia had taken Ruth on a cruise a few years back and, after a full week's time sharing the evening meal with a couple from Texas, they found themselves in a bit of an awkward moment, faced with whether to tell more of the deeper story about how the two of them came to be related.

"The evening of our first meal," Ruth said, "Patricia introduced herself, and then said, 'And this is my grandmother, Ruth.'"

"Yes, I think I've heard both the kids introduce you that way," Margaret said, unsurprised.

"But then, at the end of the week, caught in mixed messages about exactly who we really were, Patricia winked at me, smiled, and said, 'Shall we tell them?' Well, I just nodded and said, 'Yes, my dear, you can tell them,' even though I wasn't sure what she would say. But it turned out to be a wonderful moment ... one I treasure."

What Margaret learned from Ruth's story on their final evening together was that back on the cruise — over a meal shared by Ruth and Patricia with two people who were mostly strangers — what was likely a risky conversation had taken place about Patricia's small-town Kansas family, of which Ruth was the surviving member.

"As Patricia and I talked on that lovely evening with our new friends, I kept thinking to myself, 'Ruth Peterson, you are one very fortunate woman indeed. Don't ever forget this moment in your life.'"

Margaret, in tears following Ruth's story, thanked her for telling her, gave her a kiss, and said goodnight. "I'll see you in the morning before I get on the road."

As she walked away, she thought, 'Ruth Peterson. She's one amazing woman still showing me how to age openly and enjoy life to the very end, regardless. What a gift to have this woman in my life all these years — even with all her bossiness!'

Margaret ran over to give Ruth a hug in the morning. After their farewells, as she was walking out of the room and turned back to throw Ruth a kiss, Ruth put her 'pointer' finger in the air, as she had done through all the years each time Margaret left, and said, "And you will be back?" her well-known, teasing smile breaking out as she asked.

"Yes, Ruth, I will be back. You know me, I always come back," Margaret said as she smiled and turned toward the door, her eyes filling with tears.

Margaret had slept the last few nights on the couch in Pat's apartment since the final dismantling of Ruth's apartment. Now, when Margaret got back there that morning to collect her purse and say goodbye. Ruth's few women friends from the apartment hallway had gathered. They had put together a sack lunch for her and stood to wave her off. They knew their California gal faced a long road ahead, hoping—now in the middle of October—to get over the mountains before the snow flew. By now, Ruth's women friends claimed Margaret as one of their own.

Thus, off she went, with those beautiful women waving from Pat's front porch. She turned north and then west out of Elnora onto the highway, with tears streaming down her face. Somehow Margaret knew she would never see Ruth alive again.

And so it was to be.

❖ ❖ ❖

On a warm, winter January morning in Southern California, with only a few hours until Margaret would step onto the stage as Eleanor Roosevelt, the phone rang. It was Taylor. Ruth had died quietly in the night.

They thought maybe she had had another stroke, for she could no longer speak. She had closed her eyes, eventually went to sleep, and just passed away. Taylor wanted to talk about the service, when they might schedule it, and if Margaret would help organize it.

Together, the two of them made plans to check out dates with the children and grandchildren. Margaret told him that Ruth had asked her to help write the obituary.

"I have it in my computer."

"Good. I'll find and send you the address of where to send a copy of it to the paper in Essex, and send me one also. I'd like to see it."

They made a list of things that needed doing and divided up the tasks between them.

"I'll notify all the family and get in touch with the cemetery folks," Taylor offered.

"Okay, I know the pastor there; I'll work with him to plan the service and the noontime meal."

"Well, there probably will only be a few of us, but I guess it would be good to have a place to gather," Taylor said. Margaret did not try to comment, but she felt sure they should plan for a full family gathering.

Once they got the business taken care of, Taylor seemed to want to talk. He told Margaret of his trip down to see Ruth less than a week ago, the day they had taken her to the hospital.

"I hadn't seen her for some time. I knew you and Patricia were there in the fall, so when they called, I just got in the car and drove down to see her, see if there was anything I could do to help."

An ambulance had been called, and they took her to the emergency room. Upon her arrival and after their examination, the doctors confirmed for her that she had had another stroke. When they told Ruth there was nothing they could do for her, she had thanked them for explaining it to her and said, "So now, I'd like to be taken back home to my own room and bed."

The emergency room staff agreed with Ruth's request, but some logistical problem about getting her released had come up, frustrating Ruth. Taylor arrived at that moment, helped solve the problem, and got her released and back home.

By the time ECH staff had settled Ruth into her bed, winter's late afternoon darkness had filled the sky, suggesting dinnertime. Taylor stepped back into Ruth's room, "Ruth, dinner is ready. Would you like for me to ask them to bring your evening meal on a tray for you?"

"Thank you, but I'm not hungry. I'd rather visit a bit," she said easily. "And thanks for rescuing me from the hospital. If I'm going to die, I want to be right here, in my own place, in my own bed," she said, with her tired but still mischievous smile. "I'm grateful you came."

So Taylor drew up a chair next to Ruth's bed. With the door closed, a restful calm gathered around them. A small table lamp next to the window cast a warm yellow glow gently around the room and out into the cold January night beyond the windows. Ruth and Taylor alone together.

"Neither of us said anything for what felt like a long time," he told Margaret. "Actually I couldn't think of anything to say. I remember wanting to leave, but for some reason I continued to sit there close to her bedside. And just when I finally decided I would get up and leave, she said quietly, 'Perhaps … perhaps you wonder how this all came about?'"

"Me? 'Perhaps … wonder?' Her question sort of startled me, but then she said something else and suddenly there we were, talking about times long past for the two of us. I'm still amazed by her quiet strength during our long conversation. I found I had so many questions."

Somehow, slowly, these two people, whose lives had been intimately intertwined for his entire life, had their first real conversation. His dad and mother—and Ruth—had been essentially together as a threesome long before the move to Essex when he was not quite three years old, nearly seventy years ago. Throughout his childhood and youth he knew his family looked different, even if he didn't understand or acknowledge he had feelings about those differences.

Taylor had never had such a conversation with his father or with his mother. Those two had passed on from his life in silence, taking with them all the untold stories, the puzzling riddles as he experienced their lives and his life in the family home. With Ruth's gentle nudging, he must have realized he wanted to know things about his family, have answers to questions he had never dared to ask.

Margaret had watched Taylor through the years struggle alone, with what she thought of as long-hidden, worrisome concerns from his early family life. Now Taylor was telling her that he had finally found the freedom to think and care about his family and how his early life had unfolded—while he was forever working hard to escape.

Taylor had been haunted by his parents—especially Ruth. Filled with some buried resentment, beginning perhaps with an unspeakable anger toward his mother, he thought of his dad primarily as a victim. Yet, he also held anger or at least long-held disappointment about his dad, as if his dad had somehow allowed it all to happen, the disintegration of per-haps what he thought he should have had—a "normal" or "real" family.

Unwilling to blame his mother and understandably confused about the role his father may have played, Taylor had chosen to lay the blame for whatever he thought went wrong on the only other option—on Ruth. Prior to this moment, it could have been easy to view Ruth's influence primarily as a destructive presence in his family home.

Now, as he talked with Margaret on the phone the day Ruth died, it appeared Taylor had come to realize Ruth had loved them all—his mother, his father, and, perhaps, especially, him. And just maybe Taylor began to see how he might also care for her.

"Margaret, I don't know what to say other than that was the best conversation I ever had with Ruth, well, with anyone really in my immediate family. I'm so glad I got out of my chair, drove down there, and got her back home in her own bed where she could die quietly, surrounded by her friends."

❖　❖　❖

Taylor had left late that evening for his midnight drive back home to Hastings.

As Taylor departed, Ruth's women friends had stepped in, taking turns sitting by her side holding her hand through that night and the next day. Sometime the following evening, Ruth must have suffered another stroke, one that took her ability to speak … and she lingered into the night with Pat right there, her dearest woman friend from down the hall, who would not leave her side. Eventually Ruth just quietly slipped away.

Epilogue

hey all came. The family, Taylor and Nell, Margaret, the children and grandchildren, and almost everyone from the later generations of the extended Taylor clan. A full Taylor family gathering, the largest in the fourteen years since Cassandra's passing. Ruth's students came; however, by this time, she had outlived many of them. Former colleagues from the schools and the city faithfully came. And, of course, those from her church community, especially the women. They packed the church pews, and people stood in the back and along the side walls of the sanctuary for the service to celebrate the life of Ruth Peterson.

Margaret had expected this, but Taylor appeared stunned, especially by the extended Taylor family, "They are all here," he whispered to her and Nell as the service began.

The churchwomen had put together a noon meal for fifty; it worked beautifully. The family gathered in the Fellowship Hall after the service enjoying their conversations, catching up with each other, and telling stories they remembered about Ruth, enjoying a real family gathering.

After the meal, Taylor, uncharacteristically choking back his emotions, stood and acknowledged with humble gratitude his appreciation for their presence, thanking them for coming. He took his time, wanting to mention the suddenly and seemingly important fact that not a single one of them in that room for the family gathering had any blood or "real" family ties to Ruth Peterson. And yet, he reminded them of the many gifts Ruth had brought into their lives, demonstrating what it really means to be a family. "All of us sitting together in this room today are surely a testament to this fact."

Patricia and Margaret had cleaned out Ruth's room in Elnora and fixed little boxes with pieces of Ruth's jewelry, handkerchiefs, and scarves to pass around to the women of the family. Everyone stayed, sitting and standing around, enjoying a long visit.

Prior to the memorial service at the church, the immediate family had gathered at the cemetery for a brief graveside service. Taylor had let the extended family know they would be doing this but did not expect everyone to come. Yet they came. There the large Taylor family stood around together telling the family stories of other days they all remembered well, standing in that cemetery, at that very spot, to bury first Cassandra and then Ed. Now they were placing Ruth next to Cassandra as the women had planned. Cassandra still in the middle, between the other two.

Who was this woman, this Cassandra Grace Taylor Thomas—who now lay for posterity between the two who had loved her most dearly?

Who was this irascible, would-be intellectual, hard-working woman of the plains who could read only as fast as she could turn the pages of her book …

—this woman who never intended to marry, and yet a man, a husband of more than fifty years, lay in his grave beside her own in the ground …

—this uncompromising woman who took a woman lover, a lover who now had also been laid to rest beside her, a woman with whom she created an open and intimate life for more than fifty years.

Who was this woman who certainly never intended to bear a child, or be a mother, yet that child stood with his own family at the graves of all three of them now, the triangle that created his family home while testily fighting out their lives together as he grew up, watching from the sidelines, always eager to break away.

At last, this child of this unique family claimed them all instead of running away. Perhaps, for the first time, he even accepted them all, loved them all.

Fourteen years ago, when he stood on that very ground beside the new grave of his mother, Cassandra Taylor Thomas, he had misjudged the strength of his unorthodox family as he predicted the demise of what he understood to be this ill-conceived arrangement.

That death, his mother's death, had, in fact, not been the end of his family as he knew it. For his family had remained intact as the final pair stayed on, solidly together, living out old habits, old frustrations, and old loves, freshly acknowledged and newly expressed. He had not really known or understood how they could all love each other and also how they might have all loved him. He may still not have totally understood, but, at last, he now finally knew that they did.

Photo by Carol Robb

Eleanor Scott Meyers was raised by parents who came from pioneer families that settled in Kansas soon after statehood and the end of the Civil War. Her love for the hills and river valleys along with the wide prairies and big skies of her eastern Kansas upbringing now provide settings for her short stories and novels along with images for landscape paintings in Eleanor's ON THE ROAD ART STUDIO in Claremont, California.

Ms. Meyers began her teaching career in the elementary schools of Florida in 1961 and then in New Mexico. After moving back to Kansas in the late 1960s, and raising her children there, she returned to the university, first at Yale to study religion and the arts, and then to the University of Wisconsin-Madison where she completed her Ph.D. in sociology. Teaching appointments in graduate education took her to New York City and Union Theological Seminary where she taught sociology of religion and various aspects of culture related to religion—race, gender, sexual identity, politics and organized religion—and eventually to Berkeley, California where she was the first woman president of Pacific School of Religion. Years later Dr. Meyers retired from The Fielding Institute of Santa Barbara, CA where she was dean of faculty and headed one of the first, groundbreaking, fully accredited, non-campused Ph.D. programs in the U.S.

Eleanor's children live in the Midwest. An avid camper, she has followed almost every back road leading from California to the middle of the country and back, in order to partake of the joy, not only of being on the road with paint brushes in hand, but also being with her family in their homes.

In retirement Eleanor continued her studies as a student in the Art Studio Program at the University of New Mexico, Taos Branch, for several semesters. Today she calls herself a working artist, painting and writing in her California studio and home ... and is teaching watercolor and oil painting in two Claremont retirement communities.